Claws of the Golden Dragon

AIRSHIP 27 PRODUCTIONS

Claws of the Golden Dragon
© 2015 Barbara Doran

Published by Airship 27 Productions
www.airship27.com
www.airship27hangar.com

Interior illustrations © 2015 Gary Kato
Cover illustration © 2015 Shane Evans

Editor: Ron Fortier
Associate Editor: Peg Livingston
Marketing and Promotions Manager: Michael Vance
Production and design by Rob Davis.

ISBN-13: 978-0692506929 (Airship 27)
ISBN-10: 0692506926

Printed in the United States of America

10 9 8 7 6 5 4 3 2 1

By Barbara Doran

Francis clutched her tiny derringer while peering around the corner. It was too dark to see much but that worked in her favor. Not being able to see the men hunting her meant they couldn't see her.

Not for the first time she cursed her family name and every penny her ancestors had ever earned. From dozens of suitors wanting the Trendle heiress' fortune, to the occasional kidnapping attempt, the only good they'd done was to provide her a career and an education. They didn't buy her peace of mind or acceptance. A woman who took over her ailing father's place as Chief Editor and owner of the town's newspaper was a curiosity only tolerated because of her wealth.

It'd been several years since anyone had attempted an abduction and she'd become complacent. She ought to have brought a guard with her on her business trip to the Jewel Island resort. In her defense, she and its proprietor had grown up next door to each other. The island was nearly crime free and she trusted John Striker implicitly.

They'd had a productive meeting and an excellent dinner. Afterwards, not wanting anyone to think they were romantically entangled, Francis had decided to walk back to the village inn. It was a short walk along the bicycle path and it was a fine, warm evening.

Once on the trail, though, Francis felt nervous. She'd no reason to think she was in danger, yet the early evening shadows seemed darker and deeper than they ought to be. She'd almost reached the village when she realized that a shadow not far ahead of her was that of a large man behind a tree. The faint, stale, smell of cigarette smoke wafted through the air towards her.

At the same time a sudden noise roared behind her. A sound like a wildcat's scream, but louder, deeper and more terrifying. All calm lost, she'd set off running, racing along the path like a panicked sheep. The man lying in wait was just as startled as she'd been; giving her the chance she needed to escape both it and him. Pursuit had been immediate but Francis was a fast runner. She'd dodged off the path to hide among the buildings of the island's port.

There was no one to help. The port closed at night and while there was a guard, there were too many chasing Francis for one man. Fortunately, there were enough boathouses and sheds to provide her with cover. If she were lucky, those chasing her would either give up or go far enough away to give her a chance to get into the village.

Hidden behind a shed, Francis listened for her pursuit and hoped they wouldn't find her. Voices muttered angrily not far from her and she could just see their owners' shadows in the light from one lamp near the end of the dock. "Can't have gone far," one said. "Why the hell didn't you grab her?"

"Didn't you hear it? The tiger's out there, somewhere, horning in on our business."

Another voice scoffed, "That's just a story. No one's ever seen him or his partner. Now shut it and start searching. The boss'll throw us all to the Voice if he finds out we let her get away."

Francis frowned. Hadn't she read something recently about a tiger? Not a real one, of course, but some criminal going by that odd soubriquet. That was right, a letter to the editor complaining about the failure of the police to deal with local crime in Strikers Port. She'd have to ask the Chief of Police about it, the next chance she got. Given she got that chance.

Francis counted the men moving slowly and quietly among the buildings. Five and none small enough to overpower, even with a heavy pipe. No, her best bet remained staying put and waiting for a clear moment.

The trouble was that one of the men was frighteningly close, flashlight flickering as he scanned the area. "Come along, dearie," he said menacingly, "There aren't that many places to hide. Sooner or later we're going to find you. No one wants to hurt you."

As if that reassured her. Francis glanced around, searching for escape, trying not to be heard. One sound, one wrong move, and she'd be caught. The man was too close. It was as if he knew where she was already and was playing with her.

Something ran behind the man, a long shape skittering across the pavement, then up the wall behind him. He spun, the light from his flashlight catching then losing the animal's shape. Francis, who'd automatically followed the beam with her eyes, held her breath. She'd never seen a lizard that size before. Nor, for that matter, one that color or shape. It was too long, with a bright silvery sheen that caught the light before the animal had leaped onto the building above her, making small hissing noises as it ran back and forth in front of her hunter.

Annoyed, the man shot at the animal as it rushed back and forth, the noise giving Francis cover to move back and away. She couldn't see what was happening, but she could hear the other men running towards the fight.

"The hell is wrong with you?"

"Some damn critter was attacking me. Should have seen its teeth!"

"A rat? You're shooting at rats when we don't want anyone noticing us? Are you an idiot?"

"Not a rat. Some sort of lizard."

"Pull the other one. That's got bells on! Ain't no lizards running around this far north. Leastwise, none big enough to bother shooting at!"

The argument continued, loud enough that Francis thought she had a chance to escape. She snuck slowly towards the village, staying down and low, thankful that there wasn't enough moonlight to make her visible.

What she hadn't reckoned on was the guard. All the noise would draw the attention of the deafest and laziest of men and Jewel Island port's guard was neither. He caught hold of her arm, grip so tight that she dropped her pistol, and snapped, "What the hell are you.... Miss Trendle?" He released her immediately, to Francis' relief. There were advantages to being a woman of consequence in a fairly small city.

"There are men chasing me," Francis told the guard, speaking as calmly and urgently as she could. Even as she spoke, she saw the men had noticed her interrupted flight and were running straight for them.

"Run," the guard said, sounding grim. She would have protested but he shoved her in the direction of the village before she could open her mouth. Then he turned, blocking her pursuit in a vain and valiant attempt to save her. It didn't matter. There were two more of her would-be abductors coming at them from another direction.

The men surrounded them a moment later, the one who'd nearly had her earlier laughing. "Found you, girlie. Thought I heard you down that way. You come along nice and quiet and...."

His mockery was interrupted by another wild animal roar, this one shockingly close. They all stared around, trying to find the source. "THERE!" one shouted as, seemingly out of thin air, a shape appeared out of the darkness. Too big to be an animal, it moved too quietly to be a machine, seeming to float in the beams of the flashlights focused on it.

Yet machine it was, albeit one Francis had never seen before. It looked like someone had mated a motorcycle with an airplane. A black metal cover concealed the front wheel, with a clear plate over the handles, behind which the rider was just visible. Whomever he was, he wore a red mask like the brightly colored Chinese decorations hanging on the wall in her father's library.

"What the hell?" One of the men snapped off a shot at the newcomer but the bullet struck the shield covering the motorcycle and ricocheted without damaging it in the slightest. More bullets followed, but without effect.

As the men ran out of bullets the stranger leaned forward and with unnerving and impossible silence rode his bike straight at them. Given no choice but to dodge or be run over, everyone made a run for it. One man didn't move fast enough as the bike slewed sideways and mowed him down.

Another man shrieked and when Francis looked in his direction she saw something running up and down his body, biting and clawing as it went. It was the same strange lizard that she'd seen earlier, she realized, as the man dropped to the ground.

The rider of the motorcycle leaped off and twisted and flipped until he was beside Francis, catching hold of her wrist in one sharp move that pulled her out of another man's reach. He kicked the man in the face, knocking him cold with one blow.

The two remaining men turned to face the stranger, their expressions furious. "Tiger! Don't try muscling in on our territory!" one growled.

Francis held her breath. The man called Tiger was quite tall and broad shouldered, but the two men out-bulked him by a good hundred or so pounds each. "Think of it as payback," he told his enemies. "Your boss was warned about poking his nose into the Gold Dragon's territory. Now it's our turn. The only ones taking the girl will be us."

"Our? Us? There's just you. Unarmed. Against two of us." The speaker grinned, apparently regaining his confidence.

Francis stared behind the two men. A misty shape was appearing out of nowhere, a swirl of cloud and shadow that slowly coalesced into another figure. Like the one holding her arm, he wore a mask, this one blue, with a different design. From its style, Francis was sure he was the first man's partner.

"What makes you think I'm alone?" the first man asked, sounding amused as he nodded in the other's direction. At the same time, something long and silvery snaked its way up and around the newcomer's body to perch on his black-clad shoulder. Its strange resemblance to the dragons Francis had seen carved on the posts outside Strikers Port's Chinatown didn't ease her state of mind at all.

Realizing another enemy had arrived; the two men turned and stared. Then, either out of bravery or bravado, the one nearest to the newcomer aimed a punch at the smaller and slighter man. That, though, only put him in range of the lizard, for it leapt from its master's shoulder and caught the man by his nose.

As he screamed and fought with the animal the other man tried to grab Francis and pull her to him. Her new captor swung her out of reach in a single smooth motion and kicked the man in the center of his chest. "I told you, you don't get the girl," he said, although neither of the two men were awake to hear him. He turned his attention to his partner, adding, "That makes eight for me."

"I counted seven."

"It was eight. Remember the one hiding under the sink?"

"I still have nine, so I still win."

"Barely."

Angry at their sudden descent into childish one-upmanship, Francis snapped, "Let me go!" She tugged at her wrist, trying to pull free and regretting the loss of her derringer. "Don't you dare...."

"Now, Miss Trendle. Don't make me use force...." The sound of running feet drew the stranger's attention towards the village. A blown whistle, that of one of the village's tiny police force, made him sigh. "And now we have company. We'll talk later, Miss Trendle. When we won't be interrupted." He released her arm and ran for his motorcycle, leaping on it and revving its engine loudly before setting it racing up the long pier. At the same time his partner disappeared as suddenly as he'd appeared.

"Don't worry, Miss. They can't get away. Well that one can't. There's nowhere to go that...." The guard's confident voice faltered as the sound of the motorcycle faded away into the distance.

By this time the village police had arrived, led by the Chief. "Miss Trendle! Are you all right? I got a call saying someone was trying to kidnap you!"

"That's right, Chief Anderson," Francis told the older man, "But there was a falling out among thieves. One just tried to escape down the pier on a motorcycle."

The Chief sent two men down that way, their flashlights searching the darkness. When they came back, a few minutes later, they were empty handed and confused. "Nothing there. Only place to go is into the ocean."

Francis stared, not at all sure what to say, hoping no one would decide she was hysterical or delusional. Even the dock guard couldn't help. A motorcycle escape into the ocean was nothing compared to a man vanishing into thin air and a miniature dragon.

No, she decided, giving a warning look to the guard, "We must have made a mistake. Maybe he went back up the trail. Hunt for him later, though. There's these five," she indicated the men sprawled on the ground around them, "who tried to abduct me."

That settled things for the Chief. In a choice between hunting around the island in the dark and arresting the very real, very solid, load of thugs in front of him, he knew his best option.

As the Chief and his men grabbed and dragged the unconscious men away, Francis gazed in the direction the stranger had gone. He was obviously a criminal, but she owed him a debt of thanks.

Besides, she was a journalist, first and foremost. And those two were obviously a story.

(((

"Hey, Maloney? Did you see a light in that store over there? That Jeen Loon place?"

Officer Maloney's sigh said that he'd rather ignore the issue. "Nope. Not a sign." He dismissed William's concern, adding, "And if there is, them Chinee handle their own business. I told you that before, kid."

William tried not to show his irritation. Maloney could be a lazy bum with no desire to do his job. Here in Chinatown he only sprang into action if it looked like a tourist was getting mugged. Given they were patrolling long past midnight, that was an unlikely turn of events.

William had learned it didn't pay to argue. It rankled, but a rookie cop with barely six months under his belt wasn't in a position to do much. However, "Didn't Chief Michaels say he wants us doing more than looking pretty up here?

Another sigh. "Listen, Jarvis, Chief Michaels doesn't know his head from a hole in the ground when it comes to our Chinatown. Maybe things were different, down in San Francisco, but up here in Strikers Port all you get when you ask them Chinee anything is stares and babble."

That wasn't true at all. "Some of the Chinese here speak very good English."

"Oh, I'm sure they do, Jarvis. Except when it's conven.... what the hell?" The sound of something crashing inside Jeen Loon Antiques was followed by the sound of a door slamming and running feet. "Kid, wait, don't...."

Maloney's exhortation went ignored. William knew the sound of a burglar on the run when he heard one and he had the bit between his teeth. He raced into the narrow alley that went between the Jeen Loon and Uncle Ip's place. He had to turn sideways to get through but a minute later he stumbled into the dimly lit backstreet that wound its way through Chinatown.

Immediately, William regretted his impetuous rush into the fray. There were four men, none weighing less than two-hundred pounds and not an ounce of it fat. Had they noticed his presence and taken offense he wouldn't have been able to stop them. One good hook from the nearest and he would have gone down.

Fortune was on his side. The men were too busy trying to get out the back door of the Jeen Loon to notice him. From their furious and terrified argument over who was in whose way, it sounded like something inside had scared them out of several years growth.

Drawing his gun, William aimed it at the nearest of the men. "Don't move," he ordered, trying not to let his voice shake. Calm and confident, he reminded himself. Any sign of weakness would be leapt on immediately. The men were on edge already. As long as they didn't know he couldn't stop them all, they'd cooperate. Right?

Wrong. As soon as he spoke the biggest man flung something in William's direction. Although William evaded whatever it was, it startled and distracted him enough to give the man his chance. William went down and barely had enough presence of mind to tuck his chin as he landed.

William was stunned just long enough for his attacker to grab his gun and aim it straight for his face. Freezing, he stared up at the man, knowing all too well that his stupidity was about to get him killed.

Before the thug could fire, something came skittering out of the darkness, a long, lizard-like, something that snatched the gun out of his attacker's hand and ran away, its hiss sounding like derisive laughter as it disappeared into the shadows.

William recovered from the surprise before his attacker and jerked his knee upwards. It was a dirty blow, but his father had taught him that all was fair when one's life was on the line. As his attacker *oofed* and bent over, William brought his fist up hard and fast, knocking the man entirely off of him.

Rolling to his feet, William ducked another thug's blows and returned it with interest. At the same time he realized the last two thugs were fighting a black clad man wearing a strangely painted blue mask. Then he was dodging again, trying to keep his opponent from getting a blow in while simultaneously getting one in himself. No easy trick, either. This one was a boxer, with the short, sharp, strikes and quickly moving feet that characterized the better of the breed.

They circled, bobbing and weaving as they each tried to find the other's weakness. Luckily, William found his opponent's first. A peculiar twist to the man's gait as he turned that said he had a bum knee. Normally,

William wouldn't have taken advantage but his life was on the line and he had no choice. Pretending to stumble, he twisted in the very last moment and slammed his foot into his opponent's knee with all his strength.

The man screeched outrage and stumbled right into William's best uppercut. Then he crumpled, landing on top of the first man with all his weight. Which was just as well; it gave the man a soft place to land and kept the first man from moving.

Turning his attention to the other fight, William admired the newcomer's style. His father had told him that the Chinese had a different approach to boxing and watching the man fight, he saw what the old man meant.

Clawed fingers twisted and struck in sharp succession, followed by kicks that sent their victim flying across the alley. Bigger and stronger the thief might be, but he wasn't fast enough to evade nor able to withstand the force of the blows that struck him.

As the man fell, William moved slowly forward. "Good job," he said, "Thanks for helping. Can I get your name?"

"You think I'm helping you?" the black-clad man said, bending down and picking up a bag lying on the ground between them. Something gold glittered from its opening. "No honor among thieves, you know."

William reached for his pistol, only to remember that that weird lizard thing had taken it earlier. As the realization hit, the man chuckled and reached out so fast that William raised his arm to block the blow. That just amused the man as he pushed the blocking arm out of the way to pat William on the head. "Sorry. No time to fight. Maybe later, when I'm not so busy."

Before William could react, the man leapt for the nearest wall and climbed up its rough surface as if he had claws. "Tell that slowpoke friend of yours that he'd have more luck getting through alleyways if he lost some weight." A moment later the man was gone.

The sound of someone running drew William's attention then. Maloney making his slow and panting way up the small street towards him. "What... the... hell.. is... wrong... with... you?" his partner managed to gasp. Apparently Maloney had taken the long way around, being too heavy to take the direct route.

Apologetically, William told his partner, "Sorry, sir. I shouldn't have done that." He looked around at the unconscious men and added, "I wasn't the only one here, though. Another thief took down two of these guys."

"You're an... idiot, Jarvis.... Do you have... any idea what... your father would do to... me if you got hurt?"

Most likely nothing. George Jarvis had a bad temper, but he'd know that anything William did on the beat to get himself hurt would be William's own fault. At least, that was what he always told William. "I'm sorry, sir," he told Maloney again.

"Now, what happened?"

William explained, leaving out the details that he couldn't account for like the lizard and the fact that the masked man had climbed the wall like some sort of cat. Instead he finished with, "And... sorry again, sir... but I've lost my gun."

That made Maloney frown at him, looking him up and down with a dour expression. Then, narrowing his eyes, he pointed at William's belt. "No, you haven't."

William reached down and was stunned to find his weapon sitting exactly where it ought to be. Somehow he managed not to protest its return, saying, "I must have forgotten finding it in the confusion. Sorry, sir."

"Enough with the 'sorry, sir'!" Maloney snapped. "Now we'll have to figure out how to get these four back to the station. No point in winning a fight like this without taking the glory."

William sighed, certain who would be taking how much of the so-called glory. "Shouldn't we find out what's missing from the Jeen Loon?" Given most Chinatown shops had living space above them their owner might have been hurt.

"Yeah, yeah. Give me your cuffs and I'll get these sleeping beauties taken care of. You go in and see if anyone's around to tell you. And try to find a phone. Doubt they have one but it'd make getting a paddy-wagon up here a lot faster and easier."

William obeyed, shining his flashlight on a backroom full of bric-a-brac of a sort he suspected even his grandfather Krane couldn't have afforded. Lacquer gleamed and gold glittered brightly and here and there, William noticed gems like jade, rubies and sapphires.

The door into the main shop was wide open. So was a big and heavy door that led into a room with a heavy glass window looking out into the shop. There was a display cabinet in the middle with seven figurines on it, each carved from a translucent white stone, gilt with layers of gold and set with more jewels. A woman with a crown of flames, an old man clutching a young tree as a staff, a young man playing into a flute.... There was a place for an eighth figure and it hit William that that might have been what the strange thief had taken.

The light suddenly went on. "What you do here?"

The speaker was a young man with tousled brown hair and lightly tanned features. He looked only part Chinese, which only slightly startled William. Even before the anti-miscegenation law had been repealed everyone knew it happened.

William asked, "Do you work here? I'm Officer William Jarvis. Can I get your name?"

"My most honored mother is owner. This lowly person is Chou, her number two son. Your turn to answer?"

"Could you get her for me? Your shop's been robbed and I'd like to find out what might be missing."

"Mother not here. Is with father at other house. This incompetent one is in charge." Chou shook his head, smiling in a way that might have been foolish if William hadn't seen a glint of bright interest in his eyes. "Nothing missing in this room."

William indicated the cabinet, "I'm afraid you're wrong. Something's gone from here, obviously."

"Gone, yes. Stolen, no. Damaged. This useless one has taken it to repair."

Suspicious, William asked, "I don't suppose you could show me?"

"Come, come." Chou turned and walked out, his long robe dragging behind him. "Is this way, please."

They went through another door, one hidden behind a tangled passage of bookshelves, and into a small room that looked like it'd been through a hurricane. Small tools and scraps of wood and metal lay everywhere. There was a bed in the middle, with a yellow quilt and - incongruously - a stuffed black and white bear.

Ignoring William's raised brow, Chou said, "Is here. See? Meng Huang Shang, God of Dreams and Delirium. Is precious Khaitan artifact. One of Eight Gods and Prince of West. Very expensive. You like?"

William had no idea what that meant but he admitted the statue looked like one of the ones in the display case. It was made of the same material and the figure looked very similar in style. This one was of a young man lounging on the back of a tiger, a look on its tiny face that made William think it quite mad. "I see."

A shout drew William's attention towards the door. "My partner's calling. I'd better go." He pulled out his notebook and wrote the station phone number on it. "Look, if anything turns out missing, call in. Or have your mother call. There's no reason to let people get away with robbing you."

Chou took the paper William handed him, looked it over for a moment then set it down amid the chaos of his desk. "Will remember. Best go now. Is late. This incompetent one would sleep. Has had very busy night indeed."

With a last look around the room, wondering if anyone would notice if a thief had been there, William agreed. He doubted he'd hear anymore of this case but he was curious. What had happened to terrify those thugs? Who was that strange man with the odd mask? And how the hell had his gun gotten back where it belonged without his noticing?

《《《

Unlike most crooks, Perry Crogan was up and working before sunrise. A holdover from his days at the Krane Winery, it was a habit he took advantage of. Having one's plans made and set in motion long before anyone else in town was a distinct advantage. Besides, the sooner he went over his plans for the day, the sooner he could be on his way and leave the things on his wall behind. He really did need to do something about them.

He'd just had his morning cigarette and coffee when he learned he'd lost twenty-one men to the police overnight. Ten had been handling the casino at Blue Eyed Jacks, seven more on Jewel Island to bring in the little Trendle Heiress, and four more whom he'd sent to rob an antique shop in Chinatown.

That last was particularly annoying because it was the second time they'd tried and this time they'd ended up arrested by an overly enthusiastic young officer. Most of the cops who worked the Chinatown beat tended not to put much effort in the job.

The thing that annoyed Crogan the most was the fact that each arrest had been partly due to outside interference. A pair of young crooks with delusions of adequacy were horning in on his territory. The two, calling themselves the ridiculous name "Claws of the Golden Dragon", had been steadily biting into his territory for months now. It was high time, he thought, that he bit back.

"So no one has any idea where they're coming from?"

Sam Dolan, Crogan's second in command now that his old lieutenants were no longer... available, shrugged. "Well, boss, the one seems to appear and disappear out of nowhere and the other has that damned motorcycle of his."

"That everyone swears they can't even hear coming until he roars." Crogan was disgusted. "I think the lot of you are either too drunk or too stupid to notice until it's too late."

Dolan grumbled but had no answer. Even he admitted it made no sense. There wasn't a motorcycle made that rode entirely silent. One that moved as fast as the one Tiger rode had to have one hell of an engine.

The phone rang then and Crogan waved Dolan back as he answered. "Why Chief Michaels," he said, trying to sound as smooth and pleasant as a property agent should. "Whatever is it that I owe the honor to for this phone call?"

"Don't come sweet with me, Crogan. You're as sweet as arsenic and about as healthy to swallow." Michaels snapped. "What the hell is going on with your men? I'm hearing all sorts of rumors and I don't like them. Is someone moving in on your territory?"

"Territory, Chief Michaels? You make it sound like I'm some sort of gang leader or war-lord," Crogan protested. It was a long standing duel between him and the Chief. They both knew what Crogan was, but as long as Michaels couldn't prove it, he couldn't do a damn thing about it. "Though I will admit to some odd troubles lately."

"Do tell," Michaels said sourly. "I have a score of your men right now, all swearing up and down on every Bible they can find that they're innocent and they've been hard done by. Which, given Pinky Barton has at least five dead prostitutes to account for and Jonesy's probably the best safe-cracker in the business, seems about as arrant a bit of nonsense as possible."

Crogan coughed. "Now don't come all high and mighty with me, Michaels. I don't know those men. All I know is that my tavern was wrecked and that some of my employees who were vacationing on Jewel Island got themselves in a spot of trouble. Too much alcohol, Chief Michaels," he added sadly, "is a terrible thing. Which is why I never touch the stuff."

"You call yourself an Irishman?" Michaels asked. "And I already know there were a couple of outsiders poking their nose in. Pair calling themselves the Claws of the Golden Dragon. So, I'm asking again, nicely. Is someone moving in on your territory?"

"Well, it's possible someone would like to buy me out at a discount. But they haven't made any offers, so I don't really know." Crogan made a note to have a talk with his men about spilling what little they knew to the cops. "And I have no idea what "Claws of the Golden Dragon" even means. Seems like a damn-fool kind of thing to call oneself."

"Sounds like Tong trouble to me," Michaels snapped back irritably. "We both know it's a bad idea to be bothering the Tong. Tell me true, boyo, did you poke your sticky fingers into a place they don't belong?"

Crogan had to admit that his old enemy was right. He wasn't sure why he hadn't thought of it yet. Maybe because not one of those who'd met the pair had ever mentioned an accent. Besides, the local Tong was too practical to call itself the Golden Dragon. For as long as he could remember, they'd been the *Pu Gway Ren She Way*.

Still, there was one possibility he might have overlooked. "I... ah... might have... in a way. How could I know McLeod's girlfriend was a Chinee?" That was the closest he'd come to admit to having tried a bit of protection on the owner of McLeod Engines. All he'd known at the time was that Conall McLeod's company made enough money to make it worth asking for a share to keep his shop from being burned down. "I didn't find out until afterwards."

To Crogan's annoyance, Michaels laughed. "That's because you don't pay attention to the idle rich unless there's something in it for you. McLeod's girlfriend... wife, now... is Cheh Chang's only daughter. And if you don't know Cheh Chang is the biggest and richest man in Strikers Port's Chinatown then you're a complete fool."

Angry, because he could tell from Michael's tone that he'd get neither sympathy nor help from that quarter, Crogan slammed the phone down, only to have it start ringing again as soon as he did so. "Damnit, Michaels!" he started.

"And why would you be talking to Chief Michaels, Mr. Crogan?" a harsh, metallic, voice purred viciously. Crogan didn't know how the speaker, he'd long since dubbed The Voice, managed to sound like that, but he knew better than to ask.

"Michaels called me, sir," he said quickly. "I thought he was calling back after I hung up on him."

"That's good to know," The Voice said. "Best not try betraying me, Mr. Crogan. I will take great offense and you will not succeed. Remember what I can do."

Oh, Crogan remembered. He looked at the evidence of his unwanted partner's power every day and the last thing he wanted was to directly experience it. "I know," he said, staring at the wall across from him bleakly. Maybe if he had it papered?

"So tell me, did you get the thing I asked for?"

Crogan sighed. "No. The Trendle girl got away. We're going to have to let things cool down before we try again. She'll beef up her security, now she knows someone's after her."

"Get her as soon as you can," The Voice told him darkly. "I have use for her. And the other thing?"

"Also a miss. We had some overzealous cops butt in."

Silence. A disgusted silence that Crogan hoped wouldn't result in more unpleasantry. Then, "You're incompetent."

"Boss?" Dolan interrupted suddenly, before Crogan could lose his temper. "They're moving again."

The reminder of what lay within his office wall made Crogan take a deep breath, though he forced himself not to look. "I understand. We will do our best to achieve the goals you've set us."

"I have more for you to do. Listen carefully."

As Crogan took notes, he glanced up at his wall again and flinched. How, he wondered for the thousandth time, did that crazy Voice do it and how could he live with himself? Crogan was a nasty piece of work, he himself would admit it, but even he wouldn't have done what The Voice had done. Not that he could. As far as he knew, The Voice was the only man he'd ever come across who could stick a human body into a wall. Literally.

He turned away from the sight of two of his best men twisting around desperately beneath the plaster. Maybe he should just get a new office.

⟨⟨⟨

Chief Ash, "The Axe", Michaels was out of sorts. Given how many of Boss Crogan's men had been brought in overnight, he had no right to be. He ought to be glad to have those idiots dragged in by the napes of their necks. And he would be if it'd been his own cops doing the dragging, the catching, the punching and the kicking - all in accordance with their duty, mind you.

Crogan's thugs being taken down by a mysterious pair of masked thugs was annoying. Coming back to Strikers Port, after years in San Francisco and Los Angeles, he'd thought he'd gotten away from the "Mysterious Masked Vigilante" type of hooligans. One never knew what those sort were up to. Half the time he was certain they caused more trouble than they resolved. Nor was he convinced they weren't in it for the money.

Certainly these two seemed to be. Oh, the anonymous calls that he'd long since guessed came from them, warning of disturbances, kidnappings and all sorts of alarums and excursions were useful. But there hadn't been a single incident involving the pair that didn't also involve some missing goods.

There was one exception. Chou Chang had sworn up and down on a stack of Bibles that nothing had been taken from his mother's shop. Of course, the kid was incoherent at the best of times. Being brought in to talk to the Chief of Police hadn't helped. In the end, Michaels had given up and sent the kid home before he blew a gasket.

Lacking any better ideas, Michaels called in the two officers from the Jeen Loon case. Maloney was hopeless, on the force for twenty years and having grown complacent, but William Jarvis was a good, smart, kid whose biggest fault was a tendency to act before he thought. Michaels had hoped that the two would offset each other's less desirable traits and make at least one good officer between them.

"You didn't try to arrest the masked guy?"

An odd, embarrassed, look crossed William's face at the question. "No, sir. I didn't."

"It's the reason you didn't that interests me. You said you lost your gun?"

Maloney interrupted, angrily telling his junior partner, "I told you not to say that!"

"I couldn't lie," William snapped back. "Everyone would want to know why I didn't use it!"

Somehow, Michaels resisted the urge to swat the both of them. "Enough!" When they sat quiet again, he continued, "What happened to it, Jarvis?"

The kid flushed. "I let the first man I fought knock it out of my hand. I... I probably wouldn't be here if some animal hadn't attacked him while I was down."

"What sort of animal?" Michaels had a sneaking suspicion, but he was hoping that someone would have a different tale to tell this time. Or at least one that didn't sound like it was coming straight out of a bottle of Barton's finest rot-gut whiskey (est. 1849 behind the mine camp chuck-wagon).

"It must have been a cat. It was too big to be what I thought at first."

"Which was?"

"I...." William looked pleadingly from Michaels to Maloney and back again. Seeing no rescue, he sighed. "I must have hallucinated it. But it looked like the dragon on Uncle Ip's sign. Well, except this one was made of silver, not wood."

Michaels took a deep breath, expectation confirmed. Up until now, he'd been able to put stories of a real, live, Chinese dragon down to the hysterical ravings of drunken crooks. Officer William Jarvis was a teetotaler and as honest as they came. He was also the true son of his boxer father, entirely lacking the sort of imagination that would turn a cat or a rat, or even a large lizard, into a dragon.

Deciding that that particular issue was one he needed expert advice on, Michaels waved off the question, "All right. I'm sure that's what you thought you saw. Don't talk about it, right? No need to start strange rumors. We have enough already." Michaels turned to another part of the report. "You say the last thief, the one who climbed the wall, carried off a bag with something you thought was gold. But when you looked inside the store, there wasn't anything missing."

"Well, one statue seemed to be, but the man in charge, Chou Chang, said he was fixing it." William shrugged. "As far as I could tell, it looked like he was telling the truth. It certainly looked like the others in the set. Of course, I don't know much about antiques, sir. I haven't been around them since I was little."

Michaels remembered that William's mother was a Krane and that her family was once one of the richest and most noted of the elite in Strikers Port. Admittedly, Jarvis Senior was just a lowly boxer, but gossip had it that old Krane had doted on his youngest daughter and her son. "So you don't think the Chang kid had anything to do with it?"

Maloney snorted. "None of them heathen Chinee behave normally. And I don't know why we're even worrying about this job. It's not like they don't take care of themselves up in Chinatown."

Somehow, Michaels managed not to lose his temper. It was true that the Chinese in Strikers Port handled their own affairs and dealt with their own criminals. Maloney might be excused for expecting this case to be more of the same. But the criminals weren't Chinese this time, putting the ball firmly into his court. "Chinatown is part of Strikers Port," he reminded Maloney. "Besides, this is a case where they don't have the luxury of keeping to themselves. Those were Crogan's men and you know that snake doesn't let go of something once he puts his mind to it."

"Yeah," Maloney admitted. "He didn't get what he wanted from the Jeen Loon this time...."

"Or the time before," William added. When Michaels and Maloney stared he explained, "I checked the reports for the last year or so. About a month ago a group of unidentified men broke the place up. We only know about it because that time a tourist who'd been hanging around late reported it. The owner and her family never said a word."

The owner of the Jeen Loon was Mudan McLeod, formerly Mudan Chang, the one and only daughter of the richest Chinaman in town, as well as the wife of the man Crogan had just admitted targeting. Michaels shook his head. He didn't have to be a fortune-teller to see what was headed their way.

Michaels clapped his hands and rubbed his palms together. "Jarvis, do you think your grandfather's name would get you in to see Mr. Chang?"

"I... well... maybe. I don't know."

"Try. Put on some good clothes and pay him a visit. Tell him that I think his daughter's family is being targeted by a local racketeer. See if he'd put in a good word with Mrs. McLeod and convince her to ask for our help."

William nodded seriously. "Is it really that important?"

"It's looking like we have a new Tong stretching its muscles and an old racketeer who doesn't like being pushed. If something isn't done, we'll have a nice little turf war on our hands. You know, as well as I do, that when there's war, there's collateral damage."

"I'll do my best, sir."

"You do that. While you're at it, see what he thinks about something called the Golden Dragon and its claws."

The kid looked puzzled but before he opened his mouth, Michaels' door was flung open. "Sorry to interrupt, sir!" his secretary told him, sounding urgent, "There's been a bomb threat at the Sentinel!"

(((

When Francis returned to Strikers Port and to the Strikers Port Sentinel's building, it was to a scene of panic. Dozens of onlookers were gawking unabashedly, getting in the way of the police as they cordoned off the building. Off to the side she saw her reporters and her Assistant Editor, Joe Scanlon, watching the building nervously.

Pushing herself between onlookers without apologies, Francis made her way over. "Joe? What's going on?"

"Ah, Miss Trendle. I'm glad you've come. I was about to send someone to phone the island to find you." Joe waved a hand at the Sentinel building with an expression of disgust. "We received a bomb threat about an hour ago. I didn't want to risk it being real, so I sent for the police and had the building evacuated."

"It's all quite exciting. Joey had to drag me out of your office," another voice said and Francis realized that her old schoolmate, Rosamund Krane, was standing among the Sentinel's employees. "I've never seen so many people running before. It's just like in the movies! Isn't that right, Boopsie?"

Boopsie was Rosamund's big grey wolfhound, a long-suffering animal whom she dressed up in fluffy scarves and diamond collars. The only reason he wasn't given sweaters as well, was that he tended to eat them.

"Mrrrhrrr?" Boopsie said, cocking his head and looking puzzled, his usual expression when Rosamund addressed a question to him. When his mistress patted him on the head, using the glove she carried for the purpose, he sighed and lay back down on the sidewalk to wait.

Francis didn't ask why Rosamund had been in her office. Her old

"JARVIS, DO YOU THINK YOUR GRANDFATHER'S NAME WOULD GET YOU IN TO SEE MR. CHANG?"

schoolmate might own Krane Vineyard but she left its daily affairs to her mother and the family retainer, Rancourt. Instead, with nothing better to do, she often went to socialize with those she considered her circle. That she seldom consulted anyone's schedule but her own was par for the course.

Keeping her attention on Scanlon, Francis asked, "What happened?"

Ruefully, Scanlon waved a hand at the building, "Someone with a very rough voice called and told me there was a bomb in the basement. They hung up and, as I said, I called the police and evacuated. Since then an officer went in, looked around and came out looking as if all hell were on his tail. That's all I know."

A large truck with the words "McLeod's Motors" drove up, followed by the Chief of Police's car. As the drivers and passengers got out, Francis called out, "Chief Michaels? Do you have a moment to tell me the situation? Is there anything I can do to help?"

The Chief hesitated a moment then beckoned her over. "Well, lass, I'm not really sure yet, but my men did find a device of some sort down in your cellar. Trouble is, it's locked behind a fence and we can't get to it."

That would be the cage where the maintenance crew kept their more valuable tools. The wrenches and meters used to keep the paper's printers operating were specially designed and too expensive to leave lying around. "I have a master key right here," she told Chief Michaels, searching through her handbag and finding her key ring and handing it to him. She'd have asked to come in and watch the proceedings but she knew there was no way the Chief would agree.

A big, scraped up, hand reached over and took the key from her and she turned to look up. "Mr. McLeod?" she said questioningly, unsure why Conall McLeod was even there, much less taking the key to a storage room with a potential bomb in it.

"I handled armaments in the war, lass," McLeod said, grinning down at her. "Where do you think I got all these grey hairs?" He gestured at his thick, greying brush of red hair.

McLeod's son, Robby, Francis thought his name was, said, "But Dad, you always say it is Chou and I who give them to you." There was an odd lilt to his speech, an accent Francis couldn't place. "We should hurry. If it, the bomb that is, is on a timer, we cannot waste time talking." He slung a huge bag over his shoulder that looked too heavy to carry and waited expectantly.

Giving his son a dour look, Conall McLeod stuck the key in his pocket and snatched the bag from Robby's hand, "I told you, you're not coming. Understand?"

Robby didn't answer immediately, scanning the building with interested eyes. Then his dark brows drew together in a deep scowl from behind black framed glasses. After a moment he shrugged. "Yes, Dad. I understand. I'm not coming. You'd better go quickly, though. Should not keep wasting the police's time like this."

With a suspicious look for his son's sudden change of mind, McLeod turned and stalked through the big double doors, leaving Chief Michaels and Francis to look at each other with what she suspected were identically worried expressions.

Deciding there wasn't any point in just standing around, Francis turned her attention to Robby McLeod, remembering bits and pieces of the young man's story; how his father and mother had met when Cheh Chang had hired McLeod to build a mechanical lion for one of Chinatown's many festivals. How the two had become lovers denied marriage by California law until fairly recently.

Robby, the older of two sons, took after his father for the most part, being light-skinned, tall and broad-shouldered. His black hair and slightly slanted eyes were the only sign of his mother's heritage - that and the ever so slight accent that he'd no doubt learned from his mother.

Before Francis could speak, Robby suddenly turned on his heel and headed away from the building. When Michaels asked where he was going the young man shrugged. "Dad won't be needing me for a bit. I will go and get drinks and come back."

It was curiously abrupt behavior but Francis guessed that he was worried about his father and trying not to let it bother him. Rather than concern herself over it, she scanned the Sentinel building's windows, hoping that whatever trouble had found its way into its basement didn't mean this was the last time she saw the place in one piece.

Something caught her eye. "Chief? I think there's someone inside. No. I'm sure of it."

Chief Michaels wasn't the sort to assume a woman was hysterical, instead of scoffing, he asked, "Didn't Scanlon say he got everyone out?"

"He did. But I don't think everyone got the message." Francis pointed at the window where she'd seen the faintest of shadows against the ceiling. "Look, there it is again."

After a long look and with an expression that boded ill for whoever was fool enough to stay inside a building under bomb threat, Michaels turned and shouted, "JACKSON! JARVIS! MALONEY! Get over here!"

ᜰᜰᜰ

Dolan tossed another file out of the cabinet angrily. This wasn't a job for a gang boss's right hand man and if it weren't for the fact that it was The Voice who'd ordered it, he would have told Crogan just where he could shove it. Someone less important could handle this job, or, more likely, no one would. Tearing up a newsroom for the sake of making a mess was not in the job description of any organized crook.

That The Voice had sent one of his own people to 'help' didn't make Dolan feel any better. He'd never admit it but that creep scared the crap out of him. Not even the fact that he owed his promotion to the guy's weird power helped. He hadn't liked Mickey much but Dean had been a friend. Seeing the two writhing in pain behind the unmoving plaster of Crogan's office wall was enough to sicken anyone.

Glancing towards the big office at the center of the room, Dolan saw The Voice's man doing something involving lights and smoke. Dressed in an evening suit, his face concealed behind a mask, he looked like Mandrake the Magician. Whatever he was doing, though, was very real and terrifying. Dolan was an unimaginative sort but he could feel the force of the energies the man wielded.

So distracted was Dolan by what he saw that he didn't notice the intruder until it was too late. He turned back to his task, only to find himself face to face with a painted red mask whose lips suddenly and impossibly moved in a dangerous grin. "If you make a mess," Tiger said cheerfully, "you should clean it up."

Dolan's gun was in his hand before he'd even thought about it, the trigger pulled a moment later. Not that it did any good. Tiger was too fast. He caught hold of Dolan's wrist and knocked it sideways, so that the bullet hit the wall instead of its intended target. At the same time, Tiger's other hand came up, palm first, and struck Dolan in the base of his jaw. The gun went flying, skittering off out of sight.

Partially stunned, Dolan stumbled backwards, knocking a chair over and slamming into a lamp. As it shattered on the ground, he barely managed to evade Tiger's kick. Somehow, he got himself into position and swung back, his fist connecting with Tiger's raised arm.

They traded several rapid blows, Dolan regaining his equilibrium enough to get a few good punches in. In the end, though, Tiger was faster and better at what he did, twisting and evading with strikes that Dolan regarded as entirely unfair.

Dolan was just about down when The Voice's man joined the fight in his own terrifying way. Streams of black smoke roiled out from the man, stretching out like dozens of arms or tentacles, all trying to catch hold of Tiger. They failed, because as soon as the masked man realized he was in danger, he started moving faster, leaping over and under desks as he evaded The Voice's man.

If he wasn't sure The Voice would find out he'd done a runner, Dolan would have left the two to their own devices. Instead, he searched for his gun and found it stuck beneath the radiator by the window. He rushed to the wall and stuck his hand under the rough metal and was enveloped in a small cloud of dust as he pulled his weapon out.

This time, he promised himself, Tiger wouldn't stop him from firing. Turning to face the two, he realized that The Voice's man was closely engaged with their enemy. As he weighed the possibilities he wondered if it would be worth it to shoot the creep, just to get back at The Voice for what he'd had done.

As Dolan waffled over what he was going to do, his choice was taken from him as the door to the newsroom was flung open and four cops came running in. One, he recognized immediately because every crook in town knew Jack Maloney. The two younger ones he'd never seen before. As for the last, even if he didn't know the man's face, he recognized the uniform of the Chief of Police.

That tore it. Outnumbered and out-armed, the last thing Dolan wanted was to stick around. Maloney knew him as well as he knew Maloney and there was nothing he could say to make his presence in the emptied newsroom look good. Taking advantage of the fact that the four cops were busy trying to figure out how to stop the fight in front of them, Dolan dropped behind some desks and started towards another door.

《《《

Michaels would have been happy to never find himself in this sort of situation again. Mysterious Masked Vigilantes were bad enough. The sort that ended up in fights with people using what looked like magic to him were even worse. What was the probability of someone releasing some ancient demon to wander the streets of Strikers Port eating whatever suited its fancy?

Realizing his men were looking to him for guidance, Michaels sighed. "Right. Spread out. Don't let that guy with the smoke touch you."

The man who Michaels was pretty sure was called Tiger called out, "No guns. You'll just make it angry."

"It?" Michaels repeated. "It isn't human?"

"Don't think so. No pulse. No breath." The Tiger rolled out of the way again. "Probably not alive. Not a shadow, either."

Although Michaels had no idea what the Tiger meant, he decided not to ask. Somehow he knew he wouldn't get a straight answer. "What can we do?"

"There's something on its neck. I think it's a control device. If I can get behind it, I can break it with my claw" He leapt again, colliding with Officer Jarvis and dragged the kid out of the way. "Oops. Sorry. Get back further. Do NOT let it touch you."

Michaels considered their options. He could just let this fight continue until Tiger was too worn out to escape, but he was pretty sure the thing meant to kill. Distrusting Tiger's ilk though he did, something told him this creature was the worse danger. There was no guaranteeing it would stop with Tiger.

"Right," Michaels said. "How do we get its attention?"

"Noise, I think. Give it something to chase. Just half a minute. I need to get into the right position to hit it."

All three of his men looked at Michaels and, at his nod, headed for different corners of the room. As they all started yelling and hitting the walls together, the thing came to a halt towards the middle, searching around deciding which way to go. Michaels held his breath, prepared to start yelling himself and even run towards the thing if it looked like it was getting too close to his people.

As the creature moved towards William, Tiger leapt for the ceiling, clinging there by one hand. At the same time a set of metallic claws, just an inch long, jutted from his fingers and began to spark. He leapt for the creature's back in a spinning attack that landed him in just the right place to swipe his clawed fingers across the nape of its neck.

There was a screech like fingernails on a chalkboard, then Tiger pushed off from the thing's body, sending himself flying back against an outside wall. The thing began flailing wildly, twisting and turning, fighting itself and losing, stumbling backwards and forwards against desks and chairs. Typewriters crashed to the ground and papers caught fire as it struck them.

A movement caught Michaels' eye and he looked to see a man staring at the creature with wide eyes. Then, with a look of triumphant fury, the man raised a gun and fired it straight into the middle of the thing's forehead. "That's for Dean, you bastard!" he shouted.

"Dolan?" Maloney demanded, as the creature turned towards its attacker. "What the hell are you doing here?"

Maloney's question went unanswered. The creature might have been losing power, might have fallen any minute, but it had just enough energy to launch itself on the man called Dolan and slam him into the wall. Michaels choked as he realized that 'into' was all too literal. Screaming all the way, Dolan was shoved backwards, twisting and writhing as he merged with the surface behind him until only part of his face remained free.

As the creature collapsed, Officer Jackson started forward but Tiger shouted, "Stay back. It's going to blow."

He was right, too, for as Jackson got within ten feet of the thing the body began to smoke and twist. A moment later a cloud of ash filled the room. Everyone except the Tiger began choking and Michaels heard a window open nearby.

Instinctively, Michaels pulled open another window and stuck his head out. As he'd thought, Tiger was crouched on the windowsill, looking down at the crowd. His expression under the mask was almost unreadable but Michaels sensed a grin nonetheless. "An audience! How nice."

"Don't do it!"

"Sorry, Chief. I can't stay. Too many things to do and too many places to go. Ta ta." Tiger saluted him cheerfully and leapt across the street, black long-coat flaring around him as he swung around on a nearby flagpole and disappeared over a rooftop before Michaels could say another word.

When the smoke cleared enough for him to look, Michaels found that the only real casualty was Dolan. Looking at the man embedded in the plaster, body twisting and struggling against the surface and completely unable to break free, Michaels shook his head. "What the hell are we going to do with this moron?" he wondered aloud.

"Don't know, sir. But I don't think Miss Trendle is going to want to leave him here. Maybe we can chip him out?"

Michaels didn't think it would be that easy. "Jackson, go check on McLeod. If he's done, bring him here and see if he has any ideas. Maloney, tell Miss Trendle everything's all right. Jarvis? I think I'm going to want you to talk to Mr. Chang now. And remember, wash up and dress nice. Chinese or not, Chang's one of the richest men in town. It wouldn't do to look like you've been dragged through an ash pit."

Officer Jarvis was smart enough not to say that that was pretty close to the literal truth.

〈〈〈

William's best clothes were more suitable for a funeral than anything else, but they were also his only good clothing. As he left his rooms over his father's boxing club, he also regretted that he didn't have a choice but to be seen all kitted out. Whistles and catcalls followed him as he walked through the open space, ripe with the odor of sweat and echoing with the pounding of fists against leather.

Ignoring the boxers, he walked out the front door, intending to catch a cab, only to find a squad car waiting for him. Maloney grinned at him. "I figured you'd rather not walk to Chang's. You'd get your pretty dress all dirty."

Getting in, because he knew Maloney would make a scene if he didn't, William muttered, "Very funny."

"You clean up good. Look more like a D.A. than a cop. Must come from your mum's side. Your dad's one ugly S.O.B. and always was."

William just shrugged, watching the scenery go by and wondering how, exactly, he was going to persuade Mr. Chang that his daughter was in trouble. He couldn't help asking, "What do I say?"

Rather to his surprise, Maloney took the question seriously. "Honestly, best I can offer is to talk straight. Won't be easy, them Chinee don't think that way. But that Mudan chick is Chang's only daughter. He won't like it if someone's targeting her."

They'd driven into Chinatown by this time, becoming the target of dozens of dark, incurious, eyes. It was rare for police to visit this part of town and rare for it not to mean some sort of trouble. As the car rolled up to a halt in front of what was the closest thing to being Chinatown's town-hall, William hoped that his appearance would ease suspicions.

Or, he thought ruefully as he climbed out of the car, perhaps his appearance made things worse. Before he'd taken a step towards the town-hall's courtyard, a dozen or so young men appeared silently to stand between him and the building's big red doors. Each and every one of them, from the skinny fellow who kept sniffing as if he had allergies to the muscular fellow leaning against the wall with his arms folded and a confident sneer, looked forbiddingly unwelcoming.

The tallest Chinese William had ever seen opened the doors and gazed down at him seriously. "None of your laws have been broken here," he said. "Please leave." He had strong smooth features and a composed look that put William in mind of a knight from one of his mother's fairy tale books.

"I'm sorry," William apologized, "But I've been asked to come and speak with Mr. Chang. Could you please tell him the grandson of Wagner Krane is here?"

"Mr. Krane is long since dead," the man told William. "There is no reason that would convince Mr. Chang that you are worthy enough to interrupt his work."

"Now you see here...."

Before Maloney could get another word out, William spun on his heel, put his hand in front of his senior partner's mouth and hissed, "Don't!" He didn't know much about the Chinese, but he did know that blustering and threatening an obvious gang was a bad idea. "Go back to the car!"

Maloney glared at him and looked about to fight, but that was when a voice called from one of the upper windows of the building. "Tan. Bring them here. I will not have a war in my front yard." It was a pleasant sounding voice, with a light humorous quaver to it that William recognized immediately. The grammar was infinitely better, but he sounded like his grandson.

The inside of the building was attractively and simply furnished. Its walls were covered in textured red wallpaper and framed with dark wood panels from which various instruments and weapons hung. An interesting scent, flowery yet smoky at the same time, filled the air. Somewhere in the distance William could hear a flute playing and water flowing.

Tan moved too quickly for William to spend much time sightseeing and after a quick climb up heavily lacquered steps, they found themselves in a large and splendidly decorated study. A desk three times the size of the one in Chief Michaels office and ten times as ornate stood at the other end.

"So you are Gwendolyn's son." The speaker drew William's attention to the man behind the desk. Relatively small and slight, he seemed incapable of hurting anything bigger than a fly. He had pleasantly wrinkled features and the sort of smile that could only be described as infectiously inoffensive. "I was sorry to hear of her death."

Inclining his head, William said, "You sent flowers, I remember. Thank you."

"They did not find...."

Before Mr. Chang could finish his sentence, William shook his head. They might never know what brought his mother up in the old logging camp, nor how she and his uncle came to be trapped in a burning building, but neither did he want to discuss it.

"I see. Well, it is a thing I hope is avenged one day. But you did not come to see an old man you hardly know to discuss the past. If I am correct, you are now an officer of the law. I do hope you have not come in your official capacity. That seldom bodes well."

"What other way would we.... *oof*!" Maloney demanded, then broke off as William put the heel of his shoe down on his toes. "Hey!"

"Mr. Chang, I apologize for interrupting your work." When Chang leaned back, putting his fingers together in a listening pose, William continued, "You know what happened at the Jeen Loon last night."

A smile. "That is a statement and not a question because you know I know," the old man said, clearly amused. "You are a very bright young man, but not the sort to play word games. What, pray tell, does a robbery in Chinatown have to do with anything outside our sheltered walls?"

"Chief Michaels is concerned that the Jeen Loon is being targeted. Since you're its owner...."

Chang interrupted, "My daughter owns the shop now," he corrected. "I receive a stipend from the place but am no longer in charge of its operations. Nor does she disturb me with her troubles, being a filial child in all cases but her choice of husband."

Maloney snorted and might have said something but for the glare William gave him. "Your daughter, then, is being targeted. From what my Chief told me, he thinks that a man named Crogan...."

Raising a hand, Chang stopped William again. "Crogan? The owner of High Risk Insurance?" His eyes narrowed.

"I think so, yes."

"Yet can you prove it? Can you bring him in? Can you stop him?" Chang spread his hands broadly, "I keep myself informed of what happens in the world outside Chinatown's walls. I am aware that the man called Crogan, and several others of his ilk, has a way of evading arrest. That he has managed to keep his crimes well hidden. Forgive me if I say that it is hard to trust that your police can do anything in this matter that cannot be done by others. Especially where Chinatown is involved."

Although he knew Chang was right on that count, William answered, "Chinatown is part of Strikers Port, though. It does concern us when a crook like Crogan is targeting law-abiding citizens...."

"Yeah, you are law-abidin' right?"

Chang, his assistant, Tan, and William all turned and looked at Maloney. Then, as if he hadn't spoken at all, William continued, "Especially when it looks like another, new, gang might be poking its fingers into the pie. Or should I say claws?"

Chang's eyebrows shot up with surprise. "Claws?"

"Perhaps no one has mentioned to you that there was another party involved with last night's break-in. A man wearing a painted mask who calls himself one of the Claws of the Golden Dragon." William cocked his head at the older man questioningly. "He and his partner have been challenging Crogan's territory for the past few months. We think it may be a new Tong."

Both Chang and Tan went completely still and a strange expression crossed Chang's lined features. Then, very calmly, Chang said, "Claws of the Golden Dragon?" When William nodded, he continued, "They sound like outsiders with an interest in things Chinese. Have you ever heard of a Tong that did not have a true Chinese name?"

"No," William admitted. "I haven't." Not even the group of businessmen who were Chinatown's official leaders used an English name. What was it they were called? *Pu Gway Ren She Way.* A more exotic and mysterious name than "Railway Workers Association", at least.

"Well then, I assure you, Officer Jarvis, I have heard nothing of these Claws until now. Unless you believe someone here is involved, I suggest you search elsewhere for them." Suddenly he smiled, a broad, friendly smile that somehow failed to make William feel any better. "They certainly are not going to cause trouble for me or mine."

《《《

Francis gazed at the man stuck in her newsroom wall and hoped she wouldn't be sick. She'd never seen such a thing in her life. Dead bodies, what few she'd encountered, were easier to look at. They remained still and silent. This man was neither. Mostly embedded in the plaster wall, his body twisted and writhed beneath the surface, so that the solid wall appeared to move with him. Worse, though, was that half of his face protruded, allowing him to moan and beg for help.

"How could this happen?" she asked Chief Michaels. "Can we get him out?"

"How? I've no more idea than you, Miss Trendle. I've seen some weird stuff in my life, but this one takes the cake." The Chief shook his head. "As for getting him out? I've sent for tools. We'll try chipping him out first."

"I wouldn't." The speaker was the elder McLeod, his hair covered in cobwebs and dust, and his hands having acquired several more dings in the course of whatever he'd been doing down in the basement. "That looks like a phase shift of some sort."

"It might be a dimensional rift," Robby McLeod added, carrying two paper cups as he approached, one of which he handed to his father. "Have a grape nehi. Was there a bomb, by the way?"

"Not unless bombs are usually made out of plywood and black paint," Mr. McLeod said. "And have you ever seen a dimensional rift that behaves like this?"

Robby shrugged. "I've never seen a dimensional rift, Dad. You wouldn't let me build the device, remember?"

Francis and Chief Michaels looked at each other and while Francis wanted to know, the man stuck in the wall was more important. "That's fascinating, or would be, if I understood, but could you two gentlemen please stay focused on how to get this man out of here?"

A barking dog interrupted the two men before they could offer suggestions and Francis realized Rosamund had joined them, which meant Boopsie was there too. The dog didn't like what he was looking at, either, barking and lunging furiously at the man in the newsroom wall. "Oh my!" Rosamund said. "I don't like what your decorator's done to this place, Franky."

Keeping her temper, under the circumstances, was an effort. "Rose. Take your dog and go home. We can chat, gossip, whatever, later. But I have to deal with this mess and I can't concentrate...."

The wolfhound broke free of Rosamund's grip, leaping for his enemy with a snarl ill-befitting any animal named Boopsie. Putting his forepaws against the wall, he tried to catch hold of the man's throat, arched in just the right position to be ripped open.

Before anyone else could react, Robby stepped forward and caught hold of Boopsie's collar. "No," he said sternly. "Bad dog. Don't kill the nice crook. Chief Michaels will want him to talk."

For a moment Francis was sure the dog would snap in Robby's face but something changed in its attitude suddenly. Had it been any other animal, she'd think it was afraid of the young man. Certainly it dropped to all fours and hunched its neck as if embarrassed. "Good boy," Robby said, coaxing the animal back to its owner and offering her the end of its leash. "Here you are, Miss Krane. Best take him away soon, I think."

Rosamund took the leash back, wrapping it around her wrist and impatiently pulling her dog back to her side. "Well, if I'm in the way, I'll just leave," she snapped. "I don't like the company you're keeping, anyway."

"Call me later, if you like," Francis told her, more to be polite than anything else. Truth to tell, she'd have been happier not to deal with Rosamund at all.

Once Rosamund had left, her dog glancing back in an embarrassed sort of way as they walked out of the ruined room, Francis turned her attention back to the wall and stared. "Is that blood?"

"I'm afraid it is," Chief Michaels said, using a handkerchief to dab at trickles of red liquid seeping from the places where Boopsie's claws had scored the wall. The man himself was writing more desperately now and his muffled voice was panicked and horrified. "I don't think we're getting the bastard... pardon me French, Miss... free of this any time soon."

Francis didn't like that at all. "Can't we get him out of here at least?"

"Robby, go into the room on the other side. See if you can see anything," McLeod said suddenly and as his son started moving, added, "Quickly, please. More quickly than that."

It took several iterations before Robby's lackadaisical pace picked up, but once he'd gone through the door and come back to report that he'd seen no sign of the man on the other side, McLeod said, "All right. It'll mean putting a hole in the wall but I think that - if we're careful - we can cut around this man and get him out of here."

"That won't get him out of the wall, though, Chief Michaels," Robby added. "That'll take figuring out how he's stuck in there." From his tone, Francis thought he was looking forward to the challenge.

For lack of a better idea, both Francis and the Chief agreed. "We'll take him to the jail for safekeeping."

"Our equipment's at the shop," Robby argued. "Shouldn't we...."

"What will your mother say to our bringing that home?" McLeod asked, pointedly. "I wouldn't take him to the jail, Chief. Whatever we do to get him out will need a bigger place for our equipment and it might be dangerous."

"Maybe the old train yard," Francis suggested. "It hasn't been used since we moved operations closer to the port." Not only was it out of the way, having been built to service the now defunct goldmine, but it was also her property. Which meant she'd have a chance at finding out what was going on. "I can have someone open the warehouse for you.

Lacking a better plan, Chief Michaels agreed.

ᕲᕲᕲ

Crogan growled a curse and shattered his whiskey glass in the fireplace, the alcohol flaring brilliantly. "GODDAMN IT TO HELL AND BACK!" He wasn't worried that anyone would notice his fit of temper. It was mid-afternoon and the bar was practically empty. Besides, he owned the joint and if he wanted to rip it up by its floorboards he damned well would. He had good reason to be furious. The Voice had lost him yet another good man. Well, for varying definitions of good. But he needed Dolan, damnit!

"Well, that's a waste of a good drink," a voice said from behind him. It was a harsh voice, with an underlying grate that made Crogan spin around quickly. Spotting the speaker, though, he realized with relief it was just Old Uncle Gilly, starting his evening of drinking and carousing a little earlier than usual. It'd been the timber of his voice, and the abrasive bite, that had fooled Crogan into thinking The Voice had found him.

"It's Barton's hooch," Crogan told the man. "Not exactly quality stuff. Which is why we sell it here, and not down at O'Malley's." He glanced over the skinny, ill-dressed frame, trying to think why the man was called 'Old' anything. His too-long hair might be ill-kempt and shaggy, but it was as dark as a young man's. For that matter, his tanned skin - though dirty and smudged - was smooth, as if he'd never seen a day of work in his life.

Then the man raised his face and his eyes met Crogan's. Intensely black, there seemed to be a fire burning down in the depths like ancient pits of hell. Frightened despite himself, Crogan looked away and Old Uncle laughed, a harsh, terrible, laugh that mocked itself as much as those around it. "It's got alcohol in it. Isn't that enough?"

"For getting drunk, yeah." Crogan sighed. He wanted to be doing just that, but he knew only too well what happened to gangsters who lost control of themselves. "Given you don't care what happens to your liver."

Another laugh. "Been drinking the stuff for more years than I care to count. Still have the same internal organs I started with."

Crogan wanted to say Old Uncle was one of the lucky ones, but something made him hold his tongue. Whatever it was that made Old Uncle spend every free hour he had sitting at the bar sucking down whatever alcohol he could afford wasn't something Crogan wanted to know about.

Instead, Crogan reached over the bar and poured himself another drink, glad of the distraction of someone to talk to, even if that someone was a drunkard with terrifying eyes and an insatiable capacity for alcohol. "I don't think I've ever heard you talk before."

"You've never threw a perfectly good glass of whiskey into the fire, either," Old Uncle pointed out. "Now, you may call me nosy, but that's unlike you."

Crogan wasn't at all sure why, but he found himself expressing every last detail of his troubles. From the sudden interference in his affairs by a pair of would-be crooks, to The Voice and his demands. That last, especially, was something he'd later wonder at. The Voice had ordered his plans kept secret, yet there Crogan was, spilling every last bean he had to a man he barely knew.

Right then, all he could think was that here was an ear that he could tell things to without worrying about his cowardice being found out. And cowardice it was. The Voice ought never have been able to strong-arm him, Perry Crogan, into cooperating. "I'm losing my best men and I'm not getting anything to show for it," he complained. "If I knew where he was, I swear I'd find him and mute him permanently."

"Seems a tricky proposition. Finding him probably isn't that hard. Dealing with something that can stick men into walls? Troublesome. Unless you find yourself someone able to fight that sort of thing."

It occurred to Crogan that that problem might not be quite as big as he'd thought before. "Wait," he said. "Maybe I don't need to worry about it."

"Eh?"

"It wasn't The Voice who put my men in the walls. It was his man. The one that got killed, or whatever, at the Sentinel today." A sudden euphoric feeling swept over Crogan. "Yeah. That's right. The Voice doesn't have a way to stop me anymore. All I have to do is figure out where he's been calling from and I can set a trap!"

Those terrifying eyes raised and met Crogan's again, the fire in their depths burning hotter. But Crogan was so excited at the thought that he'd found a way out of his predicament that he barely noticed. "It's a little early to make assumptions," Old Uncle said. "You don't know how it was done."

"No. The Voice would have done my men in himself if he could. It would have been the best way to prove he was dangerous." Crogan got to his feet and headed for the door. He'd have to set something up at the phone company, use someone on the inside to run a trace. Then The Voice would call. And that would be his undoing. "Thanks for listening, Old Uncle. I'm off."

Behind Crogan, Old Uncle slowly rose to his feet and went to the fire blazing in the fireplace. Glancing at the bartender, who shrugged indifferently, he reached into the flames and fished out the glass of whiskey. "Humans," he said dourly. "They never bother to think. And they never, ever, listen to what they don't want to hear." Blowing out the flames burning at the top of the liquid, he drained the shot glass dry. "Another one, barkeep. And keep them coming. It's going to be a long night and it looks like I have my work cut out for me."

⊂⊂⊂

"So Chang's a no go, huh?" Chief Michaels couldn't say he was surprised. He didn't deal with the old man often but the one thing he'd learned was that Cheh Chang's idea of cooperation would make a Missouri mule look docile. "Don't look that way. It's not your fault."

William was unsettled but Michaels ignored him, looking out his window at Gold Dust River. Scanning the few small boats sailing up and down and out into the bay he reflected that it looked deceptively peaceful. The city below him and the broad expanse of newer and richer houses on the hill across the river had a picture book appearance. The mysteries beneath the surface had remained hidden and half-forgotten for so long that he'd been sure they'd never have to deal with their like again. Yet here they were.

With a sigh, Michaels turned back to face his officer. "What did he say about the Claws?"

"That he didn't know who they were and that they weren't from Chinatown." William looked thoughtful, adding, "He was surprised, but I think the name meant something. He said they weren't from Chinatown. That it was more likely someone from outside with an interest in things Chinese."

No surprise Chang denied everything. "Anything else?"

"I'm not sure, sir. But I'm afraid telling him about the Claws might have started more trouble. He might set his men on them if they show up in Chinatown again."

Michaels felt a mean-spirited desire for that to be the case. He knew Chang wouldn't send his Tong out of Chinatown but neither would he put up with outsiders interfering with his people's peace and safety. To be honest, he'd sort of hoped for that result when he'd sent William over. The trouble was, a Tong war in Chinatown might spill over into the rest of the city and if it did, he'd only have himself to blame.

Setting that thought aside, Michaels said, "Well, never mind that, Jarvis. I appreciate your going, nonetheless."

William rose, obviously expecting that he should go back to work. "Thank you, sir."

"I'm not done. Sit down."

Puzzled, William obeyed. "Should Maloney be here?" he asked, with admirable loyalty to his partner.

"No." Maloney was a good man but he was a devout and narrow-minded. This wasn't the sort of thing he was going to understand or accept. Michaels didn't want to spend the next few hours trying to get past the man's prejudices. Even William was going to have trouble with this one. "You saw Dolan earlier. Do you think that looked remotely normal?"

"Normal? No. But Mr. McLeod said...."

"I know," Michaels snapped, then stopped himself. "McLeod might be right. The whole thing might be some new devilish device. God knows there's enough out there. But there's another thing it could be and that's what I need to find out."

With a frown, William asked, "What else could it be?"

"Magic. Sorcery. Some dark art or old devil coming out of the woodwork." At the young man's disbelieving stare, Michaels sighed. "Lad, I'm taking you to meet someone but before I do, I need you to have an open mind. She doesn't like humans much as it is."

"I don't understand."

"Of course not." Michaels reflected that he wished he didn't understand either. "Look. Your mother was a Krane. She grew up here in Strikers Port. Did she tell you any old stories?" Too late, he remembered that Gwendolyn Jarvis, nee Krane, had been killed in a mysterious accident up at the family's old logging mill.

The young man's eyes went bleak. "My mother died when I was five." His voice softened and he added, "I suppose she did tell me some old stories when I was little. But what could they have to do with all this? They were just stories."

What indeed. Some of the old stories were the sort Michaels hoped weren't real. The Bone Marrow Sucker, for one. Others he'd seen himself; the gang of coyotes who acted more like men; the ghosts in the Striker mine camp; the train that replayed its destruction on Sidewinder Hill every August; the Black Beast.... And, of course, Her. "Some probably are," he agreed. "But I've seen things, here and down in San Francisco, that'd turn your blood cold. I'm needing to know if the thing we met at the Sentinel was one of those sort. I need an expert."

William looked doubtful, but was smart enough not to argue with his Chief, simply asking, "But why tell me about this at all? Even if it's true, I'm just a rookie."

"Instinct," Michaels told him. "I've learned to trust them and they're saying you'll be useful." At the look of disbelief on the kid's face, he added, "Besides, you've got a good head on your shoulders and a flexible way of thinking. You'll be needing that."

There was still doubt in William's eyes, but he agreed. "I don't pretend to understand, but I'll do what you say, sir."

"Good. Get an overnight bag. We're headed to Jewel Island to increase your worldview." Michaels glanced at the kid's feet and added, "Wear tennis shoes. There are no streets where we're going."

《《《

"LAD, I'M TAKING YOU TO MEET SOMEONE BUT BEFORE
I DO, I NEED YOU TO HAVE AN OPEN MIND."

The ferry landed at Jewel Island just short of sunset. It was postcard weather, with streaks of bright orange clouds crossing the sky and the pines and oaks of the island gleaming softly in the light. The small village around the port had an unreal appearance to William, like a Currier and Ives print brought it to life. It was too neat, too clean and too well lit.

Of course, Jewel Island's only source of income was tourism, so it looked the part. It was just that William couldn't feel comfortable in such carefully groomed surroundings. Not having grown up in the seedier part of town.

Realizing Michaels was far ahead of him, William followed quickly. To his surprise, the Chief got in the short line for bike rentals. He'd expected Michaels to borrow a car from the local police. At least neither were in uniform. It would have looked odd, he thought.

The island was barely two miles from side to side and the path around its edges was only about five miles at best. With a well paved bike path and good bikes, it was easy to reach the lighthouse on the western side of the island long before the sun had reached the horizon.

There were a few people looking over the lighthouse when they arrived. "We'll wait until they're gone, then go down there," Michaels told William as they parked their bikes.

That didn't make William feel better about their field trip. He was beginning to wonder if his Chief was going insane. All this talk of magic and monsters made him feel terribly uncomfortable. Climbing down to the rocky beach below the lighthouse, where any slip might drop them straight into the ocean, didn't help. Still, he forbore arguing, glad he'd obeyed Michaels' order to wear tennis shoes. Waiting with the older man, William watched the sunset, waiting for that moment when the light would shift to green, then disappear.

The sound of voices from above, a man and woman murmuring to each other as they made their way back to their bikes, slowly faded. At least, all that could be heard were frogs and some sort of insect. "All right," Michaels said, pulling out his flashlight and using it to scan the stone base of the lighthouse. "This way."

They made their way around the edge of the lighthouse base to a rocky area with a "Keep out" sign. Michaels climbed down past it until they reached a curtain of soaking wet seaweed. When he pushed it aside to reveal a narrow seeming crack in the wall, William protested, "We're going in there?"

"Don't worry. It's what's inside you should be afraid of." Michaels entered a carved out passage that led into the darkness. Ahead, William could hear the faint sound of water lapping against stone.

They stepped into an open chamber with a domed ceiling and a small pool at its center. A figure was there already and for a moment William wondered if this was the 'Her' Michaels meant them to meet. Then he recognized the black coat and the blue and silver mask. This was the Claw he'd met the night before.

Michaels came to a dead halt as he stared at the masked man. "Oh for the love of Pete."

"I don't know anyone by that name, Chief Michaels. But you can call me Dragon, if you'd like."

"I'd rather call you arrested," Michaels snapped. "If I had anything to arrest you for. What are you doing here?"

A voice spoke, one that echoed through the chamber in a curious, sibilant way. "The little one came to pay his respects, like any good Sorcerer should in my territory. The real question is, why are you here? Did you bring me this one for tribute?"

William swallowed; because the source of the voice was what he'd initially thought was just a peculiar rock formation sticking out of the water. It moved when it spoke and he realized it was a huge octopus resting against a large piece of timber. Remembering what the Chief had said about showing fear he answered calmly, "I sincerely hope not, Ma'am."

"Oh. The boy has manners." The creature, whatever she was, turned her attention on William in a way that made him feel distinctly like its... no, her... next meal. "More manners than his ancestor, that's for certain. And certainly more than you, my lad. Did you even remember to bring me something?"

Bowing, Michaels simply said, "Apologies, Ma'am, for the intrusion. If it makes you feel better, I've a fine package of the best livers at the market for you. I remember you liked them."

A tentacle reached out and took the package he offered with a delicate motion that put William in mind of his cousin drinking tea, with her pinky carefully extended. "Ah. Yes, I do indeed appreciate the gift. One doesn't get land meat very often down here and I do need to keep up my strength for my eggs." The octopus waved another tentacle at the masked man, adding, "His gift was better, but none can beat Uncle Ip's for seafood."

"Fried fish balls," Dragon said, grinning beneath his mask. "Finest kind."

Just as William was wondering if the conversation were going to continue on this strangely banal track, the octopus turned her attention back on Michaels. "Now I've already answered this lad's question, so I'm presuming you, too, have something to ask. No one comes here just to visit."

Michaels coughed. "I admit it," he agreed. "I am here for answers, if you're willing to share them."

"Then ask away. But remember, my dear mortal that you only get one question per visit and I don't like wasting my time."

Michaels took a deep breath, "The last time I was here, Old Smoky was creating a ruckus in town. You gave us a clue how to deal with him and it worked. We thought he was gone for good. But we just fought something blowing smoke like a chimney stack and doing things no human can. Is he back?"

The octopus tore open the package of meat and began sucking down the livers with what Williams could only describe as a thoughtful air. Another tentacle pulled a ball of something fried from another package and she ate it as well. Then, very slowly, she said, "Old Smoky, huh? You thought he was gone? You really thought that one could die?"

"I didn't think he'd stop of his own."

"You still don't understand what he is. He never died. He never left. He just... changed." Several tentacles moved in what William guessed was a shrug. "But that's not the question you really want answered, now is it?"

Michaels bit his lip. "If it wasn't, I'm too late to ask the right one."

"Wise child. Every so often you humans surprise me. And, because you've brought me something particularly special, and remembered your manners properly, I'll give you two things. One, Old Smoky still lives, burning inside for things he cannot have. Two, this one asked the right question and if you're nice to him, he might, maybe, tell you the answer."

With that, the octopus slid down into the water and disappeared, leaving Michaels and William to turn their eyes on Dragon.

"Well, now. I suppose I could be rude and just float off," the young man said, grinning broadly. "But I might have to call in a favor in the future. So what she told me was that the thing my partner fought belongs to both the old world and the new. Which, unless I miss my guess, means someone may have figured out how to use magic and technology together. If that's true, we'll need both to fight it."

(((

Francis sighed as she entered her driveway. She'd had a long day going over the damages to her newsroom and deciding what could be salvaged and what would have to be thrown away. One of the biggest disadvantages a woman faced in the business world were the men convinced she was too stupid to understand when the wool was being pulled over her eyes.

Of course, the flip-side of that coin was that she could fall back on the reliable "I'll have to talk to my father" line, rather than be browbeaten into agreeing to repairs that would cost less if she'd been a man. That her father was more interested in his sailboat was something they didn't need to know.

There was one bright spot in the mess. It'd taken hours but tomorrow's paper had been put together and edited in what she considered record time. Even now, the printers were churning out the news. Scanlon had promised to stay with the job all night if necessary, to make sure the Strikers Port Sentinel was out and ready at the appointed time. "The Sentinel hasn't been late with a printing in all its sixty years," he'd said. "I'm damned if I'm going to let it happen on my watch."

Telling her chauffeur he was free for the evening, Francis headed for the door and noticed a long pink limo in the guest parking space. She recognized it immediately and wondered where the driver, James, had gone. It wasn't like him to leave the car like that. She hoped Rosamund wouldn't find out.

After a quick glance around the yard, Francis shrugged and went inside. To her surprise, her butler, Gordon, wasn't there to meet her. Puzzled by his absence, Francis went into the sitting room to find Rosamund sitting on the couch and teaching Boopsie to fetch.

Neither Rosamund's occupation, nor her choice of ball, surprised Francis. Long experience had taught her that Rosamund had little comprehension of other people's property. Naturally she'd think an antique nested wooden ball an appropriate dog toy. Fortunately, Boopsie didn't agree. His huge jaws would have destroyed the delicate object if he'd agreed to pick it up.

"Really, Rosamund," Francis said, catching the ball as it rolled in her direction. "Don't you have anything better to do?"

"She wants to know if I have anything better to do, Boopsie. Whatever would I have to do? Timothy takes care of everything for me." Timothy Rancourt was the Krane family's butler, a quiet old man whose skill at his job was legendary in Strikers Port. He was what other butlers aspired to be, as far as Francis could tell.

Sighing, Francis poured herself a drink. Based on how little scotch was left in the bottle, she suspected Rosamund had had quite enough already.

"Is there a reason you're here, or are you just bored? And please don't answer my question by talking to Boopsie."

Wide blue eyes met Francis'. "Oh, but Boopsie likes it when I talk to him. Don't you, Boopsie?"

Francis wasn't so sure. The poor animal usually looked sadly put-upon and long-suffering to her. "He might like it, but I don't. I've had a long day and I am not in the mood."

"If you insist." Rosamund used her special glove to pat her dog. "It is boring at home, I admit, but that's not why I'm here. I came because you still haven't sent an RSVP to the society for the charity ball."

Francis took a moment to remember the invitation from the Gold Dust Philanthropic Society. It'd been addressed to her home, not her office, and had been phrased as an invitation to the Trendle Heiress, rather than the Editor-in-Chief of the Strikers Port Sentinel. "I don't know," Francis told her guest. "I don't enjoy large parties."

"Oh, but my baby brother would be so happy if you came."

Considering Peter a reason to avoid any function he graced, Francis said, "Why? He and I don't get along." Peter didn't like the fact that Francis had taken over the Sentinel and she didn't like him because he was a selfish, lazy and self-absorbed bully. Too, he was seven years her junior. Even if she were interested in marriage, he was too young for her.

"But he asked me to invite you." Seeing no sign of Francis changing her mind, Rosamund tried another tack. "The publicity for the charity would help us so much."

The doorbell rang and Francis stopped Rosamund. "Just a moment. I'm going to tell Gordon that I'd rather not have any more callers." She stepped to the sitting room door and looked out, expecting to find her butler headed down the hall to the front door. "Gordon? Where are you?"

The doorbell rang again and Francis sighed. "All right. I'm coming." Gordon would disapprove, but she went to the door to open it and found herself staring up at Robby McLeod's genial features. "Mr. McLeod?"

"Call me Robby. You asked Dad for an estimate on repairs, remember? I have it here." The young man held up a sheaf of papers. "It's not going to be cheap, especially with the damage to the printers, but I think it's a good deal."

Francis hesitated. She was tired of talking business but Robby's presence gave her the excuse she needed to get Rosamund to go away. "Come in," she said finally. "Show me what you mean."

As they walked back down the hallway, Robby continued, "Dad looked at your printers while he was there and he thinks they could be made more efficient. But that's a separate item on the list because he knew you would want to worry about repairs first. There's the wall, which we thought could be improved with a window and a remote controlled shutter for privacy. A fair number of your typewriters are ruined, too. My brother will have to handle that side. Dad and I are better at the big stuff. Chou can make them look like new and work better."

Wondering if Robby ever stopped to breathe, Francis paused at the sitting room door. "Let me tell my guest that I'm going to be busy." She opened the door and gasped. Rosamund was slumped on the sitting room floor, her dog beside her. "Oh my God!"

She and Robby rushed to the woman's side. Much to Francis' relief, Rosamund was breathing steadily. She did not, however, react to Francis' touch. Neither, when Francis shook him, did Boopsie. "What happened?"

"Just a little sleep gas," a voice said from behind Francis. "I try not to kill members of High Society. Too much legal attention." The speaker was a tall man wearing a kerchief over his face and a broad-rimmed hat. His eyes were hard beneath the rim, promising trouble. "Neither of you move an inch. And don't talk, either, McLeod."

"Of course he won't," Francis said, giving the young man a sharp look. He'd been tensed in a way that said he meant to attack any minute, but at her warning, he relaxed slightly. "You have the upper hand, after all."

"Good. Now get up against the wall. I have things to ask you."

"My father keeps the key to the safe on him," Francis answered immediately. "But there's plenty of other things you could take."

"Oh, I can see that." The man picked up a pretty little Dresden china doll from the mantel, then set it down carefully. "But that's not what I want."

Francis waited, guessing the man wanted her on-edge and frightened and while both were true, she refused to let him see it. Instead she gazed levelly into his eyes and let him fill the silence. Which, in the end, he did. "I have a problem, Miss Trendle. A partner who's caused me far more trouble than anything else. He had a way to persuade me to assist him such that I couldn't refuse."

Again Francis waited, although it was hard to remain silent. Fortunately for her rising curiosity, Robby had no trouble talking. "So? What does that have to do with this place? You surely don't think Miss Trendle is this partner of yours? Or do you think it's her father? The Sentinel's always been against racketeering. Why would he...."

A bullet hit the wall within inches of Robby's head. "Shut up. I'd heard you run at the mouth, kid. Never thought it was that bad." The man turned his attention back to Francis. "He's right, though. When my source told me that the latest calls I got from my... partner... had been coming from this house I figured it must be one of your servants. So I'm going to get each and every one of them in here and find out who it is."

Francis demanded, "Why would my servants have anything to do with you, for one thing? For another, why bring them in here?"

"Simple. The Voice wanted me to kidnap you, so I'm sure he doesn't give a damn what happens to you. Everyone says you and Striker are two of the best employers in town so your servants should care if you're hurt. I figure it won't take more than one or two cuts to get their attention."

Francis froze, terrified in a way she'd never been before. As she struggled to find a way out of her predicament, the man laughed. "Look at it this way, Miss Trendle, you'll find out just which of your servants are really loyal."

The only answer to the man's words came from an entirely unexpected source. A roar, distant but growing louder. The same roar that had accompanied that strange masked man from the night before.

Then something came crashing through the sitting room window. A big black motorcycle skidded to a halt just a few inches from the coffee table. As Francis recognized the machine, a brilliant flash of light suddenly burst from its headlight, blinding everyone in the room.

(((

Crogan stumbled backwards, stepping on something soft. The Krane woman's dog, he realized, and was glad it was still unconscious. The silly woman might treat it like a pampered lap-dog but he knew a trained attack animal when he saw one.

"Boss!" That was Donaldson, his newest second, coming in at the sound of the noise. He and the rest of Crogan's men had been tying up the servants, all of whom were unconscious as The Voice had promised. "What the hell?"

The sound of someone running down the hall and a door slamming told Crogan that his two captives were on the run. He had no idea how they'd managed to get away, but there was no point in chasing after them. The security in this part of the city was too high. It was only because The Voice had set the place up for him that he and his men had gotten in at all.

Before Crogan could think of a plan he found himself being struck in the jaw by a booted heel. The first strike was quickly followed by a fist to the belly, leaving him gasping for air and stumbling backwards. He landed against Donaldson and crashed to the ground.

As he rolled to his feet, his eyes slowly recovering from the flash, Crogan realized his attacker was a tall man dressed in black. His masked face answered the question of who had dared and Crogan managed a sneer. "Didn't get my gun, you bastard. I'm going to skin you and use it for a rug!"

"Have to catch your Tiger, first," the man said, somersaulting backwards.

Donaldson fired several shots at the man without a moment of hesitation. Crogan blinked in disbelief. Donaldson hadn't been in the room when the flash had gone off. He shouldn't have missed, but not a single bullet hit. Indeed, at least one careened off to hit the floor in front of its target, without Tiger moving an inch.

Realizing his weapon wasn't doing its job, Donaldson launched himself at Tiger, trying to grab hold of him in a tight grip. He missed again, for this time Tiger leapt upwards, grabbed hold of the chandelier and flung himself across the room.

At the same time a woman screamed and Crogan realized the Krane woman had woken up. Another scream, this one enough to break the eardrums, made him so furious that he took a step towards her and kicked her in the side. "Shut up!"

"JAMES!"

Sneering, because he knew every servant in the place had been knocked unconscious by The Voice already, Crogan kicked her again.

"Not gentlemanly," Tiger said and Crogan felt a sudden sharp pain in his leg. Looking down, he saw a thin, slightly curved, dart sticking out of his thigh. "I'm your dance partner, remember?"

Crogan didn't have a chance to tell Tiger just what he was, because another figure suddenly slammed into the room. Dressed in a chauffeur's uniform, the man rushed at Donaldson and grabbed him by the throat, lifting him high into the air.

Tiger rushed for his motorcycle with the obvious intention of escaping. Determined not to allow that, Crogan flung himself at the masked man, knocking him to the floor just as more of Crogan's men came rushing into the room.

Wrestling with his enemy, Crogan was too furious to pay attention to anything but throttling the life out of the man. They rolled across the floor, Crogan clutching on for dear life against a barrage of strikes that left him dazed and off balance. Only sheer stubborn will-power kept him from letting loose and will-power wasn't enough when a sudden shock rippled through him, starting at his hands and working its way down to his feet.

The Tiger rolled upright, electricity crackling blue around his hands, and Crogan found himself dragged to the side and leaned against a wall. Looking up, his enemy murmured, "Looks like I'm not needed anymore."

Crogan managed to look at the others and was stunned to realize that somehow the chauffeur had taken down all but one of his men. As that last man fell, a fist to his face crunching so hard that Crogan heard bone snap, the chauffeur turned to face Tiger, blue eyes calm and cold.

"James. Teach them a lesson." That was the Krane girl, her voice shaking and furious as she clambered to her feet.

"Yes, Mistress." Crogan stared now, terror flooding him in a way that he couldn't understand. The man's voice was quiet, even gentle, yet there was something about it that sent chills up Crogan's spine. It was a familiar feeling but he was damned if he could figure out why.

Tiger rose to his feet, dropping into a sideways fighting stance. His clawed fingers knocked James' hand away, ripping the outer sleeve as they passed. His kick ought to have sent the chauffeur flying. Instead, the man simply turned his head slightly, his return punch narrowly missing its target.

Suddenly, one of Crogan's men stood up and stepped between Tiger and James. "My turn," he said and Crogan was completely bewildered. What was Old Uncle doing here? "Back off, little boy."

The chauffeur halted, choosing his target. Then he stepped forward, grabbing Old Uncle by the throat. Silently, he lifted his victim into the air and Crogan saw his fingers tighten.

Old Uncle gazed at the chauffeur dourly, seeming to hardly notice the fact that he was being throttled. Then, he grasped hold of the man's arm and twisted. Bone snapped and James' hand loosened as Old Uncle dropped lightly to the floor.

For a moment the two gazed at each other, James showing no sign of pain from what ought to have been agony. Then, with a disgusted noise, Old Uncle said, "You're going to be a tough nut to crack. And I'm not getting paid enough for that. But I think it's high time you had a nice nap. So...." He spread his arms in one rapid motion and smoke poured off of him, filling the room with a cloud so black that Crogan was blinded again.

Someone grasped Crogan by the nape of the neck and lifted him in the air. "This, youngster," Old Uncle said in his ear, "is about all one whiskey buys you. Listen better, next time someone tells you something." The world spun around Crogan's ears and suddenly he was sitting on the floor in Barton's Tavern, staring blankly at a crowd of startled men and women, his men sprawled around him in a heap.

《《《

Francis stopped running halfway between her house and the nearest one up the street. Her heart raced so fast that she could hardly think straight. Leaning against the nearest fence, she watched down the street, fully expecting to see her would-be abductors in hot pursuit.

Suddenly she realized Robby was missing. After Tiger had set off that flash, the young man had grabbed her wrist and dragged her out of the building. Surely he'd been behind her the whole way? Had he been captured? Or had he gone back to save Rosamund?

Francis considered the possibility of going back. Robby had nothing to do with her troubles and she felt responsible for his involvement. But no, she didn't have a chance against that thug and his men. Just as she'd no choice but to leave Rosamund behind, she'd be an idiot to run back to the trap she'd just escaped.

Regretting her weakness, Francis hurried up to the Striker house, although it was mostly dark inside. John usually took most of his servants with him to his Jewel Island mansion, leaving the oldest behind to guard the house. Late though it was, Napier would be able to help her.

Ringing the bell over and over, Francis waited impatiently for Napier to make his way to the front. She could have sworn it took him hours, although it was probably closer to a few minutes. "Miss Trendle? Whatever are you doing here? Is there a problem? Please, come in!"

"Yes, thank you, Napier. I need to use your phone. I'll explain afterwards."

The old man bowed and quickly led Francis through to the hall table where a phone stood. Dialing quickly, Francis was soon on the line to the police, explaining the situation. "I don't know if they're still there, but I had to leave Rosamund Krane behind. They wanted me, but I'm sure they'd take her, instead."

"Don't worry, Miss Trendle. We'll have men there as soon as we can."

Relieved to have gotten help, Francis hung up the phone and turned to Napier. "You heard all that."

"Ordinarily, Miss, I try not to listen to our guests' conversations, but I'm afraid I did make an exception in this case. Would you like me to go down to your house and see if I can do anything?"

Napier was ninety if he was a day and no longer as strong as he'd been when he'd helped run the Striker mine. "No. But would you wait with me at the gate? Robby McLeod is out there too. He might need help." That was all she dared do until the police came.

"I would be glad accompany you, Miss."

They went outside and Francis climbed up on the brick column holding one side of the gate, Napier steadying her as she went. "Miss will remember that the ironwork leaves are not strong enough to stand on, I hope?"

Francis grinned back down at him. When both she and John were young they'd spent a great deal of time testing both the strength of the iron-wrought fence and their respective families' patience. "I remember."

"I believe I hear sirens, Miss. No doubt the police will be here soon."

Peering down the hillside, Francis could see the flashing lights that accompanied the wailing sirens. She turned her attention to her house, just able to see the shattered window of her sitting room. There was movement, two men fighting, but not much more. Then the lights in the room went out. "What in the world?"

The distant sound of more shattering glass followed and suddenly Tiger's motorcycle crashed out of the window. As the lights in the room behind him slowly became visible again, a woman's form, just recognizable as Rosamund Krane's, rushed to the window. "YOU'RE A DEAD MAN! I'LL HAVE YOUR HEAD!" she shrieked, reminding Francis of just how much of a termagant Rosamund could be when something was wrong in her world.

Two police cars came up the road then and stopped in front of Francis' house. Sure it was safe now, Francis allowed Napier to help her down from the fence. "I'll be all right now, Napier," she started to tell him but saw the look in his eyes. She relented, "Oh, very well. Come along."

They reached Francis' house just after the police made their way inside, leaving one to keep watch. He stopped her as she approached. "Sorry, Miss. We were too late to catch your intruders. Still, best let us make sure the house is clear before you go in." As Rosamund shrieked imprecations at everyone even remotely involved with the evening's troubles, he winced, "Hopefully soon."

Rosamund's behavior was just her way to draw attention to herself and Francis ignored it, saying, "Keep an eye out for Robby McLeod. He was with me when I ran but I lost track of him."

"They won't need to. I'm right here. I'm glad you kept going, Miss Trendle. I hoped you would." Robby's voice came out of the bushes under the sitting room window. As they watched, he climbed out, muttering Chinese imprecations at the branches catching hold of him. "I didn't want to leave Miss Krane behind, so I was looking for a chance to help her. Not that I got one, mind you."

Another shriek made everyone wince. "Just as well you didn't. She'd be furious if you took her and left her dog, and Boopsie's too big to carry."

Francis called out through the window, "Rosamund! Stop fussing and let the police do their jobs. Everything's fine now."

That didn't help, but at least Francis could say she'd tried. "Did you see what happened?" she asked, speaking over the screaming as best she could.

"It all went pretty fast," Robby admitted. "But when I came back, that man was fighting the fellow they're calling Tiger and a half dozen more were on Miss Krane's chauffeur. He's quite strong, you know. I've never seen anyone beat so many people up so quickly. Tiger knocked his opponent down and the chauffeur was going after him when another man got in the way. Something happened then and the room filled with smoke. A few seconds later, Tiger's motorcycle went flying. That's all I really know."

Once again, Francis was amazed at Robby's ability to talk without pausing for breath. She wasn't surprised James could fight, nor that he was good at it. Rancourt had probably hired him as a bodyguard. "Well, I'm glad you weren't hurt. I'm just sorry that you had to be dragged into this."

"It's quite all right. I like a little excitement now and then." Robby might have continued, but an officer leaned out of the sitting room window, beckoning Francis inside. "You'd better go find out what the damages are."

Francis agreed and went to the sitting room where Rosamund was sobbing over her poor unconscious Boopsie, ignoring her unconscious chauffer. Which, when Francis thought about it, was the way things usually went with Rosamund. "Has someone sent for an ambulance for that poor man?" There was a big black bruise in the middle of James' forehead and he probably had a concussion.

"Yes, Miss. There should be one soon," the oldest of the officers told her, introducing himself as Assistant-Chief Hamilton.

"Have you found any of the men who attacked my house?"

"We've searched the house from top to bottom, Miss Trendle," the man told her. "No sign of anyone here who shouldn't be. Your people were unconscious in the basement. Your butler awake, though, and breathing fire. He's giving a statement right now, but I'll send him to you as soon as possible."

Wondering what happened to the intruders, Francis looked at the mess. There were tire tracks on her rug, a shattered coffee table and a few broken pieces of furniture. The worst of the damage was her father's favorite antique chess set. When she spotted it the full enormity of what had just happened hit her, and she sat down hard.

Seeing just how badly the sight shook her, Robby offered, "My brother can fix those like new. He's very good at that sort of thing."

"Thank you, Robby. I appreciate that." Francis turned her attention back to the police officers. "I suppose you'll want statements from everyone?"

Assistant-Chief Hamilton agreed, "As much as we can get." Glancing at Rosamund, he added ruefully, "We may have to wait until tomorrow for some testimony, though."

Hamilton was right that they'd get no cooperation from Rosamund in her current infuriated state. Francis doubted the woman could manage a complete thought, much less a complete sentence. "I'll have her sleep here tonight and bring her to the station tomorrow morning, when she's recovered."

"If you don't mind," Robby said suddenly, "I'd appreciate it if you took my testimony now. Mother doesn't like it when I'm late for supper." He and Hamilton left the room together, closely followed by Napier, who suggested that Gordon might need some assistance.

That left Francis with Rosamund and the slowly rousing Boopsie, neither of whom were talking. Which was just as well, because Francis had too many things to think about, not the least was what that crook had told her when he'd had her in his clutches. Did someone really call him from this house? If so, who? And why?

More importantly, though, was what she could do to stop it? She had a feeling that things were going to keep getting worse otherwise.

(((

Having taken the last ferry to Jewel Island, Michaels knew they'd have to stay until morning. Fortunately, when John Striker had bought the island from the Kranes, he'd had the servants' quarters converted to a small inn. There was a standing order that any police visiting in the course of their duties could use whatever rooms were available at half-price.

The inn had a small restaurant with a quiet table to themselves where the kid could ask all the questions he liked. Not that he had, but that was because William was still processing his experience. Fair enough. Michaels had very nearly run for his life when She'd talked to him the first time, back when Chief Neil had been in charge.

At last William said, "Why did you bring me here?"

"You're not hungry?" Michaels asked, returning his attention to his companion. William gave him a dour look and he relented, "I brought you for the same reason, when I was just a youngster learning the ropes, Chief Neil brought me to meet Her. Because at least a few of us on the force know about Her. Hamilton knows. I know. And now, so do you."

"That doesn't answer my question. Why me? I can barely wrap my head around the whole thing." Wisely, even in this secluded corner, William didn't outright state what he'd just experienced. Which was exactly why Michaels had chosen him. When he said as much, though, the kid looked bewildered.

Uncertain how to explain, Michaels said, "There're things out there that most policemen never, ever, come across. Even when they do, they might not know it. Sometimes ignorance is bliss but other times.... Other times we have to deal with things coming out of the shadows at us that just aren't right."

"That Old Smoky she mentioned?"

"Exactly." Michaels remembered the days when the crazy old... whatever he was... haunted the city. Sometimes he stole. Sometimes he delivered messages. Threats, warnings and oddly enough, love letters. Sometimes he even killed. "Your mom ever tell you about the Black Beast?"

William thought about it, "I think she did, but I don't recollect much. Something about never setting a fire in the mountains without throwing something in it for the Black Beast."

Again Michaels agreed. "What little we figured out, Old Smoky either was the Black Beast himself or a relation. Give him a gift in fire and he'd do something for you, no matter what it was. Didn't matter if it were good or bad. All that mattered was the gift."

"What happened? From what you two said, it sounded like he'd stopped. And like you thought that thing in the newsroom was him."

"I didn't get the details, She said he was born of fire, so some local scientists figured water would hurt him and threw him into the ocean. Haven't seen, nor heard, from him since." Michaels shook his head. "That thing might have been him, might be something else. We'll have to see."

William looked thoughtful. "Perhaps we could lure him out again?"

Although Michaels had considered the idea, it didn't appeal to him. "It's like making wishes. You better have a good idea what you want because otherwise you could end up empty handed. And from what I heard tell, if he didn't like what you gave him, or you asked for too much, you might end up nothin' but ashes."

"I suppose that makes sense," William admitted. "But that thing in the newsroom was destroyed, or looked to be. So what now?"

"What any good cop is supposed to do. Investigate, lad. And hope our flat feet lead us on the right path before the crooks get away."

⟨⟨⟨

The rest of the meal was quiet. William recognized the trust being put in him and appreciated it, but it troubled him. As for the Chief, he seemed lost in thought. William guessed he was remembering the past, when the being he called Old Smoky had last appeared.

The waiter had just brought out the dessert menu when the manager came to speak with Chief Michaels. "I apologize for the interruption, sir, but Assistant-Chief Hamilton is calling. He says it's not an emergency, but he thinks you should know."

Michaels sighed. "Should have known we couldn't go one night without another incident. Jarvis, finish up and go to bed. We'll be on the first ferry out." He left without waiting for William's agreement.

Having eaten at the inn before, William knew that the apple pie was his mother's recipe. Even though it meant sitting alone, with nothing to do, he couldn't resist ordering it. He'd just handed the waiter the menu when a familiar voice hailed him. "Bill. How've you been? How's the Force treating you?"

William stood up immediately, recognizing his cousin-by-marriage, John Striker. They'd gone to school together and while John was his senior by two years, had gotten on well. Better, in fact, than William got on with his other cousins. Still, it was hard to forget that John was the richest man in town and William was just a poor cop.

William offered his cousin his hand. "Not bad, John. Been a bit busy, lately. You'll have heard about today's excitement, I'm sure."

"I've heard about quite a bit of excitement. Can I sit down?" At William's agreement, John added to the waiter, "I'll have the same thing he's having. With cheese, as usual."

"Yes, sir."

Sitting down, John grinned broadly at William, waited until the waiter was out of earshot and asked, "So, recovering from your meeting with Her?" At William's shocked expression, John reminded him, "With one notable exception, I own the island, Bill. Of course I know about Her. She's the only reason Michaels would drag you here."

Supposing that was true, William sighed. "This is almost too much."

"Look at it this way. At least Strikers Port isn't one of those places where this sort of thing's as common as dirt. We'd be tripping over all sorts of interesting critters all the time. Not to mention needing a whole branch of the police force dedicated to keeping them out of trouble."

It didn't help William's peace of mind to realize that there might be places where these things were common. He'd been living a simple life as a cop. A giant octopus acting like the Oracle of Delphi was bad enough. A monster who would do whatever someone wanted for the right gift, up to and including murder, was even worse. That something about the story resonated inside him and sent chills up his spine didn't help.

Changing the subject, William asked, "What brings you here, anyway? I heard you have the best chef in town working for you."

John looked thoughtfully at his utensils, then came to a decision. "Bill, did your mom ever mention the Jewel Island house to you?"

"She'd tell me stories about it, yes. But she never mentioned... Her... if that's where you're headed." Of course, even if his mother knew about the cave and its occupant she wouldn't have told him. She'd have known he'd want to sneak a look.

With a quick shake of his head, John told him, "I meant did she ever tell you it belonged to you? For that matter, did your father tell you?"

Shocked, William stared at his cousin. "To me? No. It belonged to my grandfather." When his parents had married against his grandfather's wishes, his mother had been cut from his will. They'd reconciled after William had been born, but since Gwendolyn had died before her father, the small fortune he'd meant to leave her went to the rest of the family. William's father had been too poor to contest the will.

"So I thought. So your Aunt Harriet and your Uncle Jack thought." John shook his head and met William's eyes, "The will never mentioned the house specifically. We all assumed it was part of your grandfather's property when he died. It wasn't until I bought it that we discovered that the deed had been transferred to you right after your mother died."

William's jaw dropped. On one hand, his father had never said a word. On the other hand, George Jarvis was a stubborn old soul with no trust for the Krane family. If he'd known about the deed, he'd probably decided they were better off without the place.

"Which leads me to my current problem. Harriet can't sell me the house because she doesn't own it. But I've started renovations. Legally, I haven't got a leg to stand on."

At a guess, there was another problem. "And you already paid Aunt Harriet, didn't you? Knowing her, she won't return the money."

Ruefully, John agreed. "How well you know our family." He shrugged. "That's a legal fight I can win. The question is, can you win yours? Always presuming you want to?"

"I'm not sure I do," William admitted. "I've a feeling that's not why you're telling me all this." John could have told him he'd have no chance at claiming the house. Could have told him he was better off being bought out for a meagre sum. The fact John wasn't saying anything of the sort suggested he had other ideas.

" SO, RECOVERING FROM YOUR MEETING WITH HER "

"No. It isn't. Frankly, I'd like to see Aunt Harriet taken down a notch. Her share in the Striker pie isn't enough to beat mine but she still tries to tell me how to run my business. Do I look like a man who needs that sort of advice?" Not waiting for an answer, John continued, "Besides, I liked your mom and I hated the way Aunt Harriet and Uncle Jack treated her. Not to mention how they made sure you and your dad never got a penny. Your grandfather would have wanted the money he left your mom to go to you."

"Maybe, maybe not." William was equivocating. His grandfather had been fond of him, fond enough that he'd have left enough to see to William's education. Before John could say another word, he raised a hand. "I can't decide immediately. Let me think about it. In the meantime, go ahead with your renovations. I can't afford the house's upkeep, anyway. If I get it, I'll sell it to you. And if I don't, you already made an agreement with Aunt Harriet, so it's still yours."

John looked unsatisfied but he didn't argue. "We'll talk more later. In the meantime, I thought I'd better warn you that the Sentinel got wind of the situation. Don't be at all surprised if Aunt Harriet comes down on you like a ton of bricks, trying to get you to cede the house to her. Be sure that's what you want before you sign anything."

William agreed, reflecting that this was the kind of problem he could understand. Even if he had no idea what he was going to do about it.

《《《

Crogan stepped around broken glass entering Barton's Tavern. It wasn't a break-in by his lights, just an early morning visit to a place he had part ownership in. He could hardly be blamed if Barton refused to give him a key and didn't like being woken in the early morning.

"Keep watch," he told Donaldson. "I don't want to be interrupted." Nor did he want to be seen making a fool of himself.

"Right." Donaldson parked himself in front of the door, leaning against the jam with his hat pulled down over his eyes.

Going behind the bar, Crogan scanned the bottles of whiskey and chose the biggest and fullest one he could find. Then he went to the fireplace and realized he had another problem. Barton kept the fire going even in full summer for the effect, but he didn't light it until the bar opened. If this were going to work, Crogan would have to set up a fire. Growing up in the city, the subject had never come up before.

"Hey. Donaldson. How do you start a fire?" As an afterthought, he added, "In a fireplace, that is."

"A fire? What do you want a fire for?" At Crogan's growl, Donaldson hurriedly added, "Put some kindling down, add a log, light the fire. Oh and if there's a newspaper, put it in first."

"Now you tell me." Crogan removed the wood and grabbed an old paper from the nearby stack, sticking it in the grate before putting the kindling and log back in.

"Sorry boss."

"Shut up," Crogan snapped, searching his pockets for his matches. "Now then.... light the fire...." He held the match to the closest log and waited. "Donaldson, it isn't working."

Peering through the doorway quickly, Donaldson said, "Sorry, boss. I shoulda said. Light the newspaper."

Again Crogan growled, moving the match to the paper and setting it alight. It went out half-way. He cursed bitterly, beginning to wonder if this whole thing was a waste of time.

"Put some lighter fluid on," Donaldson suggested.

That nearly singed Crogan's eyebrows. Fortunately for Donaldson's continued health, it also set the kindling alight and, finally, the log. Satisfied that he'd finally set a proper fire, Crogan pulled the whiskey bottle's cork and poured its contents onto the flames. This time he really did singe his eyebrows, setting off another round of cursing as he backed away, brushing smoke and ash off himself.

"That," a harsh voice said behind him, "has got to have been the most incompetent summoning I've ever had the misfortune to experience." Crogan turned and saw Old Uncle leaning his elbows against the bar, as disheveled as ever. "I'll also note that you can't sacrifice what you don't own and you didn't exactly pay for that bottle. On the other hand, I'll give you a few points for keeping me amused."

Crogan took a deep breath. It'd worked. It had really worked. He hadn't been sure, but after a sleepless night reviewing the fight at the Trendle house and his conversation with the man... or whatever he was... earlier, it'd hit him what the Old Uncle had meant about whiskey. Not to mention who he had to be. There wasn't a crook in town didn't know about Old Smoky.

He was about to speak when he noticed the way Old Uncle's eyebrow tilted as he looked at the empty bottle in Crogan's hand. "Right. Pay for it." He pulled out his wallet with shaking hands and found a hundred, sticking it into the till as quickly as he could.

"Better. Should have bought it first, but I'll let that pass this time." Old Uncle turned to look at Crogan, lifting his face so his eyes could be seen. Fear flooded through Crogan's veins at the sight, an icy chill that nearly dropped him to his knees. "Now, nice as it is to be acknowledged, you've had your turn already. You don't get another for at least a week. Once a fellow starts making exceptions, everyone starts expecting them. And don't tell me you don't know the rules. You were here the last time I came out to play."

Somehow, Crogan managed to look away from those horrifying eyes. "Yeah, I remember." To be honest, he hadn't believed it, despite the rumors and despite the troubles that had accompanied Old Smoky's last appearance. "Thing is there were about a hundred different stories of what would summon you and a few hundred more about what you wanted."

"Most of which were a load of guff," Old Uncle admitted. "I'm a simple man of simple pleasures. And rules really aren't something I care much about, anyway. But I don't like to be bothered, either. Last time I came out to play... well let's just say even I make mistakes."

"They drowned... tried to drown... you didn't they?"

Old Uncle laughed harshly. "Oh, that little thing? I'll admit, that had me down for a bit. But the one who told them what I am forgot to mention I come from the ocean. A little dunking won't kill the likes of me. It was how they did it that hurt and even that wasn't enough."

Crogan was about to ask what had made Old Uncle stop all those years ago if it hadn't been getting dropped in the Pacific, then he saw Old Uncle's eyes and set that thought aside for a few centuries later. Whatever had happened was not a thing Old Uncle wanted to discuss. Instead Crogan asked, "All right, what, if anything can I ask for, in return for that bottle of Barton's finest?"

"Wouldn't say it was his finest," Old Uncle corrected, grinning toothily. "Best batch they ever made was about 1872. And I say this as a connoisseur. That stuff burned all the way through for about three days straight. Tasted like hell on Earth." He looked at the fire and finally said, "You're getting the most I'm willing to offer right now, talk. I'm a lazy old sod, you know. My kind only get excited in the right conditions. But don't expect me to answer everything, either. You want answers, take a box of Uncle Ip's to Her that waits under the lighthouse. And hope she's not hungry for man meat instead."

Crogan had no idea what Old Uncle meant about Her and decided he didn't want to know. "What do I do about The Voice?"

"You need me to tell you that?" Old Uncle shook his head. "Well, obviously, you need to take him out. As for who The Voice is, I've no clue. First I heard of him was from you. You were on the right track tracing the call but don't make stupid assumptions about what he can and cannot do. Your best bet is to find out who he is and what he's got on his side, first."

Now that he was thinking more clearly, Crogan could see the logic. "One last question, then. What about my men? Got any idea how I can get them out of that wall they're stuck in?"

"Science isn't my strong point, Crogan, and there's way too much of that involved here. Best I can think is to get that McLeod fellow to fix things for you. Since he's working on it already, you don't need to do much on that count."

Agreeing, Crogan had another thought but guessed he'd better not ask, given how many questions he'd already had answered. Besides, The Tiger and The Dragon might be a thorn in his side, but his biggest problem was The Voice. He'd see to those two later. "All right. I suppose that's it then. Is there... is there anything I should do now?" It occurred to him that having no idea how these things worked meant he had no idea how to end their 'interview'.

Old Uncle laughed and tossed what looked like a gold nugget on the bar. "Pour me another drink. This one, I'm paying for."

◖◖◖

By the time Francis and Rosamund finished in the police station the next morning, the two weren't talking to each other. Rosamund, the spoilt darling of her family, didn't like it when she was scolded. Francis, on the other hand, was tired of Rosamund's selfish lack of concern for anyone except herself.

Francis usually ignored her old schoolmate's behavior. Pointing out Rosamund's flaws generally resulted in a shrieking fit that put the gulls at Strikers Port Docks to shame. But after little sleep and Rosamund's complaints about Francis' servants and the police's supposed lack of response, Francis was close to the end of her temper. The capper had been when Chief Michaels had mentioned that Rosamund's chauffeur, James, had disappeared between the house and the hospital. Rosamund's complete lack of concern had set Francis on the warpath.

The two women neither looked nor spoke to each other as they walked out of the police station. Later, Francis might attempt a more reasonable approach, but right then she'd no intention of reasoning with the woman. Instead she said tersely, "My chauffeur will take you home."

"Fine. And I hope Boopsie throws up all over the seat."

Reflecting the dog probably would, Francis chose to ignore the threat and turned towards her car. As she did so, a voice called her name from further up the sidewalk. "Francis. Young lady. I need to speak with you."

Recognizing Rosamund's mother, both women turned to face her. "Hello, Mrs. Krane. I'm glad you're here. You can take Rosamund home instead."

Harriet Krane waved off the suggestion. "Never mind that. I want to know what this is all about!" She held up the morning's Sentinel, shaking the page in Francis' face so that she was forced to step back or be hit.

Reading the headline, Francis was puzzled as to why Mrs. Krane was so furious. "'Malicious Mysterious Madman Attacks Paper'. I admit, it's a bit sensationalized and I'm still not sure Scanlon should have gone with all that alliteration but...."

This time the paper did hit Francis in the face. "Not that! This!" Outraged, Mrs. Krane put her finger on a much smaller byline at the very edge of the fold. "'Krane Deal Falls Through! Striker Strikes Out?'" That was right; one of her reporters had discovered a title problem with the old Krane house on Jewel Island. There'd been few details but enough to make it an interesting by-line. "Oh yes, John told my reporter the deal had hit a snag and that it wasn't certain the house was yours to sell. Bruce couldn't get an interview with you, so he went with what he had."

Usually Mrs. Krane and Rosamund didn't look much like each other, Rosamund having inherited her father's fine boned and elegant features rather than her mother's heavier jaw and piercing blue eyes. In that moment, though, the woman's infuriated expression made the relationship all too obvious. Before she spoke, though, Francis added, "I really am sorry you're upset, Mrs. Krane. I did make sure our reporter had all the facts, though."

"You can't possibly have. Not after that... horrible... attack on the paper. I only found out about this the day before yesterday!"

"I called the Deeds Registry, Mrs. Krane. It's a matter of public record. And everything else in the article comes from John." Francis smiled sympathetically at Rosamund's mother. "I'm sorry. I'm sure you're doing everything you can to resolve this situation. I promise, the Sentinel will be sure to print the details, once you have."

Mrs. Krane took a long, deep, breath. Her temper might be as fierce as her daughter's but she'd learned to control it. "I see. Well you'd best be careful what, exactly, your little rag says in the meantime. There are libel laws in this state, you know."

"I'm well aware of that, ma'am. I'm sure that the whole matter is a miscommunication. One you and John will speedily rectify by finding the proper owner of the house and negotiating with him." With a slight nod of her head, Francis continued, "And now, I have business elsewhere.

Rosamund, since she's here, I'll let your mother see to your ride home." Francis inclined her head to her old schoolmate and climbed into her car.

Once Lee was behind the wheel she told him, "Take me to the old workshop." With luck, McLeod had managed to get that man out of her wall. Even if he hadn't, there might be a chance she could get the prisoner to tell her his story. Either way, it was high time she found out who had it in for her.

(((

"Go to the Trendle house. Look for anything that might have something to do with yesterday's excitement. Take an unmarked car. No reason to be obvious."

William could understand why Chief Michaels was concerned. Admittedly, the attack on Miss Trendle had appeared to be your run-of-the-mill ordinary kidnapping attempt. Yet given the attack on the Sentinel, there might be a connection. "I'll go get Maloney...." The dour look on Chief Michael's face stopped him.

"Maloney and I are going to check on Mr. McLeod. The less chance he has to gossip, the better." Michaels shook his head, "Frankly, I'd send him back to patrol duty but now that he's involved, I want to keep an eye on him. His lips could sink a whole navy if we let them."

William thought Michaels exaggerated but he didn't argue. "I'll go right away."

A few minutes later William was exiting the police station when he heard a familiar voice. "You're a grown woman, Rosamund! If you can't figure out how to handle your own affairs without...." The speaker was William's Aunt Harriet, the last person on Earth he wanted to talk to right now. If he could have avoided her, he would have, but she'd already spotted him. "William, dear. Just the man I've come to see. Do be a love and come here."

Knowing arguing would only extend matters; William did as he was bade. "Can I help you, Aunt Harriet?" He paused, knowing his cousin would throw a fit if he didn't acknowledge her and added, "Good day, Rosamund."

"I don't see what's good about it," Rosamund muttered. "I'm going to the car, mumsy. Don't take forever the way you usually do."

Once Rosamund and her dog had left, Aunt Harriet smiled sweetly at William. "Now, dear boy, there's a little something I need you to do for me."

"Is it about that deed?" At her startled expression, he added, "John told me about it last night. I know it's a difficult problem for you, and I can guess what you'd like me to do, but I haven't decided. I need to find out my legal standing."

Her eyes hardened. "Don't play games with me, young man."

"Of course not. But the house is the only legacy I have from my Grandfather. I wouldn't want to go against his wishes without due consideration." William made a show of checking his watch. "Unfortunately, I'm on duty right now. If you would, please have your lawyer send me a letter detailing what you're offering."

Aware that Aunt Harriet was as close to throwing one of Rosamund's legendary fits as she'd ever been, William nodded to her and headed to the parking lot. He'd pay for that moment of rebellion but he thought it worth the earful he'd get later. In the end, Aunt Harriet would win. That didn't mean he couldn't enjoy a rare moment of contrary hard-headedness.

As he got into the unmarked sedan Chief Michaels had told him to take to Miss Trendle's house, a voice said behind him, "That's not a pleasant woman at all."

William flung himself out of his seat and spun to stare into the back seat of the sedan, where a familiar figure lounged. "Dragon? What are you doing here?" He let his hand slip away from his gun and considered whether he should call for back-up or accept this annoyance's presence. At the moment he didn't have anything to arrest the man on.

"Waiting for you to get back in the car so we can go check out Miss Trendle's place."

"You're not coming."

"Do you know how to look for signs of magic?"

William sighed and admitted, "No." He got in and started the car, then stopped and glared back at Dragon. "Wait. How did you know where I was going and how did you know about Aunt Harriet?"

In answer, Dragon whistled sharply and a long slender form appeared beside William. The dragon thing from the other night, William realized; a gorgeous silvery creature that shimmered like a rainbow. It grinned at him and slithered close, giving him a big lick with a tongue as smooth as silk. "Hey!"

"Meng. Come here. Don't startle the nice police officer while he's driving."

"How long has that thing been following me? Since last night?" William turned onto the main street and headed up the hill towards Miss Trendle's.

As Meng slithered over the seat and into Dragon's lap, its owner chuckled. "Not that long. I owe someone a favor. A certain someone believes you're in danger and requested I keep an eye on you." When William glanced at him through the rear-view mirror, he added, "Don't worry about it right now. It's probably nothing. Besides, I ought to be telling you Tiger's side of last night's entertainment."

Although William desperately wanted to interrogate Dragon further about his own supposed danger, he recognized that Tiger's testimony, albeit second-hand, was more important. "Go on."

As William drove up the hill, Dragon told him, "Primus, Tiger's pretty sure it was Crogan last night. Secundus, your cousin's chauffeur is too strong to be normal and he would have killed anyone she told him to. Tertius, it was Old Smoky who saved Tiger and Crogan's hind ends. Also, as a side note, Tiger thinks anyone who crosses Miss Rosamund had better watch their backs. She has a mean streak."

Well, that was true. William and John had long since learned to walk carefully around Rosamund Krane. He'd been quite small when he'd visited his grandfather, but could dimly remember Rosamund destroying furniture and landscape all over the place. It'd been terrifying. "I understand she was quite put out with your partner. Something about having his head."

"Stuffed and mounted, no doubt. I wouldn't worry about him, though. Tiger's a big boy and he can take care of himself. Besides, he needs a good butt-kicking sometimes, to keep him from getting cocky." Dragon chuckled at the thought, adding, "Looks like we're here."

William parked behind the Trendle house and turned to Dragon, intending to ask how he planned on explaining his masked presence to Miss Trendle's butler. Except somewhere between the last time William had looked and now, Dragon had changed his appearance. The man behind him was a young, red-headed, rookie whose uniform just barely fit him, wearing a badge reading McDougal. As for Meng, the dragon was gone.

"Right, then," William said, trying not to be impressed, "If that's how you're going to play it. Follow me, take notes and don't talk unless I ask you to. And for God's sake, don't trip over your own feet in there." It was exactly what Maloney had said to him when they'd first been partnered.

"Sir, yes, Sir!" Dragon saluted and obviously fighting down giggles, followed him to the door, standing behind him in an attitude of attention that was just barely short of exaggerated.

The Trendle family's butler looked surprised to see them. "Mr. William. It's been a very long time indeed, sir."

"So long I'm surprised you recognize me, Gordon," William told him. "I think I was five years old at the time."

Gordon looked prim. "Sir is the spitting image of his mother, and her I remember quite well." He allowed himself a slight, sad, smile. "But sir is here on official business. How may I help you? I was of the understanding that our statements had been taken last night."

William agreed, "They were, Gordon, but Chief Michaels sent me to take a closer look around the sitting room." A thought occurred to him and, a little worried, he asked, "Er... I hope you haven't cleaned the sitting room already?"

"Ordinarily, sir would be too late. But Miss Trendle ordered me to leave it alone for now. I would be glad to show you in."

William had no doubt the older man would also be glad to be permitted to clean the place up. "Thank you, Gordon. Oh, and this is Officer MacDougall. He's along to assist me."

"Of course, sir." Gordon led them through the winding back halls of the building to small servant's entrance into the living room. "I am quite out of sorts with those ruffians. Some of the antiques they destroyed are irreplaceable."

Dragon opened his mouth, then closed it quickly as he remembered his role. With a sigh, William told him, "What?"

"There's someone in Chinatown who can fix most of this. I think he works at the Jeen Loon." There was an innocent note to the man's voice, as if he were simply trying to help. "So I've heard."

"That would be Chou Chang?" Gordon asked. "Yes, Mr. McLeod said much the same thing, last night. I shall have to remember to contact this Mr. Chang. But first I need to be able to clean up."

Agreeing, William told Gordon, "We'll be as quick as we can, Gordon. After that, the room should be all yours."

"Thank you, sir. Then I will leave you to your work. Do please let me know when you're done."

Once Gordon was gone, William gave Dragon a sharp look but the innocence in the man's false features made it impossible to tell what his true intentions were. "What did you take from the Jeen Loon the other night?"

"Nothing they couldn't replace," Dragon answered, sounding slightly distracted. He was already wandering around the room, hands out as if feeling for something. As if guessing at William's confusion, he added, "I'm trying to feel the flow of energy in the room. Don't talk. This may take a while."

Lacking anything better to do, William examined the scuffs and footprints on the Oriental rug. He wasn't very good at this sort of thing but even he could tell there'd been a half-dozen men fighting at one end of the room. The smell of perfume and dog told him where Rosamund and Boopsie had probably been, sprawled together on the floor near the couch.

A tap at the door drew William's attention and he looked up to find a puzzled looking Gordon coming back into the room. "Yes?"

"Mr. William, there's a man here to see you. He says he is from Mrs. Krane's attorney. He has some important papers he needs you to sign. I asked him if they could wait, but he's quite adamant."

Surprised Aunt Harriet had worked that fast and that her man had found him so easily, William apologized. "He shouldn't have come here. But, just so I can get this over with, would you mind letting him in?"

"There is no need," a man's cold voice said from behind Gordon. "I have come." It was a soft voice, almost gentle, yet William disliked it immediately. The man was vaguely familiar, but William couldn't identify the well-tanned features or the icy blue eyes. Yet they sent a chill through him nonetheless. As he stared, the newcomer stepped past Gordon, holding out a sheath of papers. "You will take these and you will sign them. That is your aunt's desire."

Annoyed, William snapped, "My aunt will have to wait until I've read them and decided what I'm going to do."

"You are refusing to sign?"

"I am. Leave the papers with me and I'll get back with you later. This isn't the time or place for business."

"Then I have no choice but to kill you." With one long step, the man came forward, hand rising to catch William by the throat.

⟨⟨⟨

"And I don't know what's coming or going when the whole damn mess turns the department upside down. You should have Jarvis and I out on the street, keeping an eye out for trouble. Not sending the kid prancing around pretending he's a detective. Why the lad's barely had time to grow into his uniform!"

Having reminded Maloney for the twentieth time that, as Chief, it was Michaels who decided what was an officer's best job was, he sighed and nodded. Maloney was complaining for the sake of complaining at this point.

Fortunately for Michaels' temper, they reached their destination before he had to haul off and smack his subordinate. Not that the urge left him when they went to the door of the old workshop to be met by a small, fine-boned, Chinese woman dressed in a long flowing robe. Maloney had the sense to do no more than mutter under his breath, "Va voom", but even that was too much.

The woman eyed Maloney levelly and with a slight smile, dismissed him as unimportant. Instead she turned to Michaels, saying in slightly accented English, "Chief Michaels. We thought you might be coming this morning. Please, follow me and I will take you to my husband."

"Thank you, Mrs. McLeod," Michaels answered, taking off his hat to her, impressed not so much by her beauty as by her self-possession. He noticed that she'd been at the door waiting for them when they arrived, as if she'd expected them before they'd reached the entrance.

Leading them through a set of dingy abandoned offices, Mrs. McLeod brought them to a large room. McLeod had set up his laboratory towards the middle, with big lamps shining on tables filled with buzzing and beeping equipment. The rest of the warehouse was cast in shadows, so that Michaels could only make out a few shapes. The smell of rust and damp was strong in the air.

"Hello, Chief Michaels." Miss Trendle's presence didn't surprise him. He'd half-expected she'd poke her curious little nose into matters. He wasn't sure how to keep her quiet about things but he knew he'd have a fight on his hands if he tried to keep her out. "Mr. McLeod was showing me some of what he's discovered."

The gangly red-head was bent over an odd device that looked like a microscope but bigger. McLeod looked up at Michaels and Maloney's approach and beckoned them closer. "Here, take a look at this."

Peering through the device, Michaels saw an image that looked like it came from a shoe fitting device, except with colors like a Kodachrome negative. It took him a moment to recognize a hand, strangely flat as it moved restlessly in the viewfinder. "Dolan?" he asked, raising his head to look at the plaster wall laying on its side. Another device pointed down at the slab, a long thick cable running from it to the one Michaels was looking in.

"Yes. It confirms my suspicion. The man has been partially phased out of our dimension. It's unfortunate, really, that his attacker didn't finish the job." When Michaels stared at him, McLeod added, "Oh, it'd have been even better if he hadn't been phased at all. But in his current state, half in, half out, he's still subject to physical needs like eating and drinking."

Mrs. McLeod added, "I have been feeding him, but he can hardly chew. I am not sure he will survive for long if he remains there."

Maloney muttered and when Michaels looked at him, said, "Dolan's as nasty a piece o' work as his boss, Crogan. But even he doesn't deserve this." He waved his hand at the figure in the wall, looking a bit sick. "I'm hoping you can get him out, Mr. McLeod."

"Dimensional phase shifting is difficult to accomplish," McLeod continued, "I've tinkered with it but never on this scale. I'm not certain what to do yet. I've built a prototype, but I'll need a great deal of power to get this man out of his predicament alive."

Miss Trendle offered, "You can borrow a generator from the train yard."

Reflecting that it was fortunate that the young lady was a nosy little snippet, Michaels was about to thank her when he heard a sound in the darkness at the other end of the warehouse. He thought it just a stray cat or rat, but when he looked in that direction he caught a glimpse of a human figure moving quickly into the shadows.

Michaels stepped closer to the Dolan, trying to look like he was examining the man's prison. At the same time he scanned the shadows, trying to catch another glimpse of the intruder. Someone dressed in black, he thought, trying not to be seen.

Whomever it was, they weren't interested in coming close, hiding amid the old train parts as if lying in wait. Was it the fellow calling himself Tiger, nosing around in business not his own? Or perhaps a hobo, just looking for a quiet place to hide? Michaels put a hand on one of the big lamps, then spun it around to shine its beam on the intruder.

"Crogan?"

The crook blinked for several moments, then stared at him with an expression of raw fury. "Damnit, Michaels! Did you have to blind me?"

"What the hell are you doing here?" Michaels demanded. "Don't tell me you've got a conscience about your men all of a sudden."

"Yeah," Maloney added, moving cautiously towards the man, "No one would believe a word you're saying."

Crogan opened his mouth to speak, only to suddenly spin around towards the darkness behind him. "Oh no. Not you again," he gasped, backing away as a grey clad figure suddenly rushed at him. A man dressed as a chauffeur, Michaels realized, with a big black bruise spreading across his forehead. The man Miss Trendle and Miss Krane had argued about earlier? Before Michaels could open his mouth, the newcomer grabbed Crogan by the throat, picking him up off his feet and throttling him with one hand. The other arm hung in a strange position, as if it had been broken.

There was no doubt in Michaels' mind that Crogan would have been dead if another figure hadn't leapt out of the darkness as well, this one wearing a red mask. Tiger's kick struck the chauffeur across the chin and ought to have been strong enough to knock its victim down. That it didn't was just another bit of weirdness to add to all the other oddities in this case.

"That one has bitten into more than he can chew," Mrs. McLeod said in a level voice that somehow carried through the entire room.

Tiger didn't respond to the jibe, instead circling around James as the man continued throttling the life out of Crogan. Michaels ran forward and put his gun to the chauffeur's temple. "Enough," he ordered. "I need him alive."

"I need to kill him," James said evenly, ignoring the weapon. Crogan's face was turning blue and he'd stopped struggling. "Both of them."

"That'd be me, I bet," Tiger said cheerfully, grabbing hold of James' arm and digging his claws in. Electricity sparked around his gloved hands and, quite suddenly, James dropped Crogan to the ground.

James swung his broken arm, striking first Michaels, then Tiger, and sending them both flying with the force of the blow. Then the chauffeur stepped towards Crogan again. "You're nothing if not dedicated," Tiger grumbled, rolling to his feet.

Before the man could grasp his target, a sudden humming sound came from the other end of the room. Michaels rolled sideways slightly to look and saw McLeod with one of his strange machines, one end aimed directly at James. A beam of light flared and struck the chauffeur in the center of his chest, throwing him backwards and against a rusted tangle of metal.

Michaels wasn't sure he wanted to stop McLeod. There was something very wrong with the chauffeur and he had a feeling that nothing would stop James from completing his self-appointed task, if he were free. Even so, "Don't kill him!" he gasped, as James' form faded into nothingness.

"It won't kill him, Chief," McLeod said, looking grim. "But I won't be able to get him back until I get this process to reverse. He's inside that engine block and not going anywhere for now."

"Good job, Mr. McLeod. I didn't really want to have to fight that fellow again." Tiger dusted his hands off and checked his coat for tears, before bowing deeply in the engineer's direction. "I do prefer to leave killing to those who enjoy it. Besides, it's just possible that Mrs. McLeod was right about him being a bit too much for me. Maybe."

Both McLeod and his wife gave the man identical looks of disgust, but neither answered. Instead, Mrs. McLeod said, more to the open air than to Tiger, "Certain annoying young people, who think they're clever, are only fooling themselves."

Tiger was at her side before Michaels could stop him. Fortunately, all the masked man wanted was to go on one knee before her and kiss her hand. "Terribly sorry to have upset you, ma'am, but I do have other things I should be doing." He was gone in an instant, his voice echoing behind him. "Adieu!"

After a moment, staring ruefully in the direction Tiger had gone, McLeod muttered, "If only Robby moved even half that fast."

ⅭⅭⅭ

The fingers wrapped around his throat felt like solid wood to William's flailing hands. Kicking his feet, trying to get at least one good blow in before he died, he was desperately aware that he wasn't strong enough to break free.

Alone, he would never have escaped. Fortunately, though it meant revealing himself, Dragon didn't hesitate, spinning around in a series of rapid movements that somehow resulted in William landing on the floor, his attacker's hand still gripping his neck. That was easily dealt with. Without an arm to maintain its grasp, the hand easily slipped free when William tugged at it.

Looking up, William saw his attacker struggling with Meng, the metallic form wrapped tightly around him, like a boa around its prey. Meng's jaws were clenched in the man's throat, but there was no blood. At the same time Dragon spun around the man, long sleeves of his coat swirling like curls of smoke.

William pulled himself to his feet, still clutching his attacker's disembodied hand. "What the hell?" he managed to gasp, finally finding his breath.

"Don't know," Dragon said brusquely. "Quiet. I'm busy." His sleeves seemed to lengthen as William watched, becoming long strands of silver that he slowly wrapped around William's attacker, dancing around the man in a confusing whirl of motion.

Then, suddenly, the man twisted Meng free of his body and flung the dragon at its master, knocking Dragon to the floor. Turning towards William again, he stretched out his remaining hand. William dodged just in time, leaping over the couch.

A poker struck the man's head, as Gordon attempted to come to William's defense. Unfortunately, it didn't help, for while it left a dent it didn't stop the man's attack on William. It was just as well, the old man wasn't strong enough for a fight.

William backed up further, nearly running into the big round table at the other end of the room. Automatically, he rolled backwards over it, eliciting a groan of protest from Gordon as he crashed through the glass centerpiece. "Sir! Please be careful!"

Apologizing, William felt he might be forgiven for ruining more of Miss Trendle's sitting room in the interests of keeping his neck from being broken. He rolled to his feet, keeping the table between himself and the intruder. To his shock, the man stepped straight forward, right through the wood.

Staring at his attacker, realizing that he had no way of stopping him, William backed away as Dragon called, "The hand! Use the hand!"

Momentarily confused, William almost let the man grab hold of him again, then remembered he was clutching the hand that had nearly throttled him earlier. Obediently, he thrust it into his attacker's chest. A moment later the man, thing, creature, whatever, shrieked as he became solid again, his hand sticking out of his chest.

William backed against the wall and watched his would-be killer stumble backwards and forwards, smoke beginning to pour from his mouth and ears. It was a familiar sight, the same kind of smoke had accompanied the creature Tiger had fought in the newsroom. This one had no control mechanism, or if it did, it was better hidden. Nor did it matter, for his attacker suddenly fell over, crashing to the floor with a thud that reverberated through the whole house.

Taking several long deep breaths, William stared at the body. He'd looked so innocuous, short dark hair, regular features and an impeccable suit that had been exactly what one would expect an attorney's assistant to wear. There'd been nothing about him - except an oddness about his ice blue eyes - to suggest he was anything but a normal man.

William knelt down beside the limp body and turned it over to look at him more carefully. "That's strange. Weren't his eyes blue?" The empty, staring, face was the same, but somehow his eyes had gone completely black. "Gordon? Are you all right?"

Gordon was picking up the chair William had knocked down earlier. "Sir is kind to ask, but yes. That... creature... had no interest in me." He straightened and after a brief moment where curiosity warred with proper etiquette, his training won. His brief glance at Dragon did not show an ounce of interest in who this stranger was, nor why he was there. "Sir is unharmed?"

"A MOMENT LATER THE MAN, THING, CREATURE, WHATEVER, SHRIEKED AS HE BECAME SOLID AGAIN, HIS HAND STICKING OUT OF HIS CHEST. "

"A little shaken up and I think my uniform collar may never be the same but, yes." Noticing a nervous face peering in through the servant's entrance, William added, "You'd best let the others know that everything is all right. No need for another panic."

With a bow, Gordon agreed and left the room, much to Dragon's obvious relief. "I never know how to deal with butlers," he muttered. "They always look at you like they're expecting you to break something just by walking near it."

Which, given the way Dragon seemed incapable of sitting still, was probably true. It also told William something of the young man's background. He wouldn't come into contact with butlers if he was from the south end of town.

Returning to the subject at hand, William indicated the body at his feet. "What is this thing?"

"An example of what our lady friend was talking about last night. A combination of magic and science."

"And can you figure out the magic?"

The young man examined the sprawled figure for a long moment then, regretfully, said, "There's something confusing about it. It's related to God magic, but not quite." He shook his head, shrugging eloquently. "Unless you're a Sorcerer, you're not going to understand."

"Then what do we do about it?"

"Best thought is to take it to an expert in God magic. I'd suggest Mudan McLeod." There was an apologetic sense to Dragon's expression under the mask. "You'll have to take it on your own, though. I hate asking her for help. She always wants something in return. But she'll help you without an argument, because you're your mother's son."

With that, Dragon disappeared, fading out from feet to head, so that all that remained, for the briefest of moments, was his mask.

《《《

"What in the world is happening here?"

Francis turned towards the front of the warehouse, where Robby McLeod was just entering the room, carrying a cardboard box with Chinese characters covering the side. "I heard shouting. Is everything all right. Should I call for the police? Oh, hello, Chief Michaels, I guess that's your car outside? I thought it looked familiar."

Robby's mother went to him and took the box he carried. "Enough. Do not ramble. This is not the time. And I will wish to talk to you later about your behavior."

The young man looked mildly embarrassed at his mother's scolding and fell silent, following her into the laboratory as his father told him, "We had some guests. At least one of whom could do with an attitude adjustment. Did you see anyone?"

"Not really. Should I have?" Robby looked around the room, spotting the man Michaels had called Crogan. "Is he all right?"

"He's in no fit state for talking," Officer Maloney said. "But I think he'll live. He might not be liking it though."

"Call an ambulance, Maloney. He'll be liking things a whole lot less if he doesn't get medical attention." Maloney hurried off to the offices at the front of the building, while Chief Michaels shook his head, staring down at the man at his feet. "A fine how-do-you-do."

"And no one's told me what happened, still," Robby said plaintively. "I go for lunch and miss everything. That's not at all fair."

Taking pity on the young man, Francis told him the story quickly. "So now James is stuck in that engine block over there and I still don't understand anything that's going on. This man was the one at my house last night. What did he want here?"

Chief Michaels coughed. "Crogan's the boss of the gambling and protection racket in Strikers Port. Dolan's one of his men, but he usually doesn't risk getting his fingers dirty. I'm not sure why he's here at all."

"Last night he said he was after an unwanted partner he called The Voice. Could that have something to do with it?" She wasn't quite sure why she thought so. "Whomever The Voice is, he has some hold on Mr. Crogan. I almost think he's scared of him."

Returning to the workshop, Maloney scoffed. "Scared? Crogan's too damn stupid to be scared." At Chief Michaels' expression, the officer added, "Well? It's true, right?"

"I'd say that Crogan's got a one track mind and a lack of common sense," Chief Michaels admitted. "But he's no fool. Give him the right information and he can make something out of it faster than most crooks."

"You're quite right, Chief Michaels."

They all turned towards the source of the words, a shadowy figure that seemed to flow out of the darkness, a voice, a harsh crackle that sent a wave of terror through the room. Smoke billowed around the figure and two red eyes glowed amid the shadows. Francis caught a glimpse of movement out of the corner of her eye, Mrs. McLeod putting her hand on Robby's wrist to keep him put.

Maloney was the only one who reacted, shooting before anyone could speak. That only elicited laughter, a horrible sound. "Hello again, Officer Maloney. It's been a long, long, time. Long enough for you to forget that bullets don't work on me, I notice."

"So She was right. You are alive," Chief Michaels said grimly.

"I never die. It's not part of the job description," the voice said, still laughing. "She ought to have told you that. Though, granted, you probably didn't ask the right question. You humans never do." He moved closer and a shaft of light from the lamps caught his face briefly before the smoke covered it again. His features seemed familiar to Francis but in her terror she couldn't think why.

As the figure moved forward, cloak of smoke and fire billowing around him, Mrs. McLeod suddenly stepped into his path, raising her hands in a peculiar gesture. Quietly, in a tone that brooked no argument, she said something in Chinese that resonated through the entire room and set every piece of metal echoing like bells.

The stranger stepped back momentarily, laugh less confident than before. "Oh, no, Lady. I recognize this is His territory while you are here. I have no intention of challenging Him."

More ringing words, a gesture of command that Francis didn't need translated. It was obvious Mrs. McLeod was telling him to go. She didn't understand how the woman could intimidate a creature like this but she was desperately glad of it.

Bowing, the stranger managed one last chuckle. "I don't intend to stay, either. But I've come for what's mine." He bent down and picked Crogan up with one clawed hand.

Somehow, Chief Michaels managed to croak, "You're going to kill him?"

"Oh, no. I'm quite reformed in that regard, Chief Michaels. But while Crogan is, as Maloney has said, more of a fool than any man in his position has a right to be, he amuses me. And I need the entertainment." The stranger swung Crogan up onto his shoulder and backed away from Mrs. McLeod's twisting fingers. "Oh, and as an apology for intruding, you should take a look at Crogan's office. Dolan isn't The Voice's only victim."

With that, the smoke receded, leaving Francis and the others staring at nothing. Then Robby was at his mother's side, catching her to keep her from falling. "Ma!"

"I am all right, boy. I channeled more of His power than I needed." She turned to face them, managing a slight smile. "And I would appreciate it if this were not mentioned elsewhere. I do not use His gift lightly."

"I'm remembering that Old Smoky tended to avoid Chinatown," Chief Michaels said quietly. "Would you be the reason?"

"My God would be the reason, Chief Michaels. I am only a Priestess and all my power proceeds from Him. Where I am, He is."

Maloney looked as if he might explode. "Your God? One of them heathen devils?" He suddenly stopped as every eye turned on him and he suddenly realized the husband of the woman he was scolding stood within inches of him, expression strongly suggesting he'd best watch what he said. "I'm being quiet now," he muttered, flushing a bright red.

"Good, you do that," Chief Michaels told him. "And I'll believe you can hold your tongue when I see it."

While Maloney sulked, Francis turned to Mrs. McLeod. "I don't understand."

"Without a good understanding of magic and what my husband calls metaphysics, I fear I cannot easily explain." Mrs. McLeod was about to say more, but then she turned an inquiring eye towards the front of the building, where a door was opening. "Which will have to wait. We seem to have visitors."

Francis was relieved when she saw that the newcomer was another police officer, this one about her age. She recognized him immediately. Chief Michaels had taken him with him into the Sentinel building when her offices were attacked. The young man came forward and she realized he was carrying a limp figure.

"I'm sorry to interrupt, Chief Michaels," the officer said, eyes on his Chief and ignoring everyone else. "but I ran into trouble at Miss Trendle's. This man, or whatever he is, tried to kill me."

"But why bring him here, Jarvis? You should take him to the lock-up."

"I'm sorry sir. I'm not entirely sure a lock-up could hold him," Jarvis lay the man down on the floor between them, adding, "Besides, an informant who I think is expert in these matters, suggested I bring him here for Mrs. McLeod to look at."

Coming closer, Mrs. McLeod eyed the body on the floor and sighed. "Someone is being lazy again. Bring this one with us to the Jeen Loon and I will do what I can."

((((

As William dragged the body to the car and stuck it into the back seat again, he wished he'd left it there in the first place. The man seemed to weigh about three times as much as someone his height and weight ought to. If William weren't accustomed to lifting and moving the big punching bags at his father's place, handling the man would have been a struggle.

"May I come too?"

Miss Trendle's question startled him because William hadn't noticed her approach. He went to the passenger seat and held the door for Mrs. McLeod before turning to answer. "I'm not sure that would be a good idea."

"You said this man came to my house," Miss Trendle pointed out. "And you didn't bother telling us the details."

Before William objected, Mrs. McLeod touched his hand lightly. "Miss Trendle is almost as involved in this matter as you are, young man. I think it better if you share your knowledge."

With a sigh, because taking Miss Trendle meant moving the body around, William agreed. To his surprise she leaned in from the other side and did her best to help. "I could tell he was heavy," she told him when he gave her a startled look. "Actually, I'm amazed you could move him at all."

It took a minute or so to finally get everything settled but once they had, and once Miss Trendle had told her chauffeur to meet them at the Jeen Loon, William started the engine and started up the twisting road to Chinatown.

"Now," Miss Trendle said, once they were on their way. "Tell me what happened at the house. Is everyone all right?"

"Gordon nearly gave himself an aneurism trying to beat that fellow's skull in when he attacked me, but, yes. Everyone's fine." William glanced at the woman through the mirror and saw her sigh with relief. "As for what happened; I was at the house looking for clues to last night's attack. That man came to the door and demanded to see me. He had some papers, or at least claimed to have some papers, I was supposed to sign." It occurred to him then that he'd not bothered to check.

"Papers?"

"Well, yes. It's a different matter entirely. My aunt sold some property that turned out to have been put in my name. He claimed he had papers for me to sign."

Miss Trendle made a startled sound. "Wait... property.... Jarvis... You're Billy?" She sounded disgusted with herself. "I don't believe I didn't recognize you!"

"It's been over twenty years, Miss Trendle, and you're not that much older than I am," William told her. "If Gordon hadn't reminded me that I'd been at your house I wouldn't have remembered it at all." They'd been quite young when his mother would visit her oldest and best friend up on the hill, dressing him in what passed for finery and insisting that he and Francis get along. Which, he thought, they did as well as any children their age did.

"I recognized your name in Bruce's article," Miss Trendle told him. "But I didn't realize you were a police officer." She leaned over the body, searching through his pockets. When William protested, though, she told him, "I want to see if he really did have papers."

"Such a man would surely carry papers in an attaché," Mrs. McLeod said suddenly. "If he were truly from an attorney, that is. Did he have an attaché, Officer Jarvis?"

William realized with annoyance that he hadn't checked to see if anything had been left behind. "I assumed that he'd used the paper story as an excuse."

Mrs. McLeod smiled, "Even so, to fool a wise butler like Gordon, he would surely carry such a thing. It may be a good idea to examine Miss Trendle's house for anything he may have left behind. Just in case."

"For now, though, we're here," Miss Trendle said. "And I hope you don't mind, Mrs. McLeod, but after what just happened, I would like to find out more." For William's edification, she added, "A man named Crogan was attacked by someone who, now that I've had a good look this man, might be his brother. When another... person... came in to rescue Crogan, Mrs. McLeod chased him off in a way that, frankly, I'm still trying to wrap my mind around."

"Do not, please, make so much of what I did. That one is more cautious these days than he once was. He was easily frightened off." Mrs. McLeod leaned forward and pointed to the side street that went around to the alleys behind the west side of Chinatown's main street. "Take us to the back, if you will. There are delicate objects in the shop. It would be better not to bring that man in through that way. Besides, the basement is easier to reach from the back."

William obeyed, threading the big car through the narrow streets and wondering how the shopkeepers managed to get delivery trucks in and out. It was a question he'd have to ask sooner or later, he realized, if he planned on getting out himself. That, though, was something he'd think about later, because they'd soon reached the back of the shop.

Dragging the body onto his shoulder again, William followed Mrs. McLeod and Miss Trendle inside, only to hear a voice from the room Chou Chang had showed him the night before. "Customers not permitted in back. Please to go to front for service."

"Where, it is to be hoped, there is someone actually there to serve them?" Mrs. McLeod demanded in a dangerous tone.

Chou Chang appeared at the door of his workshop, eyes wide and startled. Then he was on his mother with a hug that nearly knocked her off her feet. "Ma. This insignificant child did not expect to see you here."

With a sigh, Mrs. McLeod detached her younger son from her and looked up at him. "I do not know why you would think that," she pointed out. "Nor why you would act as if you have not seen me for weeks. I distinctly remember seeing you at the dinner table last night. Eating far more noodles than is good for any one person."

He grinned impishly, dropping the broken Chinese. "And it was a wonderful meal. Thank you, Ma."

Another sigh, this one accompanied by a twitch of the lips that suggested the lady was trying not to smile, "Do not try to get out of trouble with flattery. You are supposed to be minding the store."

"You did say I could hire help if I needed it. I needed it. Tan's sister Mei is up front."

"Mei? Is she any good?"

Before the conversation could continue, because he had a feeling the two could have talked about the shop forever if permitted, William coughed. Reminded of the task at hand, Mrs. McLeod gave him an apologetic smile. "Yes, you are right, Officer. We have work to do. Chou, since you are not busy...."

"I'm always busy, Ma!"

"Not busy with the shop, then," Mrs. McLeod corrected. "Come with us. We have an interesting puzzle to consider." Without bothering to make sure they followed, she went to a door and opened it, revealing a set of stairs leading down. "This way, please. It is not far."

Following Mrs. McLeod into the basement, William reflected that the lady's idea of far and his weren't the same. They were led through a tangled maze of passages for some distance before finally reaching a larger room. Lit by candles and hung with tapestries, it was obviously a temple of some sort. But not to Buddha, despite the many similarities. Whatever God it was that was worshipped here was one he recognized only because he'd seen a much smaller version of his statue. What was the name Chou had called it? Meng Huang Shang; God of Dreams and Delirium.

⟨⟨⟨

The little temple made Francis uncomfortable. She wasn't religious, having been raised by a sceptic father, but this place felt strange. She had to admit the room was gorgeous, though, covered in tapestries with scenes of strange beasts and people doing incomprehensible things. Bright colors abounded and fine hangings of sheer cloth billowed slowly in a breeze she could just barely feel. Clouds of scented smoke drifted through the room, perfuming the air with a mix of sandalwood and jasmine.

The statue on the altar was of a delicately formed young man lounging on the back of a tiger, carved from what might have been a single block of white crystal. Despite this, there was something about the whole thing that made her feel as if he might lift his head and stare right at her at any moment. She didn't know why, but she both desired and dreaded his doing so. She looked away from the statue and the feeling faded.

Quietly, Mrs. McLeod indicated a spot on the floor in front of the statue. "If you would, please, put the body there. Also, please excuse me, but I must be rude and speak in the language my God knows best. He understands all speech, but he does not like to forget the land from which he comes." She paused, then added ruefully, "My God is not easy to comprehend. If he agrees to speak, it does not guarantee his answers will help."

Although Francis didn't understand what Mrs. McLeod meant, she bowed her head slightly. She and William moved off to the side, staring with both staring with similar expressions of curiosity and confusion.

Chou Chang sat down on the floor with a set of hand drums, tapping out a beat as Mrs. McLeod stood before the altar. She raised her hands in a series of gestures similar to those she'd used back at the workshop. At the same time she began to sing in a high pitched voice, the Chinese words utterly incomprehensible.

At first it seemed like any ceremony, albeit one performed in an unfamiliar language. Then Francis felt that strange, overwhelming, sense of dread and desire. This time it didn't fade when she tried to turn away from the statue. It grew stronger and stronger, until she felt she would break down crying from the sheer force of emotion. Inchoate needs, never expressed, nor even admitted to, struggled to break free and it took all Francis had to hold them back.

Slowly, Mrs. McLeod turned to face them, her eyes strangely dilated and her expression very nearly the same as the one on the statue; a strange, mad, look that seemed to be staring straight into Francis' mind. "I am called," she said, in a strange tone that set every metal object in the room ringing. "I have come. Ask what you would know."

Francis hesitated and before she could open her mouth, William asked, "You're... Meng Wan Shan?"

Off to the side, Chou corrected him, "Meng Huang Shang," he said. "Do not waste time. Mother cannot hold him long."

To Francis' surprise, Mrs. McLeod giggled, the hangings rippling with the soft noise. "Time flies when you're having fun." She danced around suddenly, arms rising and falling as she sang tunelessly. "I know what you want to know. Wanting's not the same as needing."

Quickly, realizing that Mrs. McLeod had been right to say her God would be difficult to understand, Francis guessed quickly and asked, "Can you tell us what we need, then?"

Mrs. McLeod was right in front of Francis in a heartbeat and it took everything Francis had not to back away. "Children should be herded in a scene... I mean, seen and not heard."

Uncertainly, Francis asked, "Do you mean me?" Should she have held her tongue after all? Maybe this 'God' or whatever it was didn't like women.

Shaking her finger in Francis' face, Mrs. McLeod told her, "You're not a child anymore." She spun around, danced in place for a moment longer and continued, pointing at William. "Neither are you, but that's when it all begins."

Francis took a deep breath, trying to work out the right thing to say. "When what all begins?"

"Spoil the rod and spare the child... no, wait, spare the child and spoil the rod...." Confused, Mrs. McLeod, or whatever was speaking through her pondered for a moment before finally saying, "Oh, right. Spare the rod, spoil the child. Children. Though I don't know how to discipline chaos. You should ask their father."

This was becoming ridiculous, Francis thought. "Why can't you just tell us straight?"

"Because," Mrs. McLeod said, sticking her finger in Francis' face, "Your language doesn't have the right thoughts. And your thoughts don't have the right language. If I could tell you what you need to know, you wouldn't need me to tell you."

Chou added, "Gods outside human understanding. If you understand them, you are a God yourself, or next thing to."

In an odd way, that made sense. Yet it left them with questions that this being couldn't answer in a way they understood and a situation they couldn't do anything about. Too, the ringing from the bells was fading, suggesting that the God couldn't stay much longer. Nor, from the way Mrs. McLeod was sweating and turning pale, was it a good idea. "Is there anything else you can tell us, then?"

The God made an effort. "The time of machines and magic isn't now. Only disaster can ensue." With that, the bells went silent and Mrs. McLeod dropped to the floor, panting as she sprawled there.

Chou left his drums to bring his mother a small bottle of something. "The God wasn't clear," he said quietly. "But I suspect the problem lies in your past." He pointed at William, who looked deeply confused. "In your childhood, God said."

Francis agreed, "Maybe it has to do with the Jewel Island house," she offered. "You did say that man claimed to be from your aunt's attorney. We should investigate that next." She was guessing, but everything had started right after John had found out that the house was William's.

William opened his mouth to protest but Chou interrupted, "Perhaps, as you have brought the body here, we should examine his belongings?"

"I searched his pockets," Francis offered and admitted, "Not very well. I didn't like to touch him." It wasn't because he'd appeared to be dead. "Something's not right about him."

Chou went to the body and opened its jacket and for the first time Francis realized what had killed the man. There was a wrist sticking out from the middle of his chest, the place where it'd been cut off looking like the cross-cut of a tree branch. The fabric of the shirt looked burned and charred.

"Wait," William said as Chou began pulling the shirt open, "I don't think you should do that. The morgue...." Before he finished the sentence Chou had finished, sitting back to frown at the sight of a chest that appeared to be carved from wood.

They all stared at the thing, not one of them sure what to do. "Never mind. The morgue isn't going to know what to do with this," William said slowly, sounding defeated.

There were screws in the wood and Chou pulled out a screwdriver. "You are correct," he said, quickly and expertly undoing each screw until he could remove the panel covering the thing's chest, prying it off carefully along with the hand stuck through it.

Inside there were delicate gears, or what had once been delicate gears. Now they were twisted and broken, some melted by the same heat that must have charred the shirt. Mounted at the center was a piece of grey crystal. Chou removed it carefully, detaching it from its connections with sure fingers.

As he raised it into the light Francis saw something flicker inside it, a movement that she would have thought was just refraction, if it hadn't seemed too nebulous. "Careful," she started to say, just as the quartz shattered in Chou's hand, shards striking his raised arm, lifted barely in time to protect his face.

A swirl of shadow twisted in the middle of the room and Mrs. McLeod was on it before it could act, catching the snake like shape right behind its head. Without hesitation and just before it twisted itself around her arm, she flung it towards the statue. "A gift for you, My Lord."

Francis squeezed her eyes shut a moment. The statue hadn't moved, she was sure it hadn't, but she swore she saw its hand reach up to catch the smoke, lift its captive high and drop it into an opened mouth as if it were a grape.

Mrs. McLeod bowed to the statue, her hands raised in thanks. Then she turned back to Francis and William. "I do not know what that thing was, nor how it came to be within that stone. But I think it is a significant portion of your troubles. Nor do I believe it is the only one."

《《《

The sound of arguing behind the door was loud enough that even the noise from the boxers in the gym couldn't drown it out entirely. So clear was it that the man standing on the other side could hear every word. Not that he needed to, to know what it was about. George Jarvis would never say or do anything to convenience his hated sister-in-law. Neither, for that matter, would Harriet Krane stop demanding he do so.

John Striker didn't know how long the argument had gone, but it wouldn't end soon, or well. Jarvis wouldn't hit a woman, no matter how much he might want to, but sooner or later John's aunt would find herself picked up and carried out kicking and screaming to the curb. Which, in turn, would lead to assault charges and William being forced to give up ownership of the Jewel Island house to save his father from prison.

That was not in John Striker's plans and he entered the office. Instantly, he regretted it. The noise had been bad enough through the door. Now he felt deafened. "Excuse me," he said, then repeated the words in the stentorian roar he'd learned from his father. That got their attention.

"John, whatever are you doing here? This isn't the sort of place for the owner of Striker Enterprises."

John eyed his aunt with a dour look. "And what of the Chief Executive Officer of Krane Winery?" He waved off her protests, adding, "We're here on the same business. To discuss the Jewel Island property with the owner's father." Deliberately, he emphasized the word 'owner', reminding her of her legal standing in the matter.

George Jarvis was a big, muscular, man with a face that showed exactly how he made a living. His jaw and his ears were thickened and solid from all the blows he'd taken over the years. "So you're ganging up on me?" he demanded. "What's it going to take to get you off my back?"

"Talk to your son," Aunt Harriet began but John put up a hand. "What is it, boy?"

"Mr. Jarvis...." John's aunt snorted at the title but John just glared at her until she was quiet, then repeated, "Mr. Jarvis isn't Bill's master, Aunt Harriet. Even if he were agreeable to what you want, he can't do much more than ask."

"He's the boy's father. William will surely listen to sense if it comes from his own father."

John said quietly, "Good sense, legal sense, would be for Bill to keep the title and for you to pay me back so I can buy it from him. You shouldn't have tried to sell the place without checking the title first." As Aunt Harriet glared at him, John added grimly, "I thought you'd try to weasel your way out of trouble. In the end, unless Bill cooperates, that property isn't yours to sell and you owe me the fifty percent down payment. And it doesn't matter to me if you already spent the five hundred thousand. You'll pay me back, one way or another."

A cold expression crossed Aunt Harriet's face as Jarvis realized just how much money was involved. Satisfied that he'd thwarted his Aunt's interference without breaking his promise not to tell Bill how much was at stake, John continued, "Now, I'd appreciate it if you were to go back to whatever bat filled cave you came from and leave me to discuss the matter with Mr. Jarvis here."

"You are a horribly rude young man and I have no desire to speak with you again until you apologize," Aunt Harriet told him. "Don't think this is over because I'm leaving. I will have my way. Or else."

Then she was gone, leaving the room in a state so close to a snit that John knew the only thing that kept her from behaving like her daughter in a tantrum was the lady's desire to maintain dignity. "That's what I'm afraid of," he muttered, as the door slammed shut behind her.

"Five-hundred thousand?" Jarvis repeated disbelievingly. "For a falling down wreck that hasn't been lived in since the old man died?"

"The structure's sound and inside isn't that bad," John told him.

"But five-hundred thousand?"

John grinned, "If things go the way I plan, the place will be the jewel in my crown. A resort to rival Hilton or Chateau Marmont."

Giving John a sharp look for his arrogance, Jarvis just said, "Given you get the property."

"Oh, the property will be mine in the end. Bill's already agreed to that, whatever he does about Aunt Harriet. And she's doing her best to make sure he doesn't cooperate, with all her screeching that he should. Even an even-tempered soul like Bill would take offense." John took a seat in the chair across from Jarvis' desk. "But I have other questions about the place. Ones Bill can't answer."

Almost innocently, Jarvis sat down behind the desk and leaned back to gaze levelly at John. "Questions?" he repeated.

"Yes. Such as exactly how Aunt Gwen died. And where."

《《《

Some time after William left for Chinatown, Michaels decided to check Crogan's office. Old Smoky might have been laying a trap for him, but Michaels doubted it. That one could go anywhere and do whatever he pleased. He didn't need a trap to hurt someone. Besides, Michaels wanted to find out what Crogan had to do with this mess.

Leaving Maloney to keep an eye on things, Michaels took McLeod with him. If there was another victim then McLeod's thoughts might be useful. Besides, he wanted to talk to the man without his subordinate interrupting. Given the damned fool's comments to McLeod's wife, that could have led to trouble.

Driving through the warehouse district, Michaels wondered how to address his questions. Deciding there was no point beating around the bush, he said, straight out, "Your wife knows magic, so I'm thinking you understand a bit about it?"

"Enough to keep out of trouble and not enough to be useful, Chief." McLeod grinned ruefully, "I let my wife handle anything of that sort where I can."

"Then I can ask you, was it magic that stuck Dolan in the block? Or science? And either way, who could be doing such a thing?"

"My wife says she thinks both science and magic are involved, but that the latter is a sort she's not accustomed to. Strictly speaking, she's not a proper Sorceress anyway, since she gets her magic from her God."

"I was told it might be a mix," Michaels admitted, "Can she help?"

"She's going to have a long discussion on the matter with her God. Near as I can tell, he's a bit flighty and it's hard to get - and keep - his attention in the best of circumstances." McLeod laughed suddenly, "I'm sure a well-raised Catholic boy like yourself is having no end of fits inside. I would be too, if my family didn't have a long tradition of magic."

Michaels managed a rueful smile. "Well, now, I won't say it isn't a strain. But I've seen things that make the whole question of religion a bit greyer than it was when I was a boy."

"Good. Mudan says the magic seems to be both very old and very young. She also thinks it's being contained somehow. Controlled. That would probably be the science."

Surprised, Michaels asked, "But that ray-gun thingy o' yours did the same thing the critter in the newsroom did." He paused, making a sharp left into the alley behind Crogan's offices and parked, "And that Tiger fellow took that out by breaking its controller."

McLeod had a sour look on his face at the mention of Tiger. Without explanation, he said, "My ray-gun thingy, as you put it, alters the atomic structure of an object, shifting it out of phase with our physical reality. But that doesn't preclude it being done with magic - it depends on the Sorcerer's abilities." He shook his head, adding, "Without a better idea of what state Dolan was phased to, I can't be sure how he got there. I could do with more samples."

"Another dimension? Like the side-step where ghosts and spirits exist?"

McLeod considered the question. "Possibly. I haven't ruled out the idea that whatever stuck Dolan in the wall is similar to my phase-shifter. I'm not the only one to experiment with the concept. Though I think the only other scientists remotely near to success are long since dead."

That made Michaels pause before opening the door to the building. "Who?"

"Fellow named Tesla, for one. He had a friend in town, though, Doctor William Jarvis." At Michaels' stunned stare, McLeod asked, "Is there something wrong?"

"The lad who brought in that other fellow just now? That can't be right. He's just a boy. And he's no doctor, either."

A look of understanding crossed McLeod's face. "Oh, I see. No, that wasn't who I meant at all. But that young man might be a relative. Is your officer's father a boxer? Yes? Then the William Jarvis I knew and worked for would have been his grandfather. It was his eternal regret that his only son wasn't at all interested in science."

Going upstairs, Michaels wondered if he should remove the kid from the case. As he reached the door and listened at it, he shook off the idea. William might have inherited his grandfather's smarts but that was no reason to assume he was behind these troubles. "I'll be troubling you to stand back," he told McLeod, focusing on the matter at hand.

Obediently, McLeod did so as Michaels kicked Crogan's door. It took several good, solid, blows to get there but at last, splintered and partially caved in, the thing gave in to his attack, half-turning, half-falling, into the room beyond.

At the same time another door opened and someone darted out at top speed, only to run straight into McLeod, who caught the man's arm and did something that flipped him head-over-heels and face down onto the floor. "Sorry," he said genially but unapologetically, "You startled me."

Michaels drew his gun and nudged the man onto his back. "You look like a dying fish, Donaldson."

"Damnit! I think he broke my wrist."

"Oh, I don't think so. More likely sprained. Put a warm compress on and keep it elevated," McLeod suggested.

Michaels dragged Donaldson back into Crogan's empty office. "Now just what exactly is going on here...." His voice trailed off as he caught sight of the wall opposite Crogan's desk. Apparently, Old Smoky had been telling nothing but the truth. Two of Crogan's men were embedded so completely in the wall that the only way one could tell they weren't paintings was because they were moving.

"McLeod," he said grimly, "I have more samples for you."

William still wasn't sure he should have let Miss Trendle, Francis, convince him to go with her to visit Aunt Harriet's solicitor. He couldn't see how his personal business could have anything to do with the attack on her paper. For that matter, William wasn't sure how Mrs. McLeod had known to call Crogan's office to get Michaels permission, nor how she'd known the number.

Their first stop had been Francis' home, where they'd found the attaché case the supposed attorney had left behind, complete with the papers that William would need to sign if he meant to hand the title to his grandfather's house over to Aunt Harriet. The sight of them gave him a chill because their presence meant the thing that had tried to kill him had told the truth about its purpose. Did that mean that his Aunt was involved in this mess? He didn't like her at all, but surely that was too much, even for her.

Feeling like he was being dragged along by the current, William entered the law offices of Harcourt Bend and introduced himself to the secretary. His name had the desired effect, persuading the woman to send him through. It took more persuading to get Francis in too, but William put his foot down on that note.

Inside, William shook Mr. Bend's hand with a grip that he realized had been a bit too strong. This despite the fact that Bend was a broad shouldered fellow who clearly prided himself on his condition. "Mr. Jarvis... I mean, Officer Jarvis. So good of you to come. And who is this young lady? Your fiancée, perhaps?"

" ...THE ONLY WAY ONE COULD TELL THEY WEREN'T
PAINTINGS WAS BECAUSE THEY WERE MOVING. "

"I'm Francis Trendle, Mr. Bend, with the Sentinel. Mr. Jarvis asked me to come because I'm more experienced with financial matters."

The solicitor gave Francis a sharp look. "I'm terribly sorry, Miss Trendle, I didn't recognize you. Your picture in the Sentinel hardly does you justice." He showed them to seats across from his, then sat and smiled at William. "Now then, I believe I know why you're here. You received the note I sent to the station? Or perhaps at your home?"

"Note?" William repeated. "No. I haven't been back to the station for most of the afternoon." The day was nearly over, he realized. "I came because your man left his attaché case, with the papers Aunt Harriet wants me to sign, at Miss Trendle's."

"Man? Attaché? Papers?" Bend appeared confused. "I sent my office boy to the police station and your house with a note for you to come here. I certainly would never have sent anyone with the... how did you get those?"

William set the papers they'd found in the attaché on the desk between them. "They were in this case." He held the thing up, adding, "The man who brought them to me was about your height, dark-haired, tanned, with blue eyes and regular features. Is that what your office boy looks like?"

"No. My office boy is a lad about eighteen. Blond-haired with grey eyes. He's gone for the day, or I'd call him in." A grim look crossed the attorney's face, "And if he took those papers and gave them to someone else... or if anyone did... I swear heads will roll. In a figurative sense of course, Officer."

William ignored the joke. "Of course. I'd appreciate it if you found out how those papers left your office, though. The man who brought them to me caused some problems at Miss Trendle's house."

Bend shook his head. "Terrible. Just terrible. Mrs. Krane will be horrified to find out what happened." He paused and looked at the papers thoughtfully, "I don't suppose I can persuade you to sign now?"

The last time William had refused to sign anything, someone had tried to choke him to death, so he felt excused for hesitating. Fortunately, Miss Trendle came to his rescue. "The only papers in the file hand Mr. Jarvis' house to Mr. and Mrs. Krane completely. There's no discussion of remuneration, or any conditions to protect Mr. Jarvis from any damages ensuing due to the house being sold without his knowledge or approval. I'm not an attorney, but I think he needs one before he does anything else."

Mr. Bend looked annoyed and William suspected he was cursing well-educated young women with the sense to ask the right questions. "Well, yes. Of course. Given these papers were all you found, I have to assume the rest are lost. We'll have to redo them and present them later. Perhaps we can make an appointment?"

"Of course," William found his voice and pretended he believed the attorney's explanation, "Miss Trendle is right. I should get my own attorney. I'm not accustomed to this and I'd hate to make a mistake in the process. It'd just cause everyone so much more trouble."

That said; Harcourt Bend couldn't wait to get rid of them. Only when William and Francis were back outside the building did the young woman say, in a voice that brooked no argument. "Bill, I want you to promise me, sign nothing, agree to nothing, until I get my attorney in on this." When he gave her a startled look, about to protest that he couldn't afford it, she added, "John may not have told you how much he's paying for the place, but it's a good deal more than you think. Trust me, your share will be more than enough to pay for a good attorney."

Perforce, William agreed. "All right. Ask him if I can make an appointment. I'd like to get this over with as soon as possible." With that, he left her with her chauffeur and headed back to the station. It was high time he and his father talked. Maybe over a steak at the diner? From the looks of things, he could afford that much.

CCCC

It took Michaels less time to persuade Donaldson to talk than it usually did. Crogan's troubles had, apparently, been such that Donaldson had been getting more and more nervous about everything.

"So some fellow called The Voice did this?" he asked, a little incredulous. In all his years of dealing with masked vigilantes and assorted villains, he'd yet to find one with a moniker quite as melodramatic as this one. Although the fellow calling himself - without a trace of irony - "The Master of Mayhem" had come close.

"That's what Crogan calls him. He never called himself anything, really." Donaldson watched McLeod as the engineer tapped at the wall where his compatriots had been embedded. "Be careful, mister! You might hurt them!"

McLeod gave the man a reassuring smile. "I promise I'm being careful. But I need to work out exactly how to get the wall back to my workshop so I can examine them."

Michaels drew the man's attention back to the matter at hand. "I don't care who named The Voice. I want to know if he's the one behind this mess."

With a gulp, Donaldson looked around guiltily. "I don't want to end up like them."

"Unless I miss my guess, Crogan's been losing Seconds for a bit now. If you'd like to end up like them, just let this Voice fellow keep bossing him around and getting him in trouble."

"If The Voice finds out, I'll be in trouble."

Michaels sighed, feeling put upon. "Look, just tell me when this started and what The Voice wanted Crogan to do and I'll try to keep you out of…." He broke off, seeing terror in his prisoner's eyes. Instinct made him grab the arms of the chair Donaldson was sitting in and throw it down sideways. At the same time he dropped to the floor beside the man and glanced over his shoulder. "McLeod! Get down!" he shouted, seeing the lamp on the desk glowing.

As Michaels curled up, fully expecting an explosion or something else horrible to happen, a strange sound fluttered in his ears, setting up a resonance that made every bone in his body feel as if they were getting ready to shatter. He was screaming, but the only thing he could hear was that god-awful sound.

Then, with a sudden jolt that almost stunned him into unconsciousness, the noise stopped. Not that he could hear anything with it gone, deafening as it had been. Slowly, expecting to find bits and pieces of himself scattered about the room, or worse, embedded in the walls, he forced himself to sit up and look around.

A man was standing in front of the desk, his hands moving in broad, smooth, gestures like a ballet dancer's. It was one of the Claws. The magic using one, Dragon. Which was exactly what was needed, because he was focused entirely on keeping a sphere of roiling black smoke contained.

McLeod was sitting up on the other side of the room and when he spotted Dragon he struggled to his feet, reaching out to catch hold of the man's arm. Except Dragon's pet rose up between him and McLeod, preventing the engineer from reaching his master.

A voice yelled something, just barely audible over the buzz in Michaels' ears. He couldn't make out the words but he thought Dragon was telling them to get out. McLeod obviously didn't want to, arguing angrily as he tried to grab hold of the young man.

Realizing their danger, Michaels got to his feet and grabbed McLeod by the elbow, dragging the man back to the door. It wasn't easy. McLeod wasn't a big man, but there was a wiry strength to him that made it impossible to move him where he didn't want to go. "I'm not leaving him!" McLeod shouted, his words becoming more audible as Michaels' hearing cleared.

"You can't help!" Michaels shouted back, grabbing the man tightly and trying to shove him away.

They might have continued until Dragon's ability to contain the smoke failed him, but that was when another roiling cloud of smoke formed into a pillar on the opposite side of the sphere. Two red eyes glowed within the darkness, sending a chill through Michaels so that he was forced to look away.

"You were supposed to watch him!" Old Smoky's voice remained a horror to listen to, the sound of a howling wind and a burning fire all wrapped into one soul-shattering package.

"I did. I saved him like you asked. You only saved Tiger once."

"He's gone where I can't follow!"

"And? You want more, earn it! This thing's yours anyway!"

Old Smoky had a command of the vernacular that would have been the envy of any dockworker. His expletives ranged from the mildly abusive to outright scurrilous. They also had no effect on Dragon, who pointed out, "Running out of time. Won't hurt you but if this breaks loose, we're fried and then where will you be?"

One last curse and Old Smoky stretched out his hands, or whatever they were, and stuck them straight into the sphere. As Dragon released his grip, Old Smoky did something that sucked the twisting darkness into himself. "I didn't bring you into this world," he growled as it fought him, "But I damn well can take you out."

Crisis over, Dragon recalled his familiar. "Where is he?" he asked.

"If I knew, I wouldn't need you to help me!"

"Right. Meng and I will do what we can." Dragon paused momentarily to glance at Michaels and McLeod and smiled ruefully. "Don't wait up." Then he was gone, fading into nothingness before anyone could speak.

Michaels turned his attention on Old Smoky, wondering what he was up to and what he would do next, and was a little surprised at the embarrassed way the old troublemaker shuffled what would have been feet if he'd had legs. "Ah. Sorry about this. Personal business."

"Where did you send him?" there was a dangerous note to McLeod's voice that niggled at Michaels; he couldn't quite put a finger on why.

"I said. It's personal." Old Smoky paused, as if listening to something, then cursed. "And more than that young fool can manage on his own. I have to go." Before McLeod could ask another question, the pillar of smoke melted backwards through the wall, leaving a burn mark in the dingy plaster behind.

⟪⟪⟪

Noticing the lights were on at John's house, Francis realized he was back from Jewel Island. After a moment's thought, she decided to ask her old friend about Bill's situation. The poor man had looked like he had been slapped in the face with every last fish in a barrel when they'd parted and she felt it was partly her fault. It'd been the right thing to do, but maybe Bill would have been happier never knowing how he'd been cheated.

Fortunately, John was not only home but available to talk, which led to the two of them sitting in his library over glasses of sherry. "So, now we're settled," John asked, "What brings you here? You're usually too busy to drop by."

"I'm here about Bill Jarvis." At John's raised brow, she asked, "The paper did an article on the problem you ran into with the Krane house. You don't think I wouldn't know about it?"

"I'm just surprised you've taken up the cause. Bill's my cousin. We even went to the same school together, thanks to my dad being too cheap to spring for a private school, so we're friends, but you haven't seen him in years. Not since his mom died."

Feeling guilty, Francis pointed out, "That wasn't my decision."

John gave her a reassuring smile, "Franky, I know that. Bill's dad is a prickly S.O.B. with no love for any of Aunt Gwen's rich and snooty family. I was lucky to get the time of day from him last time we talked. Besides, there wasn't any reason for him to bring Bill up to visit. He didn't know any of us."

"Even so…."

"I know. If I'd known about that deed, I'd never have gone through with the sale. And not just because Aunt Harriet now has five-hundred thousand of my money that I'll never see again. What really bugs me is the fact that they're trying to keep Bill from getting a penny."

Francis was glad to realize her old friend was as put out over Harriet Krane's treatment of her nephew as Francis. John could be as ruthless a businessman as any New York stockbroker and it would have been easy for him to ignore the situation and let the Krane family work out their problems without him. As long as he wound up with title to the property, that was.

When it came to that, though, she had to wonder one thing. "Why didn't you have the title checked before you paid for the house, though?"

John shook his head, looking mildly annoyed. "I did." At Francis' surprise, he continued, "My clerk told me the deed was in Rosamund's name. An outright lie that I might not have even noticed if I didn't read everything put in front of me to sign."

And a good thing, too, Francis reflected. She eyed her old friend thoughtfully. There was definitely more to the story than he'd said, but she felt certain he was telling her the truth about Bill. Still, in the years they'd known each other she'd learned to tell when John was hiding something. The question was what was it and how much trouble was it likely to be?

There was a tap at the door and John's butler, Alan, stepped in at John's invitation. "Sir, your cousin Rosamund is here to discuss the Philanthropic Society Charity Ball. I told her you had a guest already but…."

John sighed and rose to his feet, "But she insists. Fine. Let her in."

A moment later, Rosamund entered the room and - realizing Francis was the guest Alan had warned her about - came to a dramatic halt at the door. Then, with a slight sniff and shake of her head, she went to John. "I came to you about the charity ball. Will that silly house be ready?"

"Why hello, Miss Rosy. How are you tonight? Have you met my good friend Francis? Yes, I thought you had." John sat back down and gave Boopsie a quick scratch behind his ears. "To answer your question, I believe so. Fortunately, despite the unfortunate situation with the title, I've been granted permission by the house's actual owner to proceed with renovations."

Rosamund sniffed. "Actual owner. Isn't he silly, Boopsie? Of course I gave him permission. The charity ball is the whole reason I agreed to the sale anyway. Everybody knows Granddaddy always meant the house for me."

"I can't say, one way or another, what your grandfather intended," John said, "But I know what he did." Before Rosamund could protest, he shook his head. "It doesn't matter, Rosy. Whatever else, I agreed to have the main floor ready for the ball and I intend to keep that agreement."

Now that that was settled, Rosamund seemed to consider her next move and, as Francis could have predicted, she chose to do what was most inconvenient to her host. Pulling her feet up so that she was curled up in her chair, she held out a hand to John, saying, "You're a terrible host, John. If Francis gets a drink, shouldn't I?"

Somehow, John managed to keep his own temper, although Francis could tell that his cousin was pushing her luck with him. "Of course, Rosy. Sherry? Brandy?"

"Oh, I'd kill for a whiskey."

That got a sharp look from John, and Francis couldn't help saying, "Your mother doesn't like your drinking whiskey."

Ignoring Francis' comment, Rosamund held out her hand demandingly, only to receive a small, very small, glass of red wine. Before Rosamund could protest, John pointed out, "I'm under orders from your mother, Rosy. No whiskey. You'll have to get your fix elsewhere."

"Boopsie, my cousin is a mean, mean, man."

"Boopsie, your mama is even meaner when she's had whiskey."

"Boopsie, if my cousin doesn't give me a whiskey and right now, I'm going to get my own."

"Boopsie, your mama can get her own whiskey anywhere but in this house."

"Boopsie, no one in town will sell me a drop. Is that fair?"

"Boopsie, it's your mama's own damn fault for being a drunken lush."

The glass of wine went flying across the room, missing the fireplace by inches. Rosamund rose to her feet, glaring at the shattered glass and the liquid dribbling into the carpet with a furious expression. Then, before John could stop her, she ran for the sideboard and grabbed a bottle, turning and throwing it at John's head.

Fortunately, John moved fast enough to catch the bottle as it flew through the air. "Enough," he snapped. "I don't care what you drink and I don't care what you do, but it won't be here. And if you want me to keep my promise and have that house ready for your party, you'll take yourself and your pet out of here."

For a brief moment Francis was sure Rosamund would kick him. Then, with an obvious effort at self-control, the young woman turned, took her dog's leash and dragged the poor animal to the door. "Don't you dare not have it ready," she snapped as she stalked out. "I swear; you'll pay if you don't."

"I swear I'm paying for doing it at all," John muttered, going back to the sideboard to set the bottle back down.

As her friend poured himself another drink Francis went to the window to watch Rosamund leave. She wouldn't put it past the woman to wander through the house looking for whiskey elsewhere. But the sound of a slamming car door and a revving engine eased Francis' mind. She remained where she was, watching for the big pink car.

A moment later, the vehicle drove past the house and Francis frowned. The driver looked like Rosamund's usual chauffeur. But that was, or ought to be, impossible. After all, not five hours earlier, she'd seen the man thrown into another dimension by Conall McLeod's phase shifter. There was no way for him to escape. Unless, she reminded herself, Mr. McLeod had found a way to free the man.

(((

William opened his eyes groggily, his head aching as if he'd spent the night feasting on the worst Barton's tavern had to offer. Which, given he didn't drink, was impossible. He shuddered, groaning a little as he tried to sit up, and wondered why he felt so cold. For that matter, why was it so dark and why did the air smell of heavy machinery? Then there was the way the floor kept slanting one way and then the other. The last thing he remembered was leaving Mr. Bend's office and parting from Francis. How had he gotten here?

Another groan and a curse came from beside him, one he recognized as his father's. "Dad?" he managed to whisper, slowly realizing that there were heavy ropes binding him tightly. More urgently, he gasped, "Dad! Are you all right?"

His father's answer was muffled, as if he'd been gagged, but William could just understand the words, "Where are we?"

William was about to answer but a man's voice interrupted. "Where I've brought you." It was a strange voice, harsh and metallic, as if it were being forced through rusted steel.

Pulling himself together, William peered through the darkness. "So it seems," he said, as coolly as possible. At the same time his father struggled to speak. "Dad, let me handle this."

"Wise of you, boy. You, at least, have some of your grandfather's brains in your head."

William tested the ropes. They were too tight to slip out of and too strong to break, leaving him with finding something sharp. His kidnapper surely couldn't see in this darkness any better than he could. He stretched his body, searching around for some sign of something he could use.

"Don't bother," the man told him, laughing coldly. "You can't escape that easily."

William refused to give his captor the pleasure of an answer. If he wanted them dead there wasn't much William could do about it. Besides, William could guess that he'd been captured for the same reason he'd been attacked before. He'd have to give in, in the end, but he was not of a mind to make things easy.

The quiet hung on for several minutes, during which William listened closely to creaking metal and waves lapping somewhere nearby. The smell of machinery was combined with that of fish, a familiar odor to one who'd lived on the south side of Strikers Port all his life. They were in a ship's cargo hold.

At last the man spoke again, sounding annoyed at William's silence. "Don't you want to know why I brought you here?"

"I've already guessed," William told him and fell silent again.

Something cold flowed over him. Not water, though it felt much the same, more like a roiling bank of fog that chilled him to his bones. "Don't play games with me, boy!"

"Why should I cooperate with you?" William demanded. "As soon as I do, my father and I are useless to you."

That silenced his captor momentarily. Then he finally said, "Your father is useless to me already, except as hostage to your good behavior."

"And once you kill him, I have no reason to do anything for you." William hoped he sounded as calm and calculated as he needed to be. Hoped too that his father would forgive him for treating his life like a chip in a poker game.

The man laughed. "There are fates worse than death, as I'm sure you've seen." A small light flickered in the center of the room and William winced at even its dim glow. "Look at the wall, boy."

Blinking away the spots in his vision, William peered through the darkness at the wall of the cargo hold. He swallowed at the sight of three men flattened against and inside the metallic surface. "You saw Dolan, boy. You know what happens when the process is incomplete. That's what I'll do to your father, if you don't sign."

As William's father struggled to speak, William started to agree. Before he could open his mouth, a sound roared through the room, a howling shriek that resembled the screech of metal on metal, yet echoed as if it came from a living throat. It was also a familiar scream because William had heard it when Dragon's pet had attacked that man at Miss Trendle's house. This time it filled the air with deafening force. William swore that he actually felt the beast's breath blow past him, hot, metallic, and smelling just slightly of garlic.

Immediately the single light went out again and William felt as if the shadows surrounding them had somehow solidified. He could hear something against the walls of the hold, metal grinding against metal, counterpoint to the dragon's cries. Even worse than that, though, were the curses and threats of his captor, screamed in a voice that tore at the eardrums.

The pressure on William's body grew as the shadows seemed to grow deeper and stronger. Gripped tight in its hold, he was hardly able to breathe. Then the pressure was gone and the shadows seemed to flicker in and out, faint light growing brighter in the distance, a flickering motion that slowly coalesced into Dragon, riding his pet around the edges of the room, growing slowly and steadily closer to where William and his father lay.

A roiling cloud of smoke rose towards the middle of the room and William recoiled instinctively, feeling the heat pouring off of it. A figure formed at its center, a pillar of darkness whose center burned like the pits of hell. The roar of a forest fire howled as it swirled above him, arm-like tendrils raised in William's direction as if it intended to take him in its grasp. Beside him, his father made a startled sound. "You!?"

Unable to twist out of the way, William clenched his teeth, determined not to yell as the thing reached out towards him. Fully expecting to be burned to death, he suddenly found himself freed as the ropes binding him suddenly fell away, ashes blowing and drifting in the rising wind from the figure's heat.

Another touch released William's father, which proved an error on their rescuer's part. George Jarvis was in a fighting mood and the strange being's presence ignited his fury past all sense. He leapt to his feet and swung his fist with the speed that had made him famous in the boxing ring.

William gasped; sure his father would be set on fire. Instead their rescuer was flung back with the force of the blow, a very human body tossed out of the smoke containing him. He looked young, terribly young, strangely familiar, and for a moment utterly defenseless. Then he spoke and his voice - crackling with the roar of the fire - was a horror far beyond anything William had ever felt. "Temper, temper," he said, spitting a tooth out into his palm.

"I told you to stay away from my family!"

Almost casually, the stranger thrust his tooth back into his mouth, wiggling it around in a way that ought to have hurt painfully. Then, with a grin, he told William's father, "And I told you that you don't get to tell me what to do."

Again William's father tried to hit him but the stranger slipped out of reach. "Get lost! You've caused me and mine enough grief!"

The man snorted. "Stay and you'll be doing a lot worse than grieving. You're wasting my time and his." He jerked his thumb at the dragon circling around them, its rider sending spears of intense light flashing towards what appeared to be an empty spot in the air. William wasn't sure why, but it seemed to him that Dragon was trying to reach them, but that some force was holding him and his pet back.

It occurred to William that this was a rescue, albeit one far outside his understanding. That realized, he grabbed his father by the wrist and dragged him back. "Thanks," he managed to gasp as he struggled to get his furious parent to a spot where Dragon could reach them. "I owe you."

As smoke re-enveloped its master, the man whispered, "No, you don't. You're the only person in the world who will never owe me."

Then Dragon's pet caught William and his father in its claws and carried them away.

《《《

Chief Michaels surveyed the mess. The Salle Belle resembled nothing so much as a floating bonfire. One that wasn't floating very well, either. It listed to one side and Michaels thought the only blessing was that it was falling away from the docks. Not good for the other ships nearby, but better for the warehouse district. If the wooden piers caught fire, the entire port might go up in smoke. Besides, the only ship near enough to be damaged was already half-way out of its slip, escaping disaster thanks to the fast reactions of its crew.

"So you were grabbed earlier tonight and escaped just before the ship went up in smoke?" he asked William, aware that there was more to the story that couldn't be told in front of anyone else. "Kid, you live a charmed life."

William managed a weak smile, "Seems so," he agreed. "I'll try not to make it sound too unbelievable in my report."

Michaels paused as one of his other men came up to tell him, "It belongs to the Kranes, sir. Cargo ship headed to San Francisco."

"Interesting." Michaels turned to look across the river, although the Krane house was too far east to see. Then he checked his watch. "Just about 6:30pm. I think I'd better break the news, given no one else has already. Jarvis, you drive."

A rough growl drew Michaels' attention to the man seated on a nearby crate, wrapped in a blanket and looking as if he were ready to box the entire world. "My boy is not going to that place! I won't have him setting foot on Krane property. I forbid it!"

With a sigh, William pointed out, "Dad, I'm a police officer and Chief Michaels is my boss. If he wants me to go somewhere, I go. Understand?"

"You'll do as I tell you, boy!"

"I'm a grown man, Dad, not a little boy. You can't forbid me to go anywhere," William turned to Michaels and added, "I'll get the keys and bring the car around. Dad, we'll talk, later." There was a hint of threat that made Jarvis grumble, though from the look on his face, Michaels thought the man wasn't looking forward to whatever his son wanted to say.

Soon they were on the road up to Krane Winery. Once a logging camp, the family had converted the site to a vineyard back before the turn of the century. Outside Prohibition, they'd produced a steady stream of some of the better wines in Northern California.

As William drove, he told Michaels the details of what had actually happened inside the ship, finishing with, "I'm not sure why Dragon was there, but it's the other fellow that worries me. He's that one you told me about, isn't he? Old Smoky?"

"Given I saw him just a bit earlier and he made Dragon go off to handle something for him, I think so." Michaels detailed his own encounter with the two, adding, "It's obvious what he wanted Dragon doing. What I don't understand is why he wants to keep you alive. It isn't like him."

"I don't understand either." William was quiet a moment. "But my dad knows something. Wish me luck getting anything out of him, though. Dad's a stubborn old mule."

Michaels didn't know George Jarvis well, but he was sure William was right. "Why didn't he want you to go to your aunt and uncle's?"

A wry smile crossed the kid's face. "There's always been bad blood between him and them. Mom's family never accepted her marrying a boxer, even one whose father was a close associate of my grandfather's. She was disowned for a while. I suppose my being born ended that, but Dad and my aunt and uncle never got along. And when mom's body was found in the old logging camp...."

The note of pain in William's voice said more than he'd ever admit and Michaels decided he didn't need to know more. Besides, they were at their destination, a big ranch style home that sprawled along the hillside, its modern design at odds with the older buildings that constituted the winery itself.

A positively ancient butler met them at the door and gave Michaels a disapproving look. "This is not the correct entrance...." he began.

"Nonsense," Michaels snapped, "You tell Mr. and Mrs. Krane that Chief Michaels is here. I've important information about the Salle Belle and I doubt they'll want to be kept waiting."

With a look that spoke volumes, most related to the penal code, the old man went back into the house, closing the door in Michaels' face. "Lovely people, your family."

"I'm sorry, sir. Aunt Harriet has a high regard for what she considers the proprieties."

Michaels snorted and leaned on the doorbell again, guessing Jeeves, or whatever his name was, might need reminding of certain other proprieties, such as when the Chief of Police comes to your door, you let him in.

It took several minutes but the door finally opened and, with a voice dripping with disdain, the old man said, "Mrs. Krane will see you now."

They followed the butler to a large sitting room where Mrs. Krane waited, standing as straight and tall as her small frame allowed her to. "Chief Michaels. I am quite out of sorts with you. There's no need to make such a fuss."

"Your butler seemed a little deaf," Michaels told her. "Given this was important, I didn't think you'd appreciate finding out second-hand. Is your husband available? He might want to know about this, too."

"My husband has retired early. I will not have him disturbed." Mrs. Krane eyed Michaels with a look that reminded him of her daughter; querulous and impatient.

"Besides," another voice said from near the fireplace, "I'm right here. I can take care of anything Daddy could." The speaker looked very like Rosamund and Michaels guessed that he was Peter Krane, the one who'd been sent off to prep school as soon as he was old enough to go. From his slightly dissipated appearance, it hadn't done much good.

Mrs. Krane shot Peter a disgusted look before turning her attention back to Michaels. "You told Joseph you had information about the Salle Belle. I hope you're not insinuating there was anything illegal aboard."

That was an interesting thought, and Michaels wondered if he ought to have the cargo, what was left of it, investigated. "No ma'am. But if you look out your window towards the port you'll see her going up in smoke."

Her jaw dropped and she turned, staring down the hillside and a slowly growing fury grew in her expression. "What happened?"

"We haven't found out yet, but someone was using her to hold someone prisoner. When the prisoner escaped, someone set the fire. Possibly to hide the evidence." Michaels didn't mention who the prisoner was, nor what had been wanted from him. Just in case Mrs. Krane knew about William's abduction

"I... see." Mrs. Krane shook her head. "A terrible situation. I appreciate your coming to tell me personally. I'll have my people go down to see just how bad things really are." She managed a slight smile, adding, "Is there anything else?"

Michaels hesitated. "I don't suppose your husband would want to be woken? This seems like an important situation. He ought to be told."

For a moment the woman gazed at the roiling smoke far below. Then she came to a decision. "Come with me, Chief Michaels."

"Mother!"

"Silence, Peter. Chief Michaels will not discuss our family business with anyone."

The young man's finger pointed directly at William. "And what about him? Should you be letting him know?"

As if seeing the kid for the first time, Mrs. Krane smiled bitterly. "William already knows, Peter. His father will have told him. If he has not used the knowledge to his own benefit thus far, he is unlikely to do so now."

That said, she rounded on her heel and led Michaels and William thru the halls again, back into a large room with a single bed. Michaels twitched his nose at the smell; antiseptic and an underlying scent of eau de piss. A gaunt figure lay there, his features scarred and pitted, one eye covered in a white bandage. There was an odd machine attached to his head, a medical device no doubt.

Mrs. Krane went to her husband's bedside, "My husband, Chief Michaels, has been in this condition ever since he and his sister were found, badly burned, at the old logging camp. Gwendolyn, as I'm sure you know, did not survive. There are times when I wish Jack had not either." She put her hand out, touching the man's shoulder briefly, then drew it back when he moaned. "He is, as you see, quite incapable of caring about anything but his own pain."

((((

Maloney was in a sour mood, mostly because he'd been cut out of all the fun. He'd been abandoned to watch McLeod's workshop for hours. He didn't find out until his relief came that Michaels had captured one of Crogan's gang, that the Salle Belle had been half destroyed in port or, even worse, Jarvis had been aboard said ship when it had gone up in smoke, victim of an abduction for unknown reasons. Nor was there anyone to complain to. Michaels was busy and Jarvis had finally managed to go home for some much needed rest.

Unwilling to spend time cooking supper, Maloney had gone to his favorite bar and spent several hours nursing several beers and wounded feelings until almost midnight. And that, he would explain later to Michaels, was why he was in a position to spot the black motorcycle that the masked man called Tiger rode, and why he didn't bother to call for back up.

Instead, Maloney followed the motorcycle at a discreet distance, staying back so the rider wouldn't realize someone was watching him. Legally, he didn't have a leg to stand on. Tiger hadn't broken any laws that he knew of.

Not even speeding, he noted with a mix of annoyance and relief. It made it easier to follow the man but meant he had no excuse to do so.

A moment of over-confidence nearly lost the man's trail, but Maloney was canny enough to double back and glance down a narrow alley, to spot Tiger clinging to the windowsill of the second floor. Keeping hidden, he watched the man listen intently for several minutes, then slip back to his motorcycle. Taking what looked like a handset from his motorcycle, Tiger spoke into it in rapid and incomprehensible Chinese. Another voice spoke in return, too thin and tinny to recognize.

The name Crogan was mentioned several times. Then, quietly, Tiger put the handset away and climbed onto his motorcycle. A moment later he was gone and Maloney, realizing that he'd now lost his quarry entirely, made his way back to his car. Maybe if he drove around some more he'd catch the bastard?

As Maloney opened his car door he felt a presence behind him and spun around, to find Tiger standing within inches behind him. "You'd better come, Officer Maloney," the man said. "I need back-up and Dragon's busy."

A sane part of Maloney argued in vain against his answer. "Where are we going?"

"Get on and you'll find out." Tiger jumped onto his motorcycle and, once Maloney joined him, the machine roared up the street at a speed that would have given all the excuse needed to pursue him. The trouble being that there would have been no way to keep up. No land-bound vehicle had a right to move so fast.

Clutching the man tightly, Maloney barely had time to curse before the motorcycle turned and headed straight for the hill below Chinatown. They were going too fast, far too fast, and the only thing Maloney could do was hold on as they headed straight for the cliff-side. Then they'd slammed right through into a storm of colors no human ought ever see.

"Almost there," Tiger shouted. "Don't worry."

Easy for Tiger to say, Maloney thought, staring wildly around. Clouds of darkness were lit from within with a purple glow and things moved between the clouds that were like nothing he'd ever seen before or ever hoped to see again. "Dimensional phase shift!" Tiger shouted. "Don't worry, they can't touch us. We're not on the same wavelength."

Having no idea what Tiger meant, the only thing Maloney could do was hold on tight and pray they'd find their way out of this place. Then they slammed through a cloud and into a large room with a big statue at one end. Mrs. McLeod was standing there, just turning, as the motorcycle came to a stop just inches from the wall.

"You are really too much, Tiger," she said calmly. "What are you doing here?"

"Trouble. Someone's coming to steal Himself." Tiger was off his bike and up against the wall near the entrance in an instant, gesturing respectfully at the statue as he passed.

Maloney took longer, his legs like rubber from the shock of that wild trip. "Sorry, Ma'am."

"And why have you brought this man? He is not open-minded enough to be here."

That was true. Every nerve Maloney had was on edge and not just from having raced through hell. He was, or at least considered himself to be, a good Catholic boy. Why was he here and why was he helping protect a heathen idol?

Before he could open his mouth to complain, though, the door to the room slammed open and a dozen or so men crowded through. "The hell?" one complained, eyes on the statue. "How do we get this thing out of here?"

"The Voice said to break it up, remember?"

"Before you do that," Tiger said, almost casually, "I hope you won't object to a little dance? Maloney, don't let them near Mrs. McLeod!"

Ordinarily, Maloney would have retorted that he didn't take orders from masked strangers but the sight of all those crooks silenced him. This wasn't the time to argue. Instead he moved beside Mrs. McLeod, wishing he hadn't left his gun at the station when he'd gone off duty. The fact that several of the men were armed didn't make him feel any better.

Mrs. McLeod looked up at him and a slight smile crossed her lips. Then she handed him a heavy stick that he hadn't seen her pick up. "It is better than nothing," she told him gently, as several of the men started towards them. The rest were too busy with Tiger.

"Against guns?" he asked, disbelievingly and swallowed when she turned towards their attackers, her hands moving the same way they had back at her husband's workshop. This time something formed between her palms, a sphere of light and darkness that she set spinning above them. Energy filled the room, crackling around them in a display to rival Chinatown's New Year's fireworks.

Before Maloney could ask what good that had done, one of the men fired his gun straight at her, or tried to. As soon as he pulled the trigger a flare of light surrounded his weapon and sent it flying off to one side. "Their gunfire is not a problem, Officer Maloney. But you must keep them back."

"My pleasure, ma'am."

The odds weren't good, but Maloney wasn't the sort to let that stop him fighting. Instead he took up a position between Mrs. McLeod and the crooks, swinging the stick he'd been given as hard and as fast as he could. It was longer than he was used to, but he adapted quickly.

As Maloney knocked heads and poked stomachs he noted that Tiger was a handy man to have around in a brawl. Hands curled in claw like gestures, Tiger kicked and punched with the best of them, sending his attackers flying across the room and into walls with all the force he could muster. Not that Maloney could spend time admiring the other's skills; his own opponents weren't weaklings and the bastards kept getting up. "Just going to have to hit harder," he muttered, suiting action to word.

Again and again he and Tiger hit, again and again the crooks struggled to their feet, one by one getting the worst of it until they couldn't rise again. Then, almost as suddenly as the fight began, it was over and Maloney found himself face to masked face with his ally. Yielding to temptation, he reached out to grab the mask, but Tiger flipped backwards and away, landing beside his motorcycle.

"On that note," he said, bowing, "I think I'll leave. Mrs. McLeod, sorry to leave you with a mess."

"No, I do not think you are, young man." Mrs. McLeod sighed, shaking her head. "Go. I will deal with it."

Without another word, Tiger hopped onto his motorcycle and disappeared.

(((

For Crogan to admit fear would require a humility that he didn't possess. That said, he knew he was risking himself and everything he'd worked for over the years. Even before Tiger and Dragon had shown up to cause him trouble, invading Chinatown had never been worth it. Only idiots stuck their fingers into the hornets' nest known as the *Pu Gway Ren She Way.*

Right now, though, Crogan was between a rock and a hard place. The Voice was out there, still demanding he retrieve that damned idol of Meng Huang Shang. Then there was that bastard who'd chased him across town, keeping up despite everything Crogan had done to escape him. Oh, yes, and one couldn't forget Old Uncle Gilly; Crogan was still of two minds about trusting him, even though he owed the skinny bastard his life.

All of which led to where he was now, sneaking into the home of Chinatown's boss at near midnight, accompanied by a dozen men armed

" ENERGY FILLED THE ROOM, CRACKLING AROUND THEM IN A
DISPLAY TO RIVAL CHINATOWN'S NEW YEARS FIREWORKS. "

with brass knuckles and sticks. Best not to bring guns - or even knives - to this fight. Get blood in these waters and every member of the *Pu Gway* would be out for his internal organs.

Skulking through the house, Crogan was suspicious. 'What could go wrong?' echoed in his head, cheery counterpoint to all the things that could do that very thing. Thus, he wasn't surprised when, having reached the top floor of the house and slipped silently into Cheh Chang's living quarters, the lights suddenly went on and he found himself and his men surrounded by an equal number of Chinese. They didn't feel any compunction about blood in the fight, either. Each and every one was armed with two long daggers.

Cheh Chang himself was seated in a big lacquer-wood chair, dressed in a tatty robe over silk pajamas covered in embroidery. "Come now, Mr. Crogan. You did not think you could reach my sanctum without notice, did you?"

With a deep breath, Crogan managed to fight down panic. "Maybe. Maybe not," he said, glancing around at the gang surrounding him and his men. "Or maybe I'm here to negotiate."

Hundreds of tiny wrinkles shifted as the old man raised both his eyebrows, his eyes widening. "You expect me to believe that?"

"Let me handle him, boss." That was the broad-shouldered one to Chang's right. He stepped forward without waiting for an answer, dropping into a familiar stance. A smaller and skinnier fellow joined him then, sniffing and rubbing his nose with his thumb. Neither was armed, but Crogan doubted they were any less dangerous.

To Crogan's irritation, the challenge was too much for several of his men. They launched themselves at the two without hesitation and were kicked, punched and sent flying as soon as they came close. Sent rolling to the side, they soon had several men on them, blades to their throats to ensure they didn't try another move.

"Damnit!" Crogan snapped. "I told you idiots to wait for orders. Don't any of you listen?"

"I, too, am not pleased," Chang added, causing his two men to flush and back down, the taller one bowing deeply as they returned to their places. "This is not the time for nonsense, Mr. Crogan. What, exactly, have you come for?"

Crogan hesitated a moment. This was where things got tricky. There were two choices, either leading to disaster if he guessed wrong. Then, remembering the last few weeks and just how many men he'd lost, letting

The Voice tell him what to do, he said, "I'm here to warn you. Someone's trying to steal the idol of Moon Wan Shan."

There was a long moment of silence at Crogan's announcement as Chang gazed levelly at him. "Meng Huang…." he started to say, only to be interrupted by a howl of rage.

"I thought you'd betray me!" The Voice's screech of fury seemed to come from everywhere, causing Crogan to spin and stare, trying to find its source. "I'll kill you!" The air seemed to shimmer and tremble, followed by half of Crogan's men suddenly turning towards him with faces that shifted and changed as he watched. They weren't his men after all, he realized. All but one wore the face of the man who'd chased him through town. The other was the same one who'd embedded his men in those walls.

"Now you may act," Chang said, as Crogan dodged the men trying to grab him. At the same time, Chang's men rushed forward, joined by those of Crogan's men who were actually his men.

Somehow Crogan managed to get out of the way of the fight, which brought him within a few feet of the old man watching the fight. Had he wanted to hurt Chang, this would have been his moment, for the man seemed too busy to pay attention to what was right beside him.

"Do not suppose I am unaware of you," Chang said suddenly. "Nor that you have a hope of reaching me should you strike."

Crogan held up his hands to show he was weaponless. "I know," he told the old man. He didn't add why he knew, preferring to keep Old Uncle's advice to himself. He still wasn't sure he'd made the right choice, following Old Uncle's instructions. The Voice was still the worst choice, but he hadn't expected to see that creep again.

Fortunately, things weren't going well for the creep or the men The Voice had snuck into Crogan's gang. The latter were getting taken down so fast that Crogan understood why the gangsters in Strikers Port avoided annoying Chinatown's Tong. As for the creep, his attempts to get a grip on his enemies were met with utter failure. Chang's men seemed to know that letting him touch them would be, if not fatal, an end to their part in the fight.

Soon the creep was all that was left, floating in the center of the room and trying to get past the men surrounding him. They couldn't touch him, but their knives cut away much of his clothes, so that the smoke that appeared to make up his substance was drifting through the air, unable to coalesce enough to be a danger.

"Now, Tan. Remember what you've learned."

The tall man who'd been the first to attack earlier stepped forward. "Yes, sir," he said, accepting a big, brass-bound, staff from the smaller fellow. With a flurry of rapid motions the creep couldn't keep up with, he began striking and spinning. His staff moved so fast that it dissipated the smoke, weakening the creep still further and allowing him to get closer and closer. Then, with a single straight blow, he thrust the staff through the figure, right where its throat would have been.

Sparks and broken pieces of metal flew as the smoke disappeared entirely. At the same time The Voice screeched furiously, "You'll pay, Chang. You'll all pay." Then it fell silent as the last scraps of fabric forming the creep's body landed on the ground.

"Clean up this mess. I will not have my house looking like a battlefield," Chang said calmly. "Not you, Tan. Go to the Jeen Loon and help my grandson guard it, in case that one is not done."

Tan bowed and ran out the door.

Turning his attention to Crogan, Chang smiled in a way that didn't make Crogan feel at all better. "I believe it is time we talked, Mr. Crogan."

No. Not better at all.

))))((((

Breakfast in the Jarvis household was strangely quiet. William's father usually had more than enough opinions to share to make up for his son's diffidence. With George in the grimmest mood William had ever seen, the only thing discussed was how he wanted his eggs.

Putting breakfast on the table and sitting down to eat, William wondered how to ask the questions he wanted answered when his father didn't want to answer them. Perhaps a relatively innocent question, first? "How did you sleep?"

His father muttered something under his breath. When William gazed at him curiously, he said sharply, "Fine."

That was a lie. William's father had spent the night sitting in the living room, glaring at the fireplace, glass of whiskey in his hand. Whatever thoughts the man had been thinking had remained entirely inside his skull. They hadn't been good thoughts, that much William had seen. Every so often George had looked like he wanted to throw the glass into the fire in a fit of temper, only to set the glass down and mutter to himself.

In the end, William had gone to bed, sleeping so fitfully that he was sure he'd have noticed if his father had slept. All of which meant that he was too groggy to properly argue with a man he'd never been able to really talk to anyway.

At last, after a huge swallow of coffee and a few more failed attempts to get a word out of his father, William said, "You know what I think?"

George ignored him, picking at his eggs and staring at his newspaper and the headline, "Krane Wine Goes Up in Smoke" without actually reading it. His expression was hard and angry, his lips too tight to allow a single word out.

"I think you knew that the Jewel Island house was mine from the first."

"Hmph."

"I think you know something about mom's death that you're not telling."

"Grrrr."

"And I think I'll get more answers out of Old Smoky than I ever will out of you."

That got his father's attention. The man raised his eyes and glared at him furiously. "You'll stay away from that... that... that monster or else!"

It hit William that his father's behavior hid guilt. Not the guilt of a man who'd done something but of one who'd failed to. "He has something to do with this, too, doesn't he?" Remembering the interchange between his father and Old Smoky the night before, William was sure he was right. "Did he kill my mother?"

"I told you to drop it!"

No, that wasn't it, or if it was, it wasn't the whole story. What had Old Smoky said? That he was the only person in the world who didn't owe him? It made no sense and he could tell he wasn't going to get the answer from his father. Trying another tack he demanded, "Did you know about the house?"

"What if I did?"

"Why didn't you fight for it? Aunt Harriet and Uncle Jack didn't care. They left it to rot after Grandfather died." William eyed his father, trying to catch a glimpse of the truth behind his eyes and failing.

George laughed harshly. "Maybe so. But I didn't want it either. Not the place where...." His voice trailed off and he looked disgusted. "What would I do with a big old mansion, anyway?"

Knowing his father had almost revealed something, William pretended to ignore the slip. "You ought to have sold it back to her. It wasn't like Grandfather's will. The deed was registered and notarized. Aunt Harriet wouldn't need my signature now if she could fight my ownership in court."

William's father took a deep breath to calm himself and finally said, "What are you going to do? Sell it to her?"

"I haven't made up my mind. I certainly don't need the place. If John wasn't renovating it, it'd be a dump."

To William's surprise, his father looked up sharply at him. "Don't say that. Your mother grew up there. She loved that house." Then he bit off the words, realizing he'd revealed more than he'd intended. "Never mind. She wouldn't want it sitting unused, either. Maybe it's for the best that Striker's buying it."

Once again William's father fell silent and morose. William could tell he'd gotten about all he was going to get from him for the moment. Fortunately, a knock at the door made it unnecessary to try. Glad of the interruption, William went to answer. "John? Miss Trendle? What are you doing here?"

"I came to see if you could meet my attorney right now," Miss Trendle said, adding, "And I told you to call me Francis, Bill."

"Sorry… Francis. It's hard to get used to."

Miss Trendle sighed, shaking her head sadly, then indicated John, "As for this one, he feels that, as an interested party, he should be available to provide any information to my attorney that's needed."

"Not to mention moral support. I know you, Bill. You'd rather not make a fuss, and a fuss is exactly what's needed here."

Ordinarily John would be right. There'd been a point the day before when he would have signed anything he could to get Aunt Harriet out of his hair. Last night's shenanigans had put the wind up William's sails and he was in a mood to fight. "Just let me get dressed and call in. If Chief Michaels can spare me, I'm at your service."

((((

Michaels got off the phone and looked at the three men seated across from him. Two looked uncomfortable, whereas the third behaved according to stereotype and watched him with a calm and unrevealing gaze. Michaels corrected himself. Beneath the serene disinterest was an underlying humor that said Cheh Chang found the situation hilarious.

"Words fail me," Michaels said slowly. "Just what happened last night? And do not, Mr. Chang, tell me Chinatown is not my business."

"To be strictly accurate, Chief Michaels, what happens on my property is not necessarily your business. However, under the circumstances, I do consider an attempt by outsiders to steal our family idol very much a matter for the police. I would have called for assistance, but by the time I realized my house was under attack, it was far too late. Fortunately, Officer Maloney and Mr. Crogan were available to help."

Crogan looked uncomfortable. Michaels knew the man and knew he was nearly the last person in Strikers Port to come down on the side of the angels. Although, admittedly, Michaels had doubts about Chang's association with such beings. "It was the least I could do," the man offered.

"What I want to know is why? And, for that matter, I want to know why you, Maloney, went running off with that Tiger fellow to beat up a gang of thugs in a Chinatown temple? You, of all people, ought to have known better!"

Maloney muttered something about 'the heat of the moment' and 'someone had to do something'. Words that were rewarded with a gentle pat on the shoulder from Chang. "Officer Maloney was of great assistance to my daughter, Chief Michaels. He is to be commended for his dedication to his duty."

Michaels managed not to blow his top. The three were in cahoots and the fact that Chang defended Maloney's impetuous decision to join Tiger in his shenanigans was enough to make Michaels suspicious. Someone knew something they weren't telling.

At last Michaels demanded, "All right, I understand how Maloney wound up at the temple… mostly." Some of the man's story had involved an incoherent description of a ride through hell, leaving Michaels wondering what his officer had been drinking. At least it'd been off-duty. "However, I don't understand how you, Crogan, wound up at Chang's place, nor why you decided to help him out when you realized he was being robbed."

Very much to Michaels' surprise, Chang turned to the man. "I think you should tell Chief Michaels about your former patron, as well as the advice you recently received."

Now it was Crogan's turn to mutter, shuffling his feet in an embarrassed manner as he glared at the hat he held clutched in his hands. "It goes against the grain," he said finally. "I'm not used to coming clean."

"Try it," Michaels said. "Confession's good for the soul."

Suddenly, Crogan began to talk. Michaels already knew about The Voice, of course, and how the absurdly named criminal had used Crogan in his schemes. "I'm not going into details," the man told him, "Self-incrimination isn't part of my job description. But it seemed like a great deal at first. It wasn't until Tiger and Dragon interfered that The Voice got to be a problem. As long as we were giving him what he wanted, he helped us out."

"Well, that's true about most partnerships," Michaels suggested mildly.

"Maybe, but most partnerships don't end up with someone getting stuck inside a wall," Crogan told him pointedly. "So when someone suggested I do what I could to find out who he was, I went for it."

Michaels raised a brow. "And did that work for you?"

"I… may have… jumped the gun on that one. My advisor was annoyed with me." Crogan looked thoughtful, adding, "Fortunately, he's not asking for a partnership."

Given who Michaels thought Crogan's advisor probably was, Crogan had better hope Old Smoky wasn't interested in a partnership. "Was it his idea for you to help Mr. Chang last night?"

"Yeah. He said I'd be better off choosing the stronger side. Since The Voice keeps using my people to get what he wants done, that can't be him." Crogan looked around a bit nervously and added, "Plus, he thinks I'm better off with McLeod on my side. Helping Mr. Chang's part of that."

That was probably true. Given McLeod appeared to be the only person available to combat whatever weird science The Voice was using, Crogan was going to need to stay on the man's better side. Always assuming, of course, that McLeod and his father-in-law got along.

As if aware of Michaels' doubts, Chang smiled broadly. "I have sent some of my men to assist my son-in-law with moving Mr. Crogan's men, and those found in the Salle Belle to the workshop. I've no doubt that he will solve the problem of this Voice's trickery in the near future."

Michaels came to the only conclusion he could. "Then while McLeod is trying to fix the mess The Voice caused, I need to start working out what this crook's been up to and what he's trying to accomplish." He turned his attention to Crogan and smiled, "So, how about you start singing. The more choruses I hear, the more likely it is that I'll recognize the tune."

)))

Francis' lawyer was Allen Walters, a big fellow whose heavy features and slow movements often caused opponents to underestimate him. He'd worked for the Trendles for years, handling all of its business and personal affairs exclusively. Francis was glad he'd agreed to help with William's case.

"I believe we have every chance of winning some concessions from your aunt, Mr. Jarvis." As William looked doubtfully at the papers strewn on Walters' desk, the lawyer continued, "It's fortunate your grandfather put the house in your name immediately after your mother died. The biggest reason your aunt was able to contest his will was because he'd failed to mention either yourself or your father. An oversight I suspect he did not intend."

Ruefully, William told him, "My father wouldn't believe that."

Walters smiled. "I assure you, your grandfather was a good-hearted and well-meaning man. He was also not legally minded. This would not have been a problem if he hadn't also chosen to write his will without consulting his attorney."

"I see." William looked at the papers again and Francis could see the worry in his eyes. "What can I do? I don't have the money for the kind of legal fight Aunt Harriet can offer."

"Strictly speaking, you do," John pointed out. "Since the house is yours, or ought to be, the money should go to you. You could fight, and win, the entire thing. Which, if no one has mentioned it to you as yet, is enough to make you a millionaire. At least until after taxes."

William opened his mouth. Closed it. Opened it again. Then, with an expression of panic, he glared at his cousin. "No, John. No one, including you, has mentioned just how much money was involved."

Embarrassed, John said, "I suppose I haven't. I was afraid you'd run away." He turned to Francis, attempting to win her to his side. "You see how he is. The first mention of that kind of money and he starts shaking in his shoes."

"You still should have told him, John." Francis felt sorry for William. He'd always been the poor cousin to a family that treated him like dirt. The only one who didn't was John, and the difference in their wealth had surely made their friendship difficult. "Bill, I don't blame you for being upset. It's a shock."

William just gazed levelly at John. "Cousin, when and if I get this money, remind me to stick you in Dad's boxing ring and smack you around a few rounds."

"You don't have to have as much money as I have to do that, Bill."

"But it'd make me feel better."

With a cough, Walters interrupted. "Mr. Jarvis? Shall we continue?"

William looked embarrassed. "Yes. Please. What's my best course of action?"

"I believe you'd win any court battle. However, it would be an expensive fight and given Mrs. Krane's personality, it would be a long, difficult, time for you and your father. If I read you right, I think that's something you'd like to avoid." Before John could interrupt, Walters added, "Mr. Striker, I understand your concern. Mrs. Krane has been known to take as many miles as she can for every inch you give her."

William said slowly, "I won't pretend that I don't need or want money. I do admit to being incredibly uncomfortable at the idea of so much of it." He sighed. "Some concession is in order. John, how much have you paid Aunt Harriet already?"

"I gave her half the agreed on amount as soon as my lying little thief of a clerk told me that the title belonged to Rosamund free and clear. Five hundred thousand." When Francis raised her brow at him, he added, "Yes, I know, it's a huge amount of money but I've big plans for Jewel Island and I'll have to own the whole thing, not just the majority of it. Aunt Harriet knew, and drove a hard bargain."

"Do you think we could convince her to accept what you've paid her as repayment for keeping the place up and paying the property taxes?"

Francis thought 'keeping the place up' was probably a gross exaggeration, given the Kranes had practically abandoned the house and everything in it after William's grandfather had died. Even so, she said, "It sounds reasonable to me, though I can't vouch for your aunt's good sense."

With a slight cough, Walters offered, "Before we continue, I should note that Mrs. Krane, her attorney, her daughter, and her daughter's dog are waiting to discuss terms. I told her she couldn't be present while I was consulting with you but that I would let you know she was… available for negotiations."

Walters' tone made Francis suspect that Mrs. Krane's real purpose had been to bribe him to present William's legal position in the worst possible light. It was equally within Walters' character to be disgusted by the attempt and all the more determined to see to it William was well represented.

"Let's get it over with," William agreed and Walters' secretary was sent to fetch the lady and her entourage. It took some time to present the legal situation to her, for she kept huffing and puffing over the sheer effrontery of the son of a nobody-boxer, a mere policeman, laying a claim on any portion of her family's vast estate.

At last, persuaded by both Walters and her own attorney, Mrs. Krane finally agreed to have papers drawn up that would acknowledge that she had been properly paid for her part in caring for the property, that John Striker owed her nothing more, and that the house and what remained of its land was now entirely William's to do with as he wished.

"And, as John and I already discussed," William said when the last paper had been signed, "I agree to sell the property to him for the rest of the five-hundred thousand he would otherwise have paid Aunt Harriet."

John smiled. "I have that contract all ready and can write your check immediately. You'll want to start an account at a bigger bank, though. May I suggest mine? That way we can handle the whole transaction there."

Looking stressed again, William smiled. "I suppose so. Though I should stop in at the station and see if Chief Michaels needs me for anything."

"Of course." John paused and Francis knew the smile on his face only too well. He had mischief in mind. William gave him a suspicious look as his friend took a set of papers from his attaché. "But I wanted to give you this, first. There's no rush for you to decide. Look them through and make your decision when you're ready."

Mrs. Krane, who'd been gathering herself and her things with the air of one who couldn't wait to get away from the hoi polloi, narrowed her eyes at John. "What is that?"

"A contract," John said with an innocent smile at his aunt. "Now that Bill's got all that money, or will, he'll be wanting a way to help it grow. I thought he might like to form a partnership. I've got a fair number of irons in the fire and I could use some help with the Jewel Island Resort."

The only way to describe Mrs. Krane's expression was that of a dying fish. Then, with a deep and bitter sigh, she said, "It's your money, you fool boy. If you want to make the ignorant brat of a common laborer your partner, it isn't my business."

John smiled and kissed her hand with nothing but pure insolence. "Exactly, Aunt Harriet. Striker money, Striker business. Just as it always has been."

With a huff, Mrs. Krane removed herself from the room, leaving her daughter and Boopsie looking thoughtful. Had Francis still not felt out of sorts with her old schoolmate, she might have asked why. Fortunately for everyone else's curiosity, Boopsie wanted to know too. At least, that was Rosamund's assumption as she asked her dog, "Boopsie, do you think that awful boring business is over now?"

With a sigh, John answered the question, directing his words to the dog, "That's right, Boopsie. The house is no longer your mommy's property. In fact, as I told you last night, it never was."

"Well, Boopsie, if that's the case, John has to keep his promise now and have the house ready for my charity ball tonight."

"Yes, Boopsie. I plan to have...." John broke off and turned towards Rosamund with an expression of disbelief. "Tonight?"

"Boopsie, I know I sent John an invitation. Surely he read it and knows when I told everyone to be there." Rosamund shook her head sadly. "John is so forgetful, isn't he, Boopsie?"

Francis was certain the top of John's head would blow off. "I. Never. Received. Any. Invitation," he said in a flat, cold, monotone. At the same time, William put a hand on his cousin's shoulder, squeezing it warningly.

"Never received an invitation? Boopsie, you naughty dog. Was that one of the ones you ate?" From Rosamund's innocent expression, Francis was sure she'd deliberately forgotten to include John in her plans. "Well, it'll be fine. I took care of all the catering plans. They'll be there at 3pm to set up. I do hope everything is ready."

"It'll have to be, won't it?" John growled. "Go away, Rosamund. I'll have the place ready as promised. But if you say one more word, to me or to that damned dog, I swear I'll dunk you in the nearest fountain!"

"It'll be just like old times," Rosamund said, leaving the room quickly so that he couldn't make good on his promise. Which was just as well. Hopefully Walters didn't really like the statue of Michelangelo's David that John put through the wall a few inches to the left of the door.

ɔɔɔ

"Don't tell me you've never felt like braining her, yourself, Bill."

Although William would freely admit that his cousin was infuriating, he wasn't the sort to hit people smaller than himself. No matter how irritating they were. "She could do with better manners," he admitted. "But that's not the point...."

"I mean, you know as well as I do that she didn't tell me the date of the party on purpose." John flung his hands in the air, frustrated and angry. "Because she just loves seeing how high people will jump to make her happy."

"I've been lucky, John. The fact that my father and her parents won't have anything to do with each other means I haven't seen her since my mother died." Which was just as well, because the spanking William's father had promised Rosamund would have gotten him locked away years ago.

Not that spanking would have done any good. From what little William remembered of her, Rosamund had been the precious angel who could do no wrong. Her father, especially, made sure she wanted for nothing, moving heaven and earth to give her everything her heart desired. Aunt Harriet was less sympathetic to her daughter, but would give in to avoid the inevitable scene.

Which brought things back to John's own brief tantrum. "All I'm saying is that if that thing had gone a little further to the right, I'd be booking you, instead of asking Chief Michaels for time off," William told his friend as they entered the police station.

"I suppose you're right," John admitted. "It was just she makes me so hot."

Leading his friend into the Chief's outer office, William was surprised to see two of Mr. Chang's men sitting in the waiting area. Two of Crogan's thugs were with them, playing cards. The one, Tan, William thought his name was, glanced up and nodded in a composed way.

"Oh, hey there, Tan, Leung. Did the boss get in trouble again?" John asked cheerfully and, when William gave him a curious look, told him, "Tan and Leung run the construction crew renovating the house."

"I see." Although curious as to why Mr. Chang and Crogan's men were acting like the best of buddies, William decided not to ask. Instead he turned to Chief Michaels' secretary, intending to ask if he were too busy to be seen.

The woman spoke before William opened his mouth. "Go on in, Officer Jarvis. The Chief wanted to see you."

Obediently, William went through the door and stared. Crogan and Maloney were writing on a blackboard, while Mr. Chang and Chief Michaels watched and, every so often, made suggestions that caused one man or the other to erase a few words, add a few others and sometimes draw lines between circles.

"Is this modern police method, or modern art?' John asked curiously and William almost turned around to push him out. Except Chief Michaels noticed them at the door and beckoned them both in. "Can I play too?"

"Only if you have something to add," Michaels told him. "And I'm letting you in only because I don't have time to throw you out on your rear."

William ignored the by-play, examining the board curiously. Here was the attempted kidnapping of Francis Trendle. There the robbery of the Stayne house, where the only thing stolen was some old electronic equipment. A fix at the races. The take-over of several 'casinos'. A pearl encrusted choker belonging to the daughter of a local businessman. The recipe book from the Jewel Island restaurant. Other, similar, robberies and crimes filled the board, William's own abduction somewhere towards the bottom, near another incident that made him frown. "Someone tried to rob the Jeen Loon again?"

"No, young man. The first robbery was a mistake on the part of Crogan's men. They did not realize the idol of Meng Huang Shang was within the hill temple until last night." Mr. Chang leaned forward and pointed to another circle, this containing the illegal transport of liquor. "That, too, I think you should tie to The Voice."

Maloney turned and looked at the man, "Why? It's just business as usual."

"It is business as usual for Barton's men," Mr. Chang told him. "Crogan handles gambling and protection. While he and Barton work together, Crogan does not usually operate transports."

"That's right," Crogan added, apparently forgetting that he was admitting to his crimes in the middle of the Chief of Police's office. "The Voice wanted the stuff moved from a cave in the hills to my casino. It was damn good stuff, too. Kranes must have stashed it there before prohibition passed and forgot about it. Felt just like the good old days."

"I remember," Maloney told him. "We never did figure out how you people were communicating."

"Two words. Old Smoky."

Before the two men could continue the conversation, William turned to the Chief, asking, "What is all this?"

"Mr. Chang's idea. He thinks it'd be easier to connect all our problems if we draw them out." From his seat across the room, Mr. Chang bowed gracefully, expression smugly self-satisfied.

William scanned the board as best he could, given there'd been so many erasures and re-drawings that it was difficult to tell what it showed. "Who in the world is The Voice?" It sounded like something out of a comic book.

"My ex-partner, the one that got me into this fix," Crogan explained. "I don't know what he looks like, but he seems involved in almost everything up there in one way or another. I called him that because, well if you'd ever heard him talk...."

"There is still the question of the man who tried to kill you yesterday, as well as Miss Krane's chauffeur," Mr. Chang added. "We aren't sure who or what they are. They are not human, as we understand human, that much is obvious."

Still eyeing the board, William said absently, "It must have been your partner... ex-partner... who kidnapped me, then. I never did see him, but he did have a memorable voice." He frowned, "One other thing. If you ignore the jobs that fall under Crogan's venue, like the casino and the horse-race, my Krane cousins have some sort of connection to most of the items on the board."

It was John's turn to examine the board. "You know, you're right. I'd heard the electronics Stayne bought belonged to your Grandfather. And I'm pretty sure that Uncle Jack dabbled in rum-running back in the day."

That meant about the only things that didn't connect to the Krane family were either Crogan's alone or the attempted theft of that idol. Did that mean William's kinfolk were somehow involved in this mess? "I just can't see any of the Kranes getting their fingers dirty with something like this; Aunt Harriet is too conscious of her dignity, Uncle Jack is incapacitated, Cousin Rosamund is too flighty and Cousin Peter is, in a word, too stupid."

"Still, it's an interesting thought," Michaels pointed out. "We hadn't noticed that."

William examined the dates attached to each incident. They were spread out over a matter of weeks, beginning sometime in May. "This was when this Voice contacted you, right, Crogan?" At the man's agreement, he turned to Chief Michaels, "Then that's when this Voice must have started. Did anything happen around that time? I can't remember anything specific, myself."

"Not that I know of," Michaels began, but at the same time, John made a curious noise and pulled a small notebook from his jacket, going through the pages quickly. "What is it, Mr. Striker?"

John sighed. "It's hard to explain. More a hunch than anything else. But that date… is it coincidence?" As everyone looked at him, he shook himself, "All right, it's like this. Back when Aunt Harriet sold me the house, she suddenly decided that she wanted everything in the basement moved to the winery. I thought it odd; she hadn't cared before. But I didn't need a bunch of rusted old machinery, so I agreed."

"And?"

"I had Tan and his men get the stuff out of there. Apparently, while they were working they kept hearing strange noises, like something yelling."

William was disappointed. He'd hoped his cousin had a better idea than that. "You're saying the house is haunted?"

With a grin, John told him, "Oh, it's probably that too, but whatever the yelling was, it didn't start until they opened the workshop and started moving stuff. Tan never did find out where the noise came from, though."

"I still don't see how that could have anything to do with this."

John pointed to the date on the board. "The first time The Voice contacted Crogan was May 12th. I just checked and that's one day after Tan and his men delivered everything Aunt Harriet wanted from the house to the winery. Given all those other connections with the Kranes, I can't help but feel like it means something."

Michaels considered the point for a moment, looking torn. Then, "It won't be easy to investigate, much less prove," he said finally. "I'll keep that thought in mind."

"All right," John answered, then turned to his own business. "For now, though, may I ask for William's time for the rest of the day?"

Michaels turned to look at William curiously. "I don't have anything I need him doing," he admitted. "Though he's supposed to be on patrol with Maloney tonight. What do you need him for?"

Before William could stop his cousin, John grinned, "Well, for one thing, I owe Bill a rather large sum of money and we're going to have to take care of that. Then... well there's something at the house I just bought from him that I think he ought to see."

《《《

The house on Jewel Island had been the Krane's first home, back when Sebastian Krane had come west to run a logging company. Over the years it'd gone from a small wooden cabin to a slightly larger two story house to a large stone building surrounded by a carefully manicured park. After Sebastian Krane's death in 1937, its only inhabitants had been a husband and wife whose sole duty was to keep it from falling into ruin.

"The Brookes did a good job," John told his cousin as they entered the main hall of the house. "Given it was just the two of them and Aunt Harriet didn't pay them much to keep things in order."

William looked around the great hall, "Your construction crew's been working hard." He indicated the newly varnished wood flooring, the completely new paneling and the lounge area at the far end of the room.

"I had them focus on preparations for the ball," John agreed, feeling quite pleased with the result. "I didn't know it was tonight, but Tan's men are fast."

They went into the ballroom towards the back of the house and William whistled admiringly at the sight of the chandeliers, the graceful balcony overlooking the room and the huge glass doors leading out onto the patio. "This room was in bad shape even when my grandfather was alive. I remember being told to stay out because I might get hurt."

"Did you?"

"I was four. What do you think? Mr. Brooke had to climb up and get me." William indicated the railing of the balcony above.

A soft, wheezy, cough behind them drew their attention. "I remember that, Master William. I trust I will not have to repeat the effort?"

John thought Brooke might manage a rescue even now. Though in his seventies and quite grey, Brooke had a wiry strength born of years of constant exercise. He said as much, adding, "Though I don't think there's anywhere we'd have to be rescued from."

"I wouldn't try the second story of the west wing," Brooke countered. "The floor is quite completely rotted. I'm afraid it became beyond my ability to repair some years ago."

"Don't worry," John told him. "I told you I hadn't expected this place to be in as good a condition as you managed to keep it."

Brooke bowed. "Thank you, sir. I did do my best." He paused, looking worried, and added, "While I have you here, sir, I should warn you that Miss Rosamund has been...."

"As obnoxious as ever?" John couldn't help interjecting.

"I was going to say that she has been inconsiderate. Until this morning, I was of the understanding that her charity ball was to occur in two weeks. Yet her caterers have been arriving for the last few hours. My wife is quite put out at the mess they are making of her kitchen."

"Rosy told me this morning that she'd set the date for today," John agreed, still furious at his cousin's ability to make trouble for those around her. "Could you pass my apologies on to your wife and let her know I owe her for helping make this work?"

Brooke bowed slightly, smiling. "You needn't worry on our account. We remember Miss Rosamund's manners quite well. If anything, we ought to have warned you that she'd be contrary." Another bow to William and Brooke added, "Since you know, I will continue preparing for tonight's ball. Fortunately, Miss Rosamund's people came prepared to decorate."

"Of course, Brooke."

The man turned to William, "May I say what a pleasure it is to have you back, sir? It has been quite some time and I must admit to have missed you." He left the room before William could think of a thing to say.

Once the caretaker was gone, William shook himself, "It's strange," he admitted. "I do feel like I'm home. Which isn't true, since the house is yours now. I remember liking this place, though."

"You may not feel quite so comfortable when we go downstairs," John told him, remembering the main reason he'd brought William here. "Come along."

The basement consisted of an empty wine-cellar and a large storage room that went most of the length of the house. Beyond that were a set of double doors that had been firmly locked when John had first toured the house. He'd insisted on seeing what lay beyond and had been surprised to find that it contained what looked like an electrician's workshop. It'd been filled with dozens of strange devices.

"The room used to be where your grandfathers, both of them,

"THEY WENT INTO THE BALLROOM
TOWARDS THE BACK OF THE HOUSE... "

experimented," John told his cousin as they made their way to the back of the room. "At least, that's what Aunt Harriet told me."

William agreed, "Granddad Jarvis worked for Grandfather Krane back in the day. I think Uncle Jack helped out a little, too. Though he was mostly interested in ways to improve wine-making." With a frown, William added, "I don't really know what they were doing, but I remember being spanked for poking around in there once."

John laughed. "Now I know why you became a police officer. So you could poke your nose into things without getting in trouble for it."

"You might be right at that," William answered as John opened the doors to the workroom. As they stepped through, William's cheerful expression faded and he hesitated at the entrance as if frozen solid.

Looking around the empty room, with its bare brick walls and its cement floor recently washed, John wondered why his cousin was upset. John knew what was in the room beyond the next door, but William shouldn't have had any idea. Unless…. "Were you here when they carved it?" he wondered aloud.

"When they carved what?" William asked voice thin and sharp with barely controlled panic.

"You see that opening?" John asked, indicating the hole in the wall across from them. "It was bricked up when we cleared the room, so we didn't notice anything at first."

William took a deep breath, clearly just one step short of running for his life. "Was it where the yelling you mentioned came from?" He shook himself. "What am I saying? I don't believe in ghosts."

John was of the opinion that his cousin ought to. "No. That stopped as soon as we got rid of the equipment. We found this room when we were fixing the patio. It's right below there and the ceiling broke through. Tan was the first one in and I still don't know how he stayed so calm about it."

William started forward, hands clenched, entire body tense with fear. Worried, John said, "Look, you don't have to go in there. Maybe I should have kept my mouth shut."

"I'm going," William said in a flat cold voice. It obviously took everything he had, but he walked to the doorway, shining the flashlight John had given him into the room.

John didn't follow. He already knew what lay inside and that was enough. They'd have to do something about it, but right now all he could do was hope William didn't have a total breakdown.

After all, it wasn't everyday a man found a grotesque memorial to his mother's death sculpted out of solid stone.

《《《

Michaels gazed around the room, avoiding looking at the thing in the wall. Not that the rest was easier to look at; every surface, from the cement ceiling to the brick walls to the twisted and broken machinery at its center was horribly warped, melted like wax. Worse was the way the melted surfaces defied gravity, so that it looked like it had been sucked towards one point. And at the center of that point…. "Dolan wasn't the first victim, then," he said flatly. "This is the same thing, isn't it?"

"No," McLeod said as he knelt beside the wall and examined the remains, or whatever they were. "Robby, this is why I didn't let you build that dimensional rift device. Get it wrong and things go bad fast."

Before Robby could answer, William interrupted, his voice shaken, "If it isn't like Dolan then she didn't survive this, did she?" He knelt beside the figure, clutching its outstretched hands as if he'd never let go.

From what Striker had said, the kid had been that way since he'd entered the room. Michaels couldn't blame him. Bad enough finding a statue of one's mother, carved to look as if she were in torment, struggling to break free of the wall. Far worse to know, or fear, that the statue was his mother's remains.

Gently, McLeod put a hand on William's shoulder, "Son, I'm sorry, but there's no way she'd be alive. Not in this state."

Looking relieved, William released the hand. "Thank God. I was afraid she'd been stuck like this, the same way Dolan was, alive and unable to call for help. That's why I made John get you and Michaels." He touched the stone face, twisted with a mix of fear, anger and desperation.

"I don't understand any of this. Aunt Gwen alive? Dimensional rifts?" Bewildered and angry, Striker glared at William, demanding, "What's going on here?"

"Mother died here. Isn't that right, Mr. McLeod?" William's voice was calmer now, a brittle quiet that could shatter into fragments at the wrong word. "In this room. This is what's left of her."

Striker looked as if he'd had a suspicion confirmed, "I thought that might be the case. Your grandfather carved that sculpture to memorialize what really happened…." His voice trailed off as he took in William's last words. "What's left of her? What do you mean?"

Standing and dusting off his hands, McLeod explained, "Mrs. Jarvis and her brother were sucked through a dimensional rift, starting here and ending where they were found."

"A... dimensional rift?" Striker asked, obviously puzzled. "I don't understand."

"Back in the thirties, William's grandfather Jarvis was working on a discovery he'd made to transport objects from one place to another via a shortcut through another dimension. This device, in fact," McLeod put his hand on what remained of the machinery on the other side of the small room. "Unfortunately, the shortcut was extremely dangerous. A relatively minor pressure difference from one end to the other could result in everything not nailed down being sucked through. Including people."

"And," Robby added pedantically, "the greater the distance, the higher and faster the suction. The friction would have been...."

Before Robby could continue, his father put his hand over his mouth. "One, we do not require precise figures. Two, do you think Mr. Jarvis wants to know exactly how his mother died?"

For once, the kid was quelled, and Michaels was grateful. He didn't want to know the details either. Besides, the main question was "How'd she end up like that? I mean, I sort of understand this business of dimension rifts, but why would she be turned to stone?"

"We never saw this effect in our experiments," McLeod said as he examined the strangely melted walls and floor. At last he shook his head, coming back to where Mrs. Jarvis' remains were and looking around thoughtfully. "I can see what happened, but I can only speculate as to why."

When McLeod fell silent, not elaborating, William turned to him. "What happened? I need to know."

Slowly, McLeod said, "There was something incredibly hot in this room. Hot enough to melt every surface so that it was sucked into the rift and covered it. Which may have saved the house, because once you open a rift you have to close it with exactly the right sequence of vibrations. From the look of things, your mother and uncle were dragged through before anyone could reset the machine."

There was something McLeod wasn't telling William; Michaels could see it in his face. Fortunately, the kid was too dazed to be his usual observant self. Michaels coughed, drawing everyone's attention. "Is there any chance this has something to do with our other problem?"

"Maybe," McLeod said. "I'll need to go over the notes Professor Jarvis left me to be sure. But we can't do much here. The device is ruined and the rift is blocked. It shouldn't be a danger anymore. Mr. Jarvis, you should let someone fix you some lunch and try not to think too hard about what happened here."

Although he obviously hated the idea of leaving this last remnant of his mother, William nodded. He and Striker left the room and if his steps were faltering and uncertain, the kid had a determined air that gave Michaels hope that he'd be all right.

When William was gone, Michaels turned to McLeod. "Well?"

McLeod stepped back and pointed at the floor. It was covered in dirt from the hole in the roof, but McLeod had pushed enough away to show what lay beneath. The marks of two bare feet were embedded in the melted cement. Human in appearance, but longer and somewhat broader than most men's, the heels were dug deeper than the long skinny toes.

Robby stepped into the footprints and reached out, bending forward to grasp at the victim's outstretched hands and Michaels suddenly understood. Not that that stopped Robby from explaining. "Someone was here," the young man said quietly, "Someone who was trying to pull Mrs. Jarvis free. Someone who could stand, barefoot, in melted rock and not notice the heat."

Michaels had no doubt as to who that someone had been. Like McLeod, though, he couldn't guess why. "Old Smoky."

(((

When Francis reached the old Krane house she was greeted by the sight of workmen carrying flowers, ribbons and drapery in through the big double doors. Mr. Brooke was watching the parade with a dour expression and an occasional sharp command when one man nearly dropped the vase he was carrying. "Be careful, damnit! I don't want to re-polish the entire floor. And stay on the sheets!"

Seeing Francis, the old man's expression softened. "Miss Trendle, Mr. Striker said you'd be coming. So good of you to help out."

"It's a pleasure. You see, I've come ready to work," Francis told him, indicating her clothes, pants and one of her father's old shirts. "I'm not much of a cook, so I hope you'll put me onto decorating."

He smiled with an old servant's indulgence for a master's attempt to be useful. "Before anything else, you should have lunch with Mr. Striker and young Master William. They're in the blue tea-room."

Francis followed the old man through the halls, amused by how easily he'd fallen back on old habits with William. John might be the house's new owner, but William, as a member of the Krane family, remained the young master in Brooke's eyes.

When she entered the tea-room, Francis realized something was wrong. The two men were seated at the table, with a platter of small sandwiches, cookies and cakes, but neither were eating. Instead, they stared blankly, each caught up in their own thoughts. Seeing her, they both hurriedly stood.

"Come, sit down. We were just thinking," John said. "Brooke, would you… oh, good, thank you." The caretaker had already brought out a third service for Francis.

"Of course, sir." Brooke poured Francis' tea for her and, after a quick look to make sure everything was in order, excused himself.

Sipping her tea, Francis said, "You can tell me what you mean after I warn you of impending doom. Rosamund is coming. She was on the same ferry I was, and the only reason she isn't here is because she made a stop at the inn."

"Badgering the manager for that apple pie recipe again," John said resignedly. "Fortunately, no one's told her that Mrs. Brooke makes the pies for the inn."

"It was my mother's recipe," William added, and broke off, looking devastated. "Sorry, I'm not good company right now."

"With good reason," John reassured him. "Don't worry about it. Worry more about Rosy and her damned need to make everyone jump to her tune."

Francis suspected Rosy was the least of William's concerns. "We have time. Do you want to talk?"

John started to shake his head but William smiled weakly. "You already know part of it," He added for John's benefit, "I told you about what happened in the newsroom. I know this isn't the same thing as Dolan, but I can't help feeling this has something to do with everything else we've been dealing with."

"It's your story to tell," John said. "I'm just an interested onlooker at this point."

William added a spoonful of sugar to his tea. "John found something in the basement during renovations…," he told Francis and went on to explain just what that thing was. By the time he was finished, he'd put several more spoonfuls in, until the tea was slopping out of the cup and quite likely syrup. He was shaking, his voice cracking with the effort to stay calm.

When William finished, Francis took his cup from him and handed him hers. "You can't drink that," she told him when he looked startled. "And, I'm so very sorry this is happening, especially on top of everything else."

"I can't help imagining what she went through." William looked sick and as he started putting more sugar into his new cup, John took the sugar bowl away. He barely noticed, dipping his spoon into empty air and back to his cup. "It's like I can see her face, hear her screaming."

"I know you said you weren't here, but are you sure?" John asked. "You acted strangely down there, as if you knew what you'd find even before you went in that room."

William shook his head, then noticed the sugar had been moved. Automatically he reached for the dish, but John stopped him. "Why are you so sure you weren't?"

"I was home in my bed when they came to tell my father she'd been found up at the winery. Mother did bring me here to see grandfather often, but not that time." William shuddered suddenly and clenched his fists. "But... why was dad worrying about me? I remember him asking about me and..." He broke off, shaking himself.

"What is it?"

"I... can't remember. Why can't I remember?"

Francis was about to suggest that William's being barely five had something to do with it but Rosamund, walking in unannounced, had her own idea. "It's all that boxing, Boopsie. Mama says that getting hit in the head kills brain cells."

Although William and John stood politely, they all three glared at the young woman. Not that she noticed. As usual, Rosamund was oblivious to the atmosphere. She came up to the table, picked up a sandwich from the platter and fed it to Boopsie before taking one for herself. "You ran ahead of me, Francis. That was rude."

"I didn't have business at the inn, Rosamund. Besides, we weren't traveling together." Francis noted her old schoolmate was over her snit with Francis, since she was talking to her again. Too bad, really. Francis had enjoyed the peace and quiet.

"Nonsense. I said hello to you and everything. You might have waited." Rosamund took the teacup that William had overfilled with sugar and sipped the tea. Then she stared at it with a surprised expression. "Francis, you really shouldn't drink so much sugar, dear. It'll rot your teeth."

Francis shrugged. "I needed to take a bitter taste out of my mouth."

John eyed his cousin with a dour expression. "So do I." He gestured towards the door, adding, "Shouldn't you be provoking your decorators? The party's in a few hours. I'm sure you want to make sure everything is going exactly according to plan."

Shrugging off the suggestion, Rosamund sat and stole William's teacup, pouring herself more tea. "I'm sure they won't need my attention until later, when they're closer to done."

Francis suspected Rosamund intended to wait until the last minute to make as many aggravating changes and suggestions she could think of. She liked making her employees jump through hoops, after all.

Having successfully silenced her companions by her sheer lack of consideration, Rosamund nibbled a cookie, then said, "So, Billy, what do you think of the old house now? Do you approve of everything John's done to improve it?"

Distantly, with manners Rosamund didn't deserve, William told her, "I've only seen the ballroom. But everything seems fine. I'm sure your ball will be a success."

"And have you gone looking for your dog, yet? You were so unhappy last time you were here and couldn't find it."

A puzzled look crossed William's face. "My dog? I've never had a dog, Rosamund, and even if I did, I wouldn't expect to find it here."

With a smug smile, Rosamund told him, "Your stuffed toy, Billy-boy. Don't tell me you've forgotten him? You were so attached to it. Every time it went missing you spent hours crying and looking for it." Seeing William was still confused, she added as an aside to Boopsie, "You see, mama is right about boxing. His memory is like Swiss cheese."

"Rosy, do you mean a toy beagle? Named Ferdie?" John asked, brows drawn together tightly.

"That's the one," Rosamund looked smug and pleased with herself. "He was looking for it the last time he was here. When Aunt Gwennie went missing." Suddenly, she put her hand in front of her mouth, as if realizing something. "Oh, but that was just before she died. Maybe that's why he doesn't remember. Because he feels guilty for going home without her."

William turned white as a sheet and Francis realized that if his cousin said much more he was going to break, then and there. "Rosamund," she said quietly, "I think you should leave right now."

"But...."

"Now." Francis put every bit of the authority learned from editing and running her newspaper into her voice. "William's unwell and you need to go."

For once, Rosamund did as she was told, leaving the room with barely a few more words. Francis turned to her companions. "What is it? Are you all right, Bill?"

"Bill was here when his mother died," John said suddenly and at her frown, he added, "Rosamund's lies usually benefit her. There's no benefit to what she just said. And if Bill was here that day...."

"I didn't run away!" William suddenly burst out. "I didn't!" The protest sounded like one he'd had to make before, an old hurt that still stung.

"I don't know how you got from here to your house, Bill, but I'm sure of one thing. You were in the workshop, looking for your stuffed toy, because that was where we found it when we cleared the place. And if that's true, then maybe you were in that room when your mother died. Maybe you saw the whole thing and that's why you can't remember what really happened."

To neither Francis, nor John's surprise, William rose to his feet suddenly and practically ran out of the room.

《《《

"I do not believe this." Crogan set the phone receiver down and stared at it blankly.

"Don't believe what?"

Old Uncle's voice behind him nearly made Crogan jump out of his skin. "The hell is wrong with you... I mean... Good afternoon, sir." Remembering what he owed the... whatever he was... as well as what Old Uncle Gilly could do if he put his mind to it, did wonders for Crogan's manners.

Old Uncle's eyes met Crogan's and somehow he managed not to crawl backwards over the desk. Then the man chuckled. "I'm a monster, Crogan. No need for manners."

Curiosity had been raging in him ever since he'd first realized Old Uncle's true nature, and Crogan asked, "What does that mean, you're a monster?"

Brows raised, Old Uncle dropped into one of the seats across from Crogan's desk. "There's a dictionary in that shelf over there," he pointed out. "Or have you ever bothered to open it?"

Since the 'book' was actually a box Crogan used to keep a spare gun, the answer to that question was, "I try to avoid needing it." From Old Uncle's grin, he knew why. "And I know what the dictionary's definition of monster is. What I don't know is what you mean by the word."

"Unless you plan on becoming a Sorcerer at your age the dictionary definition's the closest you'd understand. An unnatural deviation from what's normal." Old Uncle glanced at the missing portion of the wall where Crogan's men had been embedded. "I see McLeod's been here."

"He and Chang's men cut the wall out early this morning," Crogan told his guest. "I didn't argue. He might be the only one who can get those two out of the mess they're in." He still found it hard to believe he was cooperating with the authorities. But he didn't have a choice if he wanted The Voice off his back. Speaking of which, "To answer your question earlier; The Voice just called."

"Threatening to stick you in the eighth dimension with your feet lodged in the twelfth for last night's debacle?"

"No," Crogan said, puzzled and irritated. "He wanted to know how things went."

"What'd you tell him?" When Crogan hesitated, unsure what he dared say in a room that might be tapped, Old Uncle added, "Don't worry. I burned out the only bug in here when I came in. No one's listening."

Relieved, Crogan continued, "I did as Chang asked and told him we got the smaller idol he wanted. I didn't think he would, but he believed me. Then he said he had another job for me. It's like he didn't even remember last night."

Old Uncle frowned, "How do you mean, another job? What does he want you to do?"

"I'm supposed to take my men to some charity ball on Jewel Island for a bit of robbery with threats." This wasn't the sort of job he usually pulled. It was one thing to rob local businesses and fellow gangsters. Quite another to go after the sort of target known to scream loudly and anxiously for protection.

"Strange," another voice said suddenly. "I understood that The Voice's actions seem to benefit the Krane family."

Startled, Crogan had his gun out before he recognized the speaker as one of the masked pair that had been plaguing him recently. "You! Tiger?"

"Dragon. Unless you're colorblind, you should be able to tell the difference between a blue and a red mask. Besides, I'm much cuter."

Without moving from his chair, Old Uncle muttered, "Debatable. What do you want, Dragon?"

"I came to present my patron's compliments and a gift." Dragon lifted a black gloved hand and an object appeared on it, a statue of a young man lounging backwards on the back of a tiger. "One you'll have a use for, I believe."

Almost immediately, Old Uncle was out of his chair and backed into a corner, tendrils of black smoke rising from his body. His arm went up over his face as he snapped angrily, "Damnit! A little warning would be nice!"

Crogan stared at the statue and demanded, "What the hell is this?"

"The statue of Meng Huang Shang that your men tried to steal from the Jeen Loon." Dragon paused, cocking his head as if listening to something and added for Old Uncle's benefit, "And He says that you are too far along the high road for this small portion of his power to affect you."

Pushing himself further into the corner, Old Uncle muttered, "Tell Him I have no idea what he's talking about. Gods and monsters do not belong in the same room."

"He says there are none so blind as those who will not see and to stop whining." Dragon placed the idol on the desk as Old Uncle slowly and unwillingly lowered his arms. "He also says that while a God of Dreams is not necessarily a God of prophecy, even He can see that if you would not have the thing you grasp for, you're better off not reaching at all."

While Old Uncle grumbled under his breath, smoke trailing with every muttered word, Dragon turned to Crogan. "You should deliver this to its would-be owner soon, before he realizes that you lied to him."

"Wait. How did you know?"

Tapping the head of the little idol, Dragon bowed slightly, "He is not all seeing, nor all knowing, but this is something that affects His servants. He wishes to end The Voice's interference in our lives, even as you do. You need not trust us, but I'd point out that none of us has put his men into another dimension, nor attempted to murder you. You're better off with us than The Voice."

Crogan admitted the man was right. Besides, "I'm cooperating with the police," he said, flinging his hands up in a gesture of surrender. "For now, I guess I'll cooperate with you, too."

"Then follow The Voice's instructions regarding the idol." Dragon stepped back from the desk, his body beginning to turn translucent. "Oh, one last thing, Old One. He says that if you do not want to go where a road ends, you ought not follow the one who leads you there."

"You tell Him that there's always the option of jumping off at the last moment," Old Uncle snapped in return.

"True," Dragon answered, "But He would remind you that the fall is a long one and the landing could be quite painful." Before Old Uncle could react, the man disappeared entirely, leaving Crogan to wonder if he'd be better off moving to Chicago.

⟨⟨⟨

There was something restful about the surf, William thought, leaning against the railing of the lighthouse. As long as he stared at the water, he felt as if he could handle the images in his head. Had he been in that room when his mother had been killed? An overwhelming sense of guilt confirmed it. The same overwhelming sense of guilt that made him certain it was his fault his mother had died.

If so, why hadn't he remembered this before? Why hadn't he told his father, or someone, what he'd seen? Or had he and they hadn't believed him? His grandfather would have, surely, but perhaps he'd chosen not to admit his knowledge, not wanting William to be blamed. Was that why the old man had left the house to him? So that, one day, he'd remember what he'd done?

"No. That isn't it." William muttered, certain there was something important that he needed to remember. "It can't be it."

"What can't be it?" The voice came from above him and looking up, William saw the man called Tiger perched on the lighthouse roof. "Your cousin's looking for you."

Glad of the distraction, William shrugged off John's worries. "Why are you here? Are you looking for trouble?"

Tiger slid down to the walkway and leaned on the railing beside him. "Trouble finds me without my having to look for it." His lips twitched in a wry smile beneath his mask. "Want to talk?"

"I don't think there's anything to say. I was here, I saw my mother die and I may be why she died." William didn't know why he'd said so much. Perhaps it was because they hardly knew each other. He didn't have to worry about Tiger trying to reassure him.

"Doubt you were." At Tiger's succinct comment, William frowned and the man continued, "You were five. Scientists like your grandfathers know how dangerous their experiments are. Their workshops get locked up tight if their owners have any sense, trust me. Neither Doctor Jarvis or Sebastian Krane were fools. You shouldn't have been able to get in."

Although William wondered how Tiger knew about what they'd found in his grandfathers' workshop, he knew he wouldn't get a straight answer if he asked. "It doesn't matter how I got in. I was and mother must have gone in to find me. I just wish I could remember why."

"Understandable," Tiger agreed. "I'd want to know, myself."

"And why was Grandfather's device running without anyone else there?" William had been thinking hard about the whole thing and it seemed obvious to him that the accident would never have happened if anyone who knew what they were doing had been in that room.

"Given it was an accident," Tiger agreed and at William's stare, he added, "I'd look at the floor of that room sometime. You and your mother weren't alone."

"How do you know?"

"I'm that good," Tiger said succinctly. Then he turned serious again.

"I'd love to stay and chat but I can hear Mr. Striker headed this way and I have things to do to before tonight."

"Tonight?"

"The Voice isn't done. My partner says he ordered Crogan to pull off a heist. If Crogan comes, it won't be to obey orders, but I'm sure The Voice has a backup plan." With that, Tiger jumped up on the railing and leaped towards the ocean, landing on the seat of his motorcycle as it flew past. By the time John appeared in the doorway of the lighthouse, the masked man was gone.

((((

Maloney shifted uncomfortably in his only suit. He wasn't cut out for this and he wished he'd kept his nose out of this nonsense. He wanted his uniform back and the only thing that made him happy was the fact that he'd been allowed to keep his gun.

"Tell me again why I'm here? And who is that kid anyway?"

Crogan sighed. "We're here to see who takes the bag he's putting in the locker. And you don't want to know."

The kid in question turned towards them grinning as if he'd heard their conversation, an impossibility given he was all the way across the train station from the little hotdog stand where they stood. It was hard to tell through the young man's tinted glasses, but Maloney could have sworn that he winked at them.

Stuffing the bag in a locker, the kid disappeared among the crowd waiting for the next train to San Francisco. It was a pretty good trick, Maloney had to admit. One moment he was there, then Maloney blinked and their courier was gone, like a puff of smoke.

Crogan looked relieved. "I guess he didn't have any trouble with the bag after all."

Unsure why the kid would, Maloney shrugged. "Now we wait?"

"No. You wait, remember? The Voice knows what I look like. If I hang around he'll know something's up." Crogan grimaced. "Besides, I'm supposed to be going to Jewel Island. I've a feeling The Voice would notice if I didn't."

If Michaels hadn't ordered him to help Crogan out, Maloney would have told the crook just where he could go and it wasn't Jewel Island. "So you're leaving me on my own?"

"Oh, no, sweetness. I'll be here with you."

The kid's voice, harsh as a smoker's and deeply amused, startled Maloney so that relish went flying when he spun around. When it hit the kid in the face, Crogan gasped. Thin fingers rose, wiped the relish from tanned features and tasted it. "Nice, but not as good as a bottle of whiskey," he said calmly. "Crogan, run along. And be careful."

Before Maloney could say a word, Crogan was gone, leaving Maloney with the kid. Except, now that he was face to face with the man, Maloney wasn't so sure he was as young as he looked. Nineteen year olds might pretend to be confident but this man knew what he was doing and what he could do. Moreover, he'd talked to Crogan like an equal... no, like a superior... and Crogan had accepted the treatment without complaint. "What am I supposed to be calling you?"

"Gilly will do," the man said, going to purchase a hotdog. As he slathered it with enough hot sauce to set a house on fire, he added, "Did Crogan tell you what to do when our quarry gets that bag?"

"We're supposed to follow at a discreet distance and be finding out where it goes."

"As long as the bag stays in this world, where it belongs, I could follow it without your help. Given our quarry has demonstrated a talent for shifting into another dimension; however, I'm probably going to need someone to handle that receiver McLeod loaned us. I burn things like that out if I try to use them for long."

Now that made less sense than anything Maloney had heard in the last few days. "How are we supposed to be following the thing if it goes into another dimension?" He still couldn't quite believe he was saying that. "McLeod's good, but is he good enough for that?"

"Our quarry may move through dimensions but I'm damned sure he has a base in our world." Gilly bit into his hotdog, looked thoughtful and added another large helping of hot sauce. "Could do with a bit more char."

Ignoring the man's behavior, Maloney asked, "And what is in the bag, then? Gold bars? Jewelry?"

"A bloody nuisance, among other things." Gilly grimaced. "Also, unless I miss my guess, a bite too big for The Voice to chew. Monsters, even man-made ones, should know their place."

Maloney didn't understand at all, but he didn't have time to ask. Something strange was going on near the lockers. An odd kind of wavering in the air that almost had a human shape. The only reason he'd seen it at all was because the late afternoon sunlight had struck the long hall in just the right way. "Hey."

To his surprise, he found he was talking to empty air, Gilly having disappeared as quickly as he'd appeared earlier. He stared around, seeing only cigarette smoke from a nearby ashtray. "The devil?" he muttered. "What do I do now?"

Once again Gilly was there. "Like I expected, he went beyond my reach. Grab that thing and let's go."

In the car, a few minutes later, Maloney demanded, "If he's out of your reach how do we find him when he comes back?" He didn't understand this stuff, but it was obvious that their quarry wouldn't come back right where he'd left.

"I have a sense of where the thing in the bag is," Gilly told him and pointed north, across the river and up the hill. "No surprise. It's somewhere up that way. Don't bother turning that box of McLeod's on yet, though. I doubt it has the range."

Maloney drove on in silence, crossing the bridge that led into the upper class neighborhoods. "Higher up. Towards the winery," Gilly said after several minutes. "He can't be that obvious, can he?"

The last was more to himself than to Maloney, but given curiosity was raging in him by now, Maloney went ahead and asked, "And who is he, then? One of the Kranes?"

"What do you think?"

Remembering what William had said about his kinfolk, Maloney shook his head. "There isn't a one among them could be behind this."

"Would you stake your life on that?"

That gave Maloney a moment's pause. "Maybe not," he admitted. "Are they, then?"

Gilly laughed sardonically. "Why ask me?"

For the briefest of moments, sense warred with Maloney's usual tendency to say what he thought. The latter, as usual, won. "You're Old Smoky, right? You know every dirty deed done in this town, don't you?"

Now Gilly was laughing in earnest, smoke pouring out his nose and mouth as he chortled. Startled, Maloney barely managed not to veer off the twisting road leading up the hill. "Damnit! Don't do that! You're getting ash everywhere."

Slowly the smoke subsided as Gilly drew himself back together. "Not afraid of me?"

"Not a bit of it," Maloney lied. "I'm a good Catholic boy."

"That you are," Gilly said, grinning broadly. "St. Christopher's medal and faith pouring off you like a river. Doesn't mean I couldn't hurt you if I wanted." As Maloney slowed the car, he added, "Didn't say I wanted."

Maloney returned to driving. "You didn't answer my question."

"That's because I don't actually know every dirty deed done in this town. Never have, never did. I'm a monster, Maloney, not a God." Gilly glared out the window. "I can go anywhere fire can. But that doesn't mean I'm everywhere. Or that I want to be."

"I'm not pretending to be understanding that," Maloney muttered. "And it still doesn't tell me what I'm wanting to know."

"That makes two of us," Gilly grumbled. "What you folk figured out is probably right. The Voice and the Kranes are like peas in a pod. But I'm blessed if I can work out how he's doing the half of what he's doing. Only thing I do know is he's using some of my power to do it and I don't like that one bit."

They were almost to the winery, so Maloney pulled over and switched McLeod's radio receiver on. "Is it working?" he asked, peering at the thing curiously. There was a blip of light at the top of the little circle of glass but he had no idea how far away that was or what it meant.

"I think so. McLeod said it'd have a light like that when it picked up the signal. Keep driving. As long as I don't touch the thing I can keep an eye on it."

The road twisted and turned and suddenly Gilly said, "I'll be damned. Not the winery."

"Eh?" Maloney glanced down and saw the blip was pointed off towards the north-east, while the winery was exactly north of them. "Where is it, then?"

"Must be the old logging camp, the first one Krane built, before he realized he couldn't get the wood out," Gilly told him. "That's the only thing left up that way."

"Well then, that's where we'll have to be going," Maloney said, trying to sound cheerful and failing. He wished he had back-up right then and the fact that he had one of the oldest and meanest monsters ever to walk the hills of Strikers Port on his side didn't feel like a substitute. At least he knew he could trust Jarvis.

(((

Michaels watched the men leaving the ferry with a jaundiced eye. Half were from Chinatown, the other from the docks and none were men he could trust. It wasn't just that most had been in and out of jail for one reason or another, either. The Voice must have put ringers in the lot as well. The question was, where was The Voice himself?

A skinny figure twisted and bounced through the crowd, easily recognizable by the way he moved. "McLeod, isn't that…."

" IS IT WORKING? HE ASKED,
PEERING AT THE THING CURIOUSLY. "

Chou Chang was there before Michaels could finish his sentence, coming up to where his father stood and bowing deeply. "Honored father, this foolish child is glad to see you."

With a sigh, McLeod ruffled his son's hair. "I know you speak better English, boy. What are you doing here?"

"My most honored and honorable mother has called for my help in the kitchens of the Krane House, beloved father." Chou grinned at Michaels, adding, "As a cook, that is. She doesn't need any help with ghosts, demons or monsters."

"I'll take your word for it, son," Michaels told the young man, amused because this was about the most coherent he'd ever seen the kid. "Better get moving then. That party starts in an hour and your mother probably needs all the help she can get."

Bowing, Chou said, "This one's revered mother is capable of great feats when she puts her mind to it. However, she has also commanded her humble and incompetent child to be at her side quickly, therefore...." he ran off before his father could open his mouth to tell him to get moving.

"Those boys of mine are enough to make any father crazy," McLeod muttered and as Michaels chuckled, added, "Although I'll admit to being proud of them, too, despite all the trouble they cause me."

"A better sort of trouble than what's brewing tonight," Michaels agreed. "Tell me something, McLeod, do you know much about Old Smoky? Your wife seemed to know him, back at your workshop."

A wry smile crossed McLeod's face as they turned back to head to the Krane house. "I don't know much about him, no. Just what Mr. Krane and his son Jack told me when we helped banish him the first time."

Startled, because this was the first Michaels had heard of the Kranes' involvement, Michaels said, "Wait, I hadn't heard any of this before."

"Didn't your Chief tell you?" At Michaels' shake of his head, McLeod sighed. "Maybe he didn't want anyone to know what a mess we made."

"And now you've said that, you'd best explain," Michaels grumbled.

"There's not much to say. Old Smoky's a kind of Fire Elemental, so Mr. Krane and my boss thought the best way to get rid of him was to drop him in the ocean. That part you knew?"

Michaels agreed. "Come to think of it, the Chief never really did say exactly how they did it."

"We used the rift device. Remember what I said about how it worked? We built a pressurized chamber in the far end of the room and Jack summoned Old Smoky into it. Then we opened a rift between the chamber and the ocean." McLeod looked pained, "We knew what happened when there was a pressure difference. The plan was to put the other end high enough that Old Smoky would be pulled through."

"She, the Lady under the lighthouse, did say he was injured," Michaels said. "And he hasn't been active, so it must have done some good."

"It did more harm than good," McLeod told him grimly. "The trouble was that we hadn't known about the effect of greater distance. The chamber imploded and came close to sucking everyone in the room out with Old Smoky. I managed to close the rift but one of the men your Chief had sent to help us was halfway through at the time. The results weren't pretty."

Seeing the guilt in the man's eyes, Michaels shook his head. "You did what you had to," he said. "You couldn't know what would happen."

McLeod smiled ruefully, "No, I couldn't. But it doesn't make it any easier." He sighed. "It's in the past; I try not to dwell on it too much. And to teach Robby to be far more careful with what he does than we ever were. I'm not sure I've succeeded."

Michaels returned to the subject, "So you and the others threw Old Smoky into the ocean and it didn't kill him. Granted, both he and Herself says he can't be killed that easily, maybe not at all. So why'd he stop showing up after that? And why was he in that room with Mrs. Jarvis when she died? Trying to save her?"

"I've been thinking about that ever since I saw those footprints," McLeod said as they turned the last corner leading up to the Krane house. "Did you know that it was Old Smoky who aided and abetted George Jarvis' courtship? That if he hadn't helped them send letters to each other, Gwendolyn Krane might have married someone her father approved of?"

Michaels stared. "It was their love letters the Chief told me about? How in the hell could that have happened? They had to be crazy, using a devil like Old Smoky for a courier!"

McLeod looked into the brightly lit ballroom and shrugged. "I know what it's like to have everyone against your marriage. So I can understand why George would have been glad of any help, even the devil's, to get a chance at the woman he loved. As for Gwendolyn, she was too kind and trusting for her own good. She might not have thought Old Smoky was a bad sort."

"But why would he do it?"

"What was the old line, 'a drop or a dram and your dreams come true'?" McLeod started up the stairs towards the door, "I've a feeling that it started with a dash of whiskey in the right place, with the right words and the right desire. And from there.... well, Mudan says that when monsters try to do decent things, or start feeling things they're not built to feel, they start changing."

"Wait? Are you saying Old Smoky had feelings for Gwendolyn Jarvis? That he was in love with her?" Michaels stopped, remembering something William had said the other night about his rescue. That Old Smoky had told him that he was the one person in the world who would never owe him. Maybe McLeod was onto something.

Just as he was about to say as much, an enraged screech drew his attention towards the ballroom. "I SAID IT NEEDS TO HANG FROM THE MIDDLE OF THE CEILING!" Miss Krane, having one of her moments.

⟨⟨⟨

William watched Rosamund's belligerence increase with every sip of wine. Perhaps it was because he was an outsider, but it seemed to him that she'd be tossed in a cell to dry out if she were anyone but the favored daughter of the Krane family. It troubled him. He could understand how and why the men and women he dealt with as a policeman got where they were. Poverty and desperation created pressures some could only handle by lubricating their lives with whatever alcohol they could find.

Rosamund had neither excuse. She was well fed, well cared for and given every last thing she needed. William corrected himself, not what she needed but what she wanted. Perhaps that was the clue. What was missing in her life that made her try to drown her sorrows from the moment she woke until she fell into bed? And was it a mystery he could solve, given her family would never see him as anything but the unwanted son of an unfortunate marriage?

"Miss Rosamund," Brooke was saying as gently as he could, "We don't have a ladder long enough to reach the ceiling."

"I DON'T CARE... WHAT IS IT?"

The last had been directed at the immensely calm and collected Mrs. McLeod, who stood behind Rosamund with a small steaming cup in hand. The woman smiled, "Miss Rosamund, forgive the interruption, but have you eaten?"

"What?" Rosamund stared at Mrs. McLeod with a confused expression.

"I think that you have been here since noon and have not eaten properly. That is not healthy. At the very least, have some tea." Mrs. McLeod smiled gently at William's cousin and there was something in her voice that seemed immensely persuasive. It was also unexpectedly effective. Rosamund took the teacup and drank its contents without seeming to taste it.

Only after she'd finished the drink did she blink and stare into it, "That was tea?"

"A special tea," Mrs. McLeod told her. "With lotus root, fruit and other simple herbs. They are very good for you. Very healthy. Very sustaining."

William didn't know much about Chinese herbs but whatever it was in the tea had a calming effect on his cousin's temper. She looked less tense than she had before. "It's good. Can you get me the recipe?"

"I will be glad to do so, Miss Rosamund. I think it would do you good to drink more. I also think you should eat now; just a small snack to tide you over before the party." Mrs. McLeod took the teacup back, adding, "If you come with me, I shall persuade Mrs. Brooke to find you something."

Rosamund hesitated, looking at the crystal chandelier that one of the workers held in his hand. "But my decorations?"

With a slight incline of her head to acknowledge Rosamund's concern, Mrs. McLeod turned and called out to the Chinese men who were setting up the buffet. "Tan. Leung. Come." Both men, Chang's seconds-in-command, if William had guessed right, were at Mrs. McLeod's side without hesitation and she ordered, "Take care of that thing. Miss Rosamund would like it hanging in the very center of the room."

Bowing, Tan took the chandelier and called his men over.

"There now. My cousin and his friends will make sure it gets where you want, Miss Rosamund. Now, if you would come this way?" By sheer force of personality, Mrs. McLeod escorted her charge out of the room.

Behind her, the dozen or so Chinese performed a feat of acrobatics worthy of a circus act, one by one climbing atop each other's shoulders until they were high enough to reach the ceiling. So awed was he by the performance that he barely noticed Chief Michaels and McLeod approach.

"How did she do that?" the Chief asked, staring after the pair as they left. "I've never seen anyone calm your cousin down so fast."

"Most likely with the aid of a medicine the Chinese use for alcohol poisoning," McLeod told him. "That and she's had quite a bit of practice keeping obstreperous young people in line."

At a guess, McLeod meant his sons, and William grinned. "They do seem to be a bit lively," he told the man. "Although I suppose it'd be even more interesting if all of this lot were involved as well." He gestured at the men - and one woman - who were carefully raising the chandelier to its appointed place and making sure it was properly attached.

"You have no idea." McLeod was about to say more but that was when Francis came into the room from the direction of the kitchen, her eyes wide and worried, looking like she'd been running. "Miss Trendle? What is it?"

"That man who was in my house the other night. He's here. I just knocked him out."

⟪⟪⟪

They were a few hundred yards from the logging camp when Gilly suddenly sat upright and made a disgusted noise. "Oh for... I told him to be careful over there."

"What?" Maloney focused on not winding up being thrown off the road and down the hill below. "What are you talking about?"

"Crogan. The idiot's gotten himself knocked out cold." Gilly shook his head sadly, "He can't say I didn't warn him, either."

Maloney slowed down so he could look at his companion. "Crogan? What happened and how do you know?"

"Crogan's pretending to do what The Voice wants. So he went over to Jewel Island with a crew to 'help' with that party of Little Miss Perfect's. I told him he should be careful because Miss Francis would be there too and she doesn't know about his cooperating with the police yet. She's a fast one with a poker, it seems."

On one hand, Maloney would freely admit that Crogan probably deserved having his head knocked in by the woman he'd threatened with grievous bodily harm. On the other, "You still didn't say how you know."

"Crogan's poured enough whiskey into my fire to keep my attention for at least another month," Gilly answered. "Not that that's going to make me come to his rescue this time. If he's stupid enough to forget someone has good reason to be afraid of him, he can take his lumps. Besides, I'm no one's guardian angel."

It sounded to Maloney as if the monster were protesting too much but he didn't ask more. Instead he glanced at the radio receiver. "Looks like we're almost there." The blip was almost to the center of the screen.

"Yep. As expected, we're just short of the old logging camp. Better stop the car here."

Maloney considered dropping his companion off where they were and letting him do whatever it was he did alone. That would have left his curiosity, itching like a newly acquired mosquito bite, unrelieved. He didn't trust Gilly, but if he was to find out who was behind all this nonsense he was going to have to go along with the monster's plans. Without a word he pulled the car over onto the side of the road and got out.

Grinning as if he knew perfectly well what Maloney was thinking, Gilly headed up the road, sniffing the air appreciatively. "Ah, memories," he commented. "The Kranes'd build a logging camp and I'd burn it down. Good times."

"If I thought for an instant you could be made to stay there," Maloney countered, "I'd put you in jail for arson."

Thoughtfully, Gilly considered the idea. "Nah. It'd be boring. Besides, I think the statute of limitations may have run out by now. Last act of violence I committed was twenty-one years ago."

"You don't do math very well, do you?" Maloney pointed out. "Way I figure, you stopped your games back in '32."

"I had one last encore in me since that time," Gilly responded, almost absent-mindedly. "After that, I gave up killing for Lent." Strangely, and to his own surprise, Maloney believed him.

They were near the old logging camp, so Maloney fell silent. He was too busy trying to see where he was walking in the twilight. If he didn't want to keep whoever was hiding out up there from noticing them he would have used a flashlight.

The camp was almost completely dark, but that made it easier to tell where their quarry had to be. A building at the far end. There wasn't much, just the tiniest seam of light from beneath what was probably a door, but it was enough.

Moving as quietly as he could, Maloney followed behind Gilly, envying the monster's ability to walk soundlessly across broken pavement. Somehow, Maloney made it to the door without tripping over his own feet or crashing into something, but it was a tense few minutes.

Gilly cocked his head as he listened at the door, his eyes glowing behind his glasses and his expression intent. Someone was there, that much was certain, moving in a slow and deliberate manner.

A voice spoke, sounding tinny, as if coming through a speaker, and a bad one at that. "Did my proxy come back this time?"

"It did, sir." The second voice was that of an old man. "And I believe Mr. Crogan has finally achieved, or at least partially achieved, the goal you set him."

"Excellent. Then we have at least some small portion of that so-called God's power?"

Beside Maloney, Gilly smirked, as if he knew something the voices beyond the door didn't. Whatever he thought, however, would have to remain unsaid for now. The question Maloney had was what they were going to do.

Unfortunately, someone else had the answer to that question. Maloney suddenly felt the pressure of a gun placed at the back of his head. "Don't move," a quiet, almost gentlemanly voice said behind him. "Either of you."

"Why not just kill them?" a younger man's voice said suddenly, sounding petulant.

"That's for your father to decide, Master Peter. We aren't allowed to take such actions without orders." A pair of hands searched Maloney and found both his gun and flashlight, then moved on to Gilly. The same voice said, "This one is unarmed."

Maloney might have acted as soon as he'd felt two hands searching him but some instinct kept him from moving. It was a good thing, too, for while the next voice sounded like the first, it came from several feet away. "We'll bring them inside for Mr. Krane to decide." Strong hands shoved Maloney through the door.

Inside the building, with a set-up that seemed strangely similar to McLeod's down at the workshop, he could just see the sardonic grin on Gilly's face as they were pushed to the center of the room. Of course, he didn't have to worry, being immune to bullets.

The monster's expression changed as he spotted something at the center of the work area, an odd machine with a set of bent metal bars attached to one side, looking like something out of a Flash Gordon serial. "Oh hell," Gilly muttered, actually sounding frightened, "Not that thing again."

《《《

"It's your own fault, Crogan."

Rubbing his head and glaring at his captors, Crogan admitted that he had been warned. The trouble was, he hadn't expected to find Miss Trendle cleaning dishes in the kitchen. She was too rich and important to be doing something so mundane. "What sort of newspaper editor stands around doing housework?" he demanded. "And you know you could have killed me?"

"Considering you were threatening me the other night, I think the jury would regard it as self-defense," Miss Trendle countered. "Chief Michaels, are you sure this man can be trusted?" Behind her, both the cook and the butler nodded agreement, both clearly ready to brain him if he made so much as a single false move.

Michaels snorted, "No. Not really. But right now, I think his skin is more important to him than anything else. Besides, he's warned us that there's going to be trouble and I have my men, as well as Chang's, ready and waiting for it."

Miss Trendle didn't look convinced, which was fine with Crogan. All this cooperation made him uncomfortable, and he was looking forward to the day The Voice was out of his life. "Now that that's settled, I don't suppose I could get that sandwich I came in here for?"

The cook sniffed. "Good luck with that," she told him. "The only food in this place is hors d'œuvres, most of them Chinese and all of them intended to feed the horde Miss Rosamund's invited. And I'm not feeding you out of my refrigerator."

Suddenly and unexpectedly, Miss Trendle took pity on him. "At least let him have some of the cookies from tea."

Not at all sure what to make of the lady's change in attitude, Crogan eyed her mistrustfully. "What's in them? Arsenic?"

"Just figure it's an apology for bashing your head in," Miss Trendle answered. "Besides, the sooner you've eaten, the sooner you're out of here."

Michaels eyed Crogan, "Afterwards, you can be keeping your men out of trouble. Miss Rosamund's guests have too much loot on them for my comfort and I don't want your thugs getting sticky fingers."

Waving off the warning, Crogan accepted the plate of cookies the cook gave him gratefully. They were damned good cookies, he'd give the woman that much. "Don't suppose you'd like a job at a tavern in town when this gig is over?"

"I have every intention of remaining in this house until I die," Mrs. Brooke said dourly. "And absolutely none of working in a devil's playground like a low-class booze hall."

Crogan shrugged. "Your loss," he told her, finishing off the cookies. "Right, I'll be off to check on my men, then."

As he rose, wincing at the pain in his head, Miss Trendle stepped forward. "I'll go with you."

"Eh?"

"Rosamund saw you too, right?" At his agreement, she continued, "She's in a state getting ready for this party. If she sees you I'm not going to be responsible for what she does. A poker to the noggin might be the least of your worries."

Admitting that was true, Crogan answered. "After you, then. Especially if you're armed."

Suddenly, the old man was there, opening the door. "I shall accompany you," he told them. "So that this man does not try anything... foolish." He glared at Crogan, daring him to argue the point.

"Thank you, Brooke," Miss Trendle told him.

"Whatever," Crogan added, not caring at all. "Shall we, Milady?"

Miss Trendle ignored the jibe, heading into the hall outside the kitchen and asking, "Which way?"

"My men are moving the wine and drinks out into the bar," Crogan told her. "I've got Donaldson, who knows what he's doing with a bottle, handling the bar itself."

Thoughtfully, Miss Trendle suggested, "Best warn him to water down anything he gives Rosamund." At his frown, she told him, "She's not a pleasant woman to be around when she's thwarted. She's even worse when she's drunk."

Remembering Miss Krane's enraged screeches when he'd met her the other night, Crogan believed it. "And some people complain about low-class booze halls," he muttered. "You'd think her family would have done something about that sort of problem by now."

To Crogan's surprise, the old man murmured, "It is regrettable that no one has ever tried to curb Miss Krane's temper. But then, the Rancourts have always tended to indulge their charges."

That didn't make any sense. "What do you mean? Rancourts?"

"I've said too much," Brooke said, looking embarrassed. "Please, pardon my loose tongue. I shouldn't speak of my employers, or my superiors, so readily."

Miss Trendle added, "Besides, I know who he means. The Rancourts have served the Kranes in some capacity for generations. I've heard it said that the family wouldn't be anything if the Rancourts weren't there to keep them in order."

"The Rancourts, Timothy especially, are very loyal and committed to the Kranes," Brooke said firmly, in a way that suggested that if he had any criticism of how the Rancourts handled their duties neither Miss Trendle, nor Crogan, would ever know it. Which, in itself, told Crogan that the old man had his doubts.

A voice hailed them as they turned the last corner towards the storage area where Crogan's men were. The last time he'd heard it, that voice had been yelling fit to break every eardrum in reach, but this time it was almost sweet. "Franky, dear! Aren't you going to dress for the party? Everyone's starting to arrive."

Crogan dodged sideways into an alcove and pretended to adjust the decorations. Fortunately, Brooke helped cover for him, saying, "A little to the left. No, up."

Miss Krane and her dog arrived a moment later and if the dog muttered under its breath in a distrusting fashion, his owner was too used to him to notice. It was only when the animal goosed Crogan that she said, "Boopsie, leave the servants alone. We have things to do."

"Be careful, man," Brooke added, partly to make his role look right and partly because Crogan had nearly dropped the shield when he'd noticed something around the dog's neck.

"I did bring better clothing, Rosamund," Miss Trendle agreed, distracting her friend from her dog's behavior. "I'll have to ask Mrs. Brooke what room they're in."

"Oh, good. I was hoping. Are you wearing green? Your red hair always goes so well with green."

"So I've been told," Miss Trendle replied. "Do you want to see?"

The two women left the hallway and Crogan breathed a sigh of relief. "Smart woman, that Miss Trendle," he muttered, glad now that she'd come along. Then, after getting the shield back where it belonged, he turned to Brooke. "I'm going to go back to my men. And I have a task for you, too."

"Excuse me? You have a task for me... sir?" The epithet held a world of doubt.

"Yeah. Go find Chief Michaels and tell him that that pearl choker we were talking about earlier today is being worn by a very large and possibly vicious Russian wolfhound."

⟪⟪⟪

Francis adjusted her petticoats and straightened to show off her dress. "What do you think?"

Clapping her hands delightedly, Rosamund circled Francis, readjusting the furbelows attached to the collar. "I've always told you green's your color. You should wear it more often. And I love that pin." She touched the emerald and green lacquer brooch attached to Francis' shoulder. "What is it? A bee? Where did you get it?"

"I'm not sure what it is, really. Father got it for me in Chicago. He said it matched my personality." Francis smiled ruefully.

"I'll have to ask Timothy to find one for me."

As Rosamund went to the mirror to check her own appearance, Francis asked, "Timothy? Your butler?"

"Oh, he's more than just a butler, Franky. He takes care of everything. Mummy and Daddy supply the money of course." A slightly discontented look crossed Rosamund's face, quickly wiped away. "But he sees to everything. He hires all the servants, too."

"I see." A thought occurred to Francis; Timothy would surely know something about James. "Is he going to be here tonight?"

Rosamund shook her head, "I told him I wanted to take care of this party. It's mine and I don't need his help."

Hesitantly, because she didn't want another fight, Francis asked, "Then maybe you know, was that James' brother I saw driving your car last night?" She'd wanted to ask for some time now but she and Rosamund hadn't been talking to each other since their spat.

"No, silly. That was James of course.... I think...." A puzzled look crossed Rosamund's face. "You know, I'm not really sure. He's downstairs, of course, if you're still worried about that bump he took."

Francis was sure it couldn't be James, but she wasn't going to argue. Instead she asked, "Does he have any brothers? I'd swear I saw someone who looked just like him recently." Of course, that someone hadn't been a real person at all, just a wooden figure that managed to act like a human being.

Considering the question as she teased her hair into exactly the position she wanted it, Rosamund asked, "How should I know? He's a chauffeur. I'm not supposed to talk to the chauffeurs. Except to tell them where I want to go." She paused and actually thought, "Although I think maybe he must, because mummy's chauffeur looks like him and so does Peter's. Timothy must have hired them together, so we'd have a matched set."

It would be like the Kranes to want all their chauffeurs to look exactly alike. "When did he hire them?" Rosamund was behaving almost sensibly and Francis wanted to take advantage of it.

Rosamund thought about it, "I think it was a month or so back, around the time we sold the house to John. Timothy didn't like our old chauffeurs - they talked too much - and brought James and the other two in to replace them."

A knock at the door interrupted their conversation, although Francis doubted she'd learned anything useful. She went to the door and peeked out, "Chief Michaels? William? Is something wrong?"

"No," Michaels said, smiling at her. "I just need to ask Miss Rosamund something."

Turning from the mirror and twisting slightly to show off her lovely pink gown, Rosamund said, "Everyone just seems full of questions tonight. But I'd be glad to talk to you if it's that important. Just, my party will be starting soon and I'd hate not to be ready to greet my guests."

"This won't be long," Michaels answered, coming into the room. William followed behind, looking surprisingly comfortable in the tuxedo John had found for him. Fortunately, the two men were of similar build. "Jarvis, would you check out the dog, please?"

"Boopsie?" Rosamund asked, for the first time looking worried. "He's been with me all this time. I'm sure he hasn't bitten anyone tonight."

"That's not the problem, Rosamund," William told her gently as he approached the big animal slowly and went to one knee. "Hallo, Boopsie. Would you mind letting me look at your collar? I have some chicken for you."

Apparently William had said the magic words because Boopsie, who had been lying in elegant and bored splendor on the nearest couch, got down quickly and came over to William without hesitation, accepting the treat with a neat and delicate touch. William held out his hand, letting the dog smell his palm, then stroked Boopsie's head. After a moment, he rose to his feet and told the Chief, "It looks like it might be the same one."

"What might be the same one?" Rosamund asked, actually seeming to realize there was a problem.

"Miss Krane, I hesitate to ask, but where did you get your dog's collar? The pearls are real, aren't they?"

Rosamund blinked. "Why does that matter? It's my dog and if I want to give him real pearls...."

"Rosamund, it's important, we need to know who gave you the collar," William interrupted and Francis was amused to note he used the same tone on her as he'd used on Boopsie. "You didn't buy it for yourself, did you?"

"Of course not. Daddy gave it to me. It's just like Margo's choker."

That made William blink. "Uncle Jack gave it to you?"

"He always gives me things, Billy. Everything I want."

"I understand. He loves you very much." William looked thoughtful. "But Uncle Jack's been sick for a long time, so he didn't go out to buy it for you? When you say he gave it to you, you mean someone else got the choker and handed it to you for Uncle Jack?"

Looking as if she thought he was silly for even needing to ask, Rosamund told her cousin, "Naturally, Billy. You know Timothy takes care of everything for the family."

"I didn't," William said gently, "I haven't been around much, remember?"

With a sigh and a shake of her head, Rosamund said, "But Timothy was taking care of us even before your mother died, Billy. You should remember that."

William chuckled, "I was five, Rosamund." Chief Michaels coughed, which caused William to smile wryly. "I'm sorry, Rosamund, Francis, but I'm still a working man and my boss has things for me to do. Thank you for letting us in. I'll see you downstairs in a little while."

Once they were gone, Rosamund turned to Francis, "Now what was all that about?" she wondered.

Francis had no idea, but one thing seemed obvious. Timothy Rancourt, the latest in a long line of Krane family retainers, appeared to be involved. She'd have to find a chance to tell William about the man's involvement with James, and possibly the man who'd tried to kill him.

⫷⫷⫷

Maloney was puzzled by Gilly's behavior. He'd been overwhelmingly confident just a few minutes earlier. Now, having seen the strange machine of The Voice's, the monster looked just about ready to make a run for it.

"What is all that noise? Ah, Master Peter, you've returned. Who are these men?" Dragged into the light, Maloney was momentarily blinded. When the spots faded from his eyes, he found himself looking at an old, fragile-looking, man dressed in a neat black suit. He didn't know the man, but something about his dress and speech made him think 'butler' or 'valet'.

"They were hanging around outside, sneaking. The Jameses caught them for me." The speaker was a young man with a discontented air and washed out features that reminded Maloney of his partner. What had the butler called him? Peter? This must be Jarvis' cousin, then. "I figured we should bring them in and see what Dad wanted to do with them."

The old man glanced back at the machine that made Gilly so nervous and to Maloney's surprise, the strange mechanical voice he'd heard earlier came out of a speaker attached to the thing. "What is it, Timothy?"

"We have guests. An older man and a boy."

One of the men holding Gilly said, "This one is not what he seems." He shook his captive slightly, eliciting a snarl. "He saw the rift device and tried to escape as smoke. I got him into range before he escaped."

Timothy's eyes widened as he looked at Gilly. "So you're the one they call Old Smoky?" The monster didn't have to answer, for the old man obviously knew he was right. "Master, we are in luck tonight. We've captured another of the beings you desired."

As if to prove his identity, a thin trail of smoke trailed from Gilly's mouth, dissipating quickly like breath in icy air. He gasped, struggling against his captor, then very nearly collapsed from the effort. "What... have you... done?"

The voice, and by now Maloney was certain this was The Voice himself, said, "The same thing that allows me to exist in this world creates a field around us that neither monsters, nor false gods, beings spawned of belief, can escape."

"What the devil are you talking about?" Maloney decided to add his two cents to distract them from Gilly. Maybe, if he played his cards right, he could give the monster the chance he needed to work out an escape. Besides, any information they could get might help.

"Who was that?" The Voice demanded in a querulous way that sounded just like Peter. Maloney was getting an inkling as to who its source might be. Of course, the Krane kid's big mouth had a lot to do with that.

"The other man, sir. A mere ruffian, no doubt a denizen of the city's south side whom this being we've captured inveigled into assisting him."

Realizing that their captors hadn't recognized him was a relief. The idea was to get as much information as Maloney could while revealing as little of his own. "Damnit, he didn't pay me enough for this crap!"

"Shut up, you idiot," Gilly gasped, but the look he shot Maloney was pleased. "You got paid plenty." More smoke escaped his lips and he dropped his head again, hanging loose in his captor's arms.

"Find out more about the other man. See if he can be used. We can certainly pay him more than this monster did."

"Sir, may I suggest that it's unwise to trust someone whose loyalties are so easily persuaded?"

"No. I'm in charge here. Do as I say."

Timothy sighed and gestured to the man holding Maloney. Released, Maloney stepped forward a few feet, then halted quickly when the old man drew a gun. "Hey, easy. I'm not going to try anything stupid."

"That is to be determined," Timothy replied, his aim calm and steady. "Now then, your name?"

"Ashford," Maloney offered quickly, choosing a name he'd used in another undercover operation.

"And what is this creature here paying you?"

With a laugh straight from his belly, Maloney told the old man, "You're nuts, right? I tell you how much he's paying so you can just barely outbid him? I don't work that way. You tell me what you'll pay and I'll be telling you if it's enough."

Gilly managed to whisper, "Stupid... idiot.... I'll burn you to ashes...." Hopefully he was playing along, though, because this was the only thing Maloney could think to do. He probably was. Maloney remembered what the monster had said about killing earlier and how strangely honest his words had felt.

Turning towards Gilly, intending to tell him something snappy and hopefully convincing to their captors, Maloney spotted the men who'd grabbed them and the only thing he could say was, "Who are they? The

Bobbsey twins?" The two men were dead ringers for the man McLeod had phased into an engine block and the man Jarvis had brought in not an hour later.

That made Gilly lift his head, peering over his shoulder weakly to look at the two men, while Timothy said, "They're very useful employees. No need to trouble yourself over their resemblance."

Suddenly and resentfully, Peter added, "They're not all that impressive, either. Just puppets. There's more of them where they came from."

"Puppets?" Gilly repeated and a smile lit his face. "Not alive?"

"Peter, you should not say another word...."

Having begun spilling the beans, the young man seemed unable to stop. "Of course not." He kicked the one closest to him, eliciting no response whatsoever. "I helped put them together."

The man, or puppet, holding Gilly's arms looked down at his captive. "He is becoming quite hot. My hands are catching fire." He was calm, incredibly so, for a being about to be immolated, which only proved Peter had been telling the truth. So was the puppet; smoke rose from his hands, quickly followed by flames. The scent of burning wood filled the air.

"Peter, you idiot!" The Voice snapped. "Timothy, use our second line of defense. If it works on our tools, it'll work on their source!"

"Yes, sir." Timothy picked up a silver bottle from the nearby table, its side engraved with the Blessed Mary. Unstopping it, he flung its contents onto Gilly, just as the arms of the puppet, holding the monster captive burned to ash.

Gilly, who had just straightened, staggered backwards as the holy water hit him. He gasped sharply, dropping to one knee and for a moment his eyes went wide and startled. Then he began to scream as his face and hands began to burn as if seared with acid. "No. Stop. Don't!" he screeched. "Please. Don't."

"Timothy, put him in the empty chamber. Even if the effect of the holy water eases, smoke can't escape that so easily. We don't have time to deal with him right now. His kind can't handle the rift the way that false god can. Besides, our tool has reached the other end and has begun breaking through."

"And the other man?"

"Put him in, too. He's not important right now."

Before Maloney could protest he was dragged into a glass room and shoved to the floor. Gilly was thrown in a moment later, still whining with pain, and the door slammed shut behind them.

(((

The last of the guests arrived, leaving William with little to do. He only knew these people from the papers; the Stayne heir and his fiancée; Blake Adams of West Manufacturing; Simone Trent, names that read like a who's who of Strikers Port's elite. People far out of his class. He hardly knew what to say.

Given that, he felt he could be forgiven for slipping away from the noisy crowd in the ballroom to take a breather. If nothing else, he could check the room where his mother had died for whatever it was Tiger had told him to look for.

He'd just entered the room when Rosamund called out to him from behind, following him with a determined look on her face. "Billy, whatever are you doing down here instead of talking to our guests?"

Turning to look at his cousin, surprised to find that her tone, usually right on the edge of mockery, actually sounded as if she wanted his company. Which was, he thought, more a tribute to whatever Mrs. McLeod had given Rosamund than a true change of heart. "They're not really my guests, Rosamund. They're yours."

"You and Jack are partners, that means you're partly responsible for...," Rosamund's scold paused and she sighed. "Oh, never mind. It's not like you know anyone upstairs, anyway."

Ruefully, William told her, "Well, no, I don't, and I'd probably offend someone accidentally. Besides, there was something I needed to check down here."

She frowned, "Billy, John said he found that stuffed dog of yours already. It isn't in here anymore."

Now he couldn't help laughing, even though he was standing within a few short feet of what remained of his mother. "I know that, Rosamund. Even if it were down here still, it'd be a complete mess. The rats or something would have turned it into a nest."

"But I put it in one of the lockers. I'm sure the rats...." Rosamund faltered and looked distinctly embarrassed. "Er... Well... I...."

Feeling almost fond of his cousin, William waved off her stammered attempt at an explanation. "I guessed this afternoon that you were the one who took it." Given her earlier insistence on reminding him, it was obvious she'd stolen the toy in a snit over something. "It's over and done. Don't worry about it."

Looking relieved, Rosamund and Boopsie came closer to the door. "Then why are you here? There's nothing here, right? Daddy wanted all the machinery months ago."

" UNSTOPPING IT,
HE FLUNG ITS CONTENTS ONTO GILLY..."

Rosamund's father had been the one wanting the machinery? That didn't make sense and William was about to ask more when he realized that his cousin was just about to look into the room behind him. "Rosamund, I don't think you want to...."

He was too late to stop her from stepping up to peer past him at the ruined room. "Oh! That's...," She looked sick, her eyes wide as she swayed and almost stumbled into his arms. To his surprise, though, she pulled herself together, and clutched the doorway instead. "That's Aunt Gwen...."

"It looks like her, yes," William agreed, deciding not to explain that it really was what little remained of his mother.

"No," Rosamund said, shaking her head and sounding sick. "That's her. That's... I remember... That man... turned her to stone...."

William stared at Rosamund, who was white as a sheet and covered with a fine sheen of sweat, then at the stone figure reaching out of the wall. At last, afraid to do so because of the memories breaking their way into his consciousness, he looked at the floor. The marks of feet, a man's bare feet, imprinted in the melted stone. A voice in his ear, harsh and full of rage, "I can't do it!" Another voice, so full of pain and terror that he could barely hear his mother in it, "You have to! Save him. Please! You have to save him!"

Suddenly Boopsie started to bark furiously and Rosamund screamed, causing William to look up again, his fugue broken. The wall around his mother's remains was shattering, a strange, terrible, light glowing from the center of the cracks. Then, with a sound that shook the entire house, a man's fist broke through, crumbling the wall to dust and sending broken chunks of Gwendolyn's stone figure flying.

William did the only thing he could. He grabbed Rosamund by the waist and flung her over his shoulder. Then, Boopsie close behind, he ran.

《《《

"Can you hear them?"

Gilly's whisper drew Maloney's attention down to the curled up figure at his feet. He'd been too busy looking for a way out of their prison to pay the monster any mind. "What?"

"I said, can you hear them talking?"

"No," Maloney snapped. "Why?"

Gilly sat up, leaning against the side of the room closer to the door so he couldn't be seen and shook water off his arm. He was looking strangely healthy for a creature who'd been sizzling and screaming with pain not two minutes earlier. "Because that means they can't hear us and I need you to tell me what they're doing. Can't have them see I'm not hurt."

Maloney eyed the men crowded at the other end of the room. "Timothy is fiddling with that statue from the Jeen Loon. Hooking it up to something," he said, then asked, "So holy water doesn't hurt you after all?"

"Trust me, it ought to have." There was a rueful note to Gilly's tone. "Guess there are some perks to riding the high road. Go on, tell me everything you see, even if you don't know what it is."

Although Maloney wanted an explanation, this wasn't the time. "Most of the work area looks like McLeod's set-up. Loads of machines and lights, nothing I can understand. The machine that talked to us is on the other side of the room from us, facing another room like this one. There's a weird... light... inside it. Almost looks like a tunnel of some sort."

"Another room like this? No wonder the thing isn't imploding. Can you see the other end?"

"Not really. No, wait, I see someone moving." The sight made him sick, reminding him of his trip through whatever place it was Tiger had taken him earlier.

Gilly sighed sharply, smoke trailing and dissipating rapidly from his breath, "Damn. I was afraid that was what he was up to. What else?"

"Just Timothy and the kid fiddling with the statue. And those things, what did the kid call them? The Jameses. About five of them all just hanging around doing nothing. What are they, anyway?"

Ruefully, Gilly said, "If I'm right, they're puppets powered with small bits of my substance. From back when they tried to kill me in '32." When Maloney gave him a confused glance, he added, "Long story short, they used a rift like this one to toss me in the ocean. Didn't kill me, but a good portion of my Self was torn off when I tried to keep from being pulled through. They must have found a way to contain the pieces and use them. May have got more the last time a rift and I got together and argued."

"If they're part of you, does that mean you can control them?" Maloney asked hopefully.

"No more than anyone can control their kids. Less so, since I didn't have the raising of them," Gilly grumbled. "They're entirely under Krane, or Timothy's, control. No bets on what happens if that's lost."

Maloney was about to ask if Krane was The Voice when he noticed what Timothy was doing. "That's weird. They're arguing with the statue. At least, that's what it looks like."

Gilly laughed weakly, "Thought that might happen. Even an itty-bitty God like Meng Huang Shang's more than he can handle."

"I don't understand."

"We don't have time for a lesson in metaphysics. Suffice it to say that Krane's understanding that the old Gods depend on the magic of human minds to exist is flawed. Monsters are a different story, but I'm no use to him with the rift. I try anything with all this inter-dimensional energy in here and I'm going to end up ripped apart again."

By which Maloney guessed that that meant Gilly couldn't escape this place any more than he could. "So, what are we going to do?"

"You're going to keep watch," Gilly told him, grinning broadly, and leaned so Maloney could see what was happening behind his body. The metal wall was slowly melting away, red hot and dripping. He was halfway through already. "They forgot something important when they put me in here. Where there's smoke, there's fire. And there isn't a metal on Earth that can stand up to the heat from the heart of the world."

))((

Michaels peeked through the kitchen doorway to see how things were going amongst the rich and famous of Strikers Port. Fairly well, as far as he could tell. Mrs. McLeod's cooking was apparently a hit and Donaldson was handling the bar with the skill of one long accustomed to dealing with demanding customers. It didn't matter to him, after all, if the alcohol he served had been distilled in an aluminum pot or aged in oak.

That quiet calm was suddenly broken by William and Rosamund appearing at the large double doors across the room. As the guests stared at the two, who sported similar expressions of panic, William rushed to the glass doors overlooking the patio. "Everyone get off of there!" he shouted. "The floor's collapsing."

Michaels and McLeod ran out and arrived just as the few dozen men and women who'd been enjoying the evening air demanded an explanation. At first, Michaels couldn't see the problem, then he realized that the stone pavement below them was shaking ever so slightly. Had they been in San Francisco he would have thought it was a quake.

Given all the troubles they'd had, a quake was the least of their worries. The kid didn't panic for no reason and Michaels didn't hesitate to add his own voice to the hubbub. "OFF THIS PATIO QUICKLY!"

There were startled shouts behind Michaels but he focused on getting the people in the most danger out of the way first. Then he heard a gunshot behind him and turned to see five men, as alike as peas in a pod, all standing at the center of the room with weapons raised.

At the very same moment, the floor of the patio cracked and shattered, revealing a blaze of something that was neither light nor darkness but a terrifying combination of the two. "A rift?" McLeod gasped, "It can't be."

More men, looking exactly like the ones in the center of the room, were climbing up out of the hole created in the floor. People were screaming and running, dodging bullets and trying to find an exit. Michaels grabbed McLeod, intending to drag him outside.

That was when two roars split the air - the one a wild animal hunting its prey, the other the shriek of metal on metal. A motorcycle appeared out of the night, its masked rider swinging a chain that caught hold of the nearest of the men who'd climbed from the hole and sent him flying.

At the same time, a silver beast dove down from the sky, snatching up two of the men and carrying them off almost before Michaels had a chance to say, "What are those two doing here?"

"Never mind that! We have to get everyone away from that rift." Together with William, McLeod was grabbing and shoving people down the steps as fast as he could, ignoring the fight inside the ballroom, where Tan and his men were making an escape route for the guests.

One of the attackers got within Michaels' reach and he tried punching the man in the face. It was like hitting a block of wood, and had just as much effect. The man raised his gun, aiming it for Michaels, only to have it knocked from his hand by a sudden flash of green and red. Miss Trendle again, showing a fine skill with a poker.

Tiger appeared, his chain slamming into the man's face and splintering it. Then he was gone again. So was Miss Trendle, headed after another man. This one didn't look like the first intruders, but he was obviously one of their allies. He was grabbing jewelry off everyone he could reach. Before Miss Trendle reached him, Miss Krane was there with her dog, the animal leaping at the man and snapping at him angrily.

"This is a mess," Crogan snarled from behind Michaels, "Those guys are impossible to fight." Even as he spoke, Dragon came flying through, his pet grabbing two more men and carrying them out the doors.

"Where are you taking them?" Michaels shouted.

"Hanging them up outside!" Dragon shouted back. "Cut 'em down later, after the rift's closed!"

The fight continued in that fashion, with Tiger and Dragon dealing with the strangers and Crogan and Tan's men handling those thugs who'd snuck into their own gangs. Then, as suddenly as it began, it was over and Michaels was glad to see that there seemed to be no real casualties. Oh, a few of the guests who hadn't moved fast enough had been knocked about some, but at least no one was dead.

Deciding that Crogan and Tan could handle things inside, Michaels went out on the porch to find McLeod peering down into the hole in the floor. "You said that's a rift?"

"It looks like a rift," McLeod said grimly. "But if it is, it isn't working the way they did before. I don't understand."

"The pressure must be the same at both ends," Tiger said, rolling up to the edge of the hole on his motorcycle.

McLeod gave the masked man a sharp glance, as if expecting him to say more, but when Tiger remained quiet, looking grimly down, he agreed. "You're probably right. I had some success with using a compression chamber to maintain the same pressure at both ends. But it doesn't work for long."

"Then the device has to be switched off." Tiger settled himself on his motorcycle, adjusting a knob.

"The device is on the other side of that rift, young man. How do you expect... oh, no, you're not!"

"No choice. Even if I knew where the other end is, I can't get there in time, even on Yuan here. Don't worry, my shielding can handle rift energies. Mostly." The engine revved and the motorcycle moved backwards, away from the hole. Before Tiger could start forward, though, McLeod was behind Tiger, hands on his shoulders. "Hey!"

"If it's the same device as before, I know what to do with it. You don't - at least, you'd better not - so I'm coming."

Tiger sighed. "Yes, sir." Looking up towards the sky, where Dragon and his pet were looping in a lazy figure eight, keeping watch on the men hanging off the tower's crenellations, he shouted, "Keep an eye on things here." Then, without waiting for an answer, he sent his motorcycle flying forward and down into the hole, through the rift.

〔〔〔

The hole Gilly melted in the wall of their chamber was big enough to let them hear what was going on outside. Not that it made any sense to Maloney. Someone was speaking, in a manner similar to Krane's, but all it did was repeat the word 'she', over and over, in different tones and styles.

"In a stone den was a poet called *Shi Shi*, who was a lion addict, and had resolved to eat ten lions," Gilly said, chuckling. "There's nothing like a God of Madness for making things difficult."

"What?"

"It's a poem using homonyms," Gilly explained, gleefully. "Chinese is a wonderful language for puns, you know."

Maloney wasn't certain what that meant but understood that the

God in the idol wasn't cooperating with Krane's plans. Indeed, from the frustrated voices of those trying to control him, they were completely unable to make him obey.

"I have all the power I need over you, Meng Huang Shang!" Krane's voice echoed through the room. "You're nothing but a thing born of belief! All I need to do is throw you into the rift and you will be lost forever!"

Gilly chuckled, the heat rising from his body increasing as he took advantage of their captor's distraction. Especially when the other voice answered, "Oh, noes, massa! Don't be throwin' me in no briar patch!"

"Sir," Timothy said, sounding tense, "I'm not sure things are going well on the other side of the rift."

"What do you mean?"

"The puppets ought to have finished their work and begun setting up the machinery. I don't see any sign of a connection."

Peter scoffed. "I told you those things are too stupid to handle things. You should have let me go to the party and set it up before they broke through."

Reassuringly, Timothy told the young man, "That's quite all right, Master Peter. You're too valuable to waste on a little thing like that. I could have gone myself, but someone needs to run the equipment on this side, too."

Maloney saw annoyance on the petulant features. At the same time Gilly said what he, himself, was thinking. "If the kid could be trusted with any sort of machine, Timothy could have left him here and gone. Just as well. If the kid could be trusted, I wouldn't have realized the thing holding me was a puppet, instead of a living being."

"You did say something about giving up killing," Maloney answered, peering down the tunnel of shadows that led to the other side of the rift. "What happened? Did you grow a conscience?"

"There's no need to be insulting," Gilly snapped, then sighed softly, "Yeah, maybe."

Maloney might have asked more, but then he noticed movement at the other end of the tunnel. Something dark and bulky, rushing forward at a high rate of speed. "Something's coming," he said, trying to make out what it was. "It looks like a motorcycle."

"Tiger," Gilly said grinning. "Thought he'd be the one. That bike of his may be the only thing that can go through a rift without its riders being burnt to a crisp, or turned into something unseemly by all the magic."

A moment later the cycle and its two riders screeched to a halt just inside the chamber containing the rift. Krane's voice mocked Tiger as he paused, examining the situation. "Nice try, Tiger. But if you break that glass you'll have everything on the other end of the rift coming in to join us!"

If Tiger answered, his voice couldn't be heard through the chamber's glass. Not that it mattered, because he leaned forward on his motorcycle, the man behind him clinging tightly, and sent it straight through the wall. Having ridden it before, Maloney wasn't surprised when it passed through as if it were made of light and air.

"I'm sorry," Tiger said as he and his companion, McLeod, dismounted. "Did you speak?"

"Timothy! Use the idol and stop them!"

The old man turned and hit a switch on the machine containing the idol, creating an intense white glow that shaped itself into a larger version of the statue. Except this image moved, the man's figure sitting up and reaching out towards Tiger with a mad little smile.

Immediately, both Tiger and McLeod bowed, though Tiger bowed much more deeply and reverently. "Greetings, My Lord," he said. "Shall I withdraw and leave these creatures to your tender mercy?"

The metallic voice that had been repeating the same word over and over suddenly spoke in English. "This is not my battle to fight. I leave it to those better suited to such things."

"That's what you think!" Krane shouted, "Timothy, do it!"

Timothy flung another switch and energy flared through the idol, black and fiery. That only made the God chuckle. "That tickles."

"Timothy!"

"I'm sorry, sir, I have the energy setting at full. It doesn't seem to have any effect."

At the same time, Peter, having had enough of doing nothing, grabbed hold of the idol, "I'll throw you through the rift!"

Laughing, the God told him, "I triple-dog dare you!"

As Peter reached for the door to the chamber, McLeod and Timothy simultaneously shouted "No!" They were too late, for the young man hit the button controlling the door and was immediately thrown across the room by the force of the wind coming out of the rift. Bricks and smoke followed, flying past so fast McLeod barely had time to duck.

As suddenly as it sprang up, the wind died down and McLeod gasped, "What?"

"Dragon," Tiger said grimly. "He's holding the rift his own way. He won't be able to do it for long. Close it. Quickly."

McLeod rushed towards the machine Krane's voice had been coming out of, stopping when two more puppets stepped in his path.

"Unhcegila, are you going to sit on your dead ass or help out?" That was the God's voice again, still coming out of the device the idol had been connected to. "Oh, I do like this machine. It actually lets me talk."

Gilly sighed. "Won't last for you any more than it would for me," he muttered, standing up and kicking the last bits of molten metal out of his way. "Fine, then."

As Gilly rushed one of the puppets, hands burning as if they were made of lava, Tiger rushed the second, swinging a chain in one hand and slicing with the clawed fingers of the other. Maloney slipped through the hole, burning himself on the metal but too angry to pay any attention.

As quickly as he could, Maloney got to Timothy's side and put his hands on the old man's arms. He didn't like having to deal with someone so weak he could be broken with a touch, but Timothy was the only one he could handle. Peter had been knocked cold and the puppets were just too damned strong.

"Look out!"

Tiger's shout warned Maloney just in time as strange smoky figure like the one that had nearly destroyed the newsroom appeared inches behind him. He dodged and the figure missed, grabbing Timothy instead and embedding him into the nearest table. The old man started screaming immediately, struggling to break free, blood seeping from his lips.

"The control device," Tiger shouted, reminding Maloney of the thing the masked man had destroyed before, the box that apparently allowed the creature to exist.

Maloney spotted his gun on the table across from him and flung himself forward, catching hold of it and spinning around. As the thing's hand reached out, within inches of his face, he fired, shattering the control device. Immediately, the smoke dissipated, leaving Maloney lying amid scattered bits of metal and plastic.

Krane was shouting angrily at McLeod, but his words were incoherent as the engineer shifted and twisted the dials as fast as his fingers could move. "Sorry, Jack, but I'm going to have to close it. We'll try to get you out another way, but not this. Too many people could die." Then there was silence.

Once again the God spoke. "Unhcegila. It's time for you to choose."

Gilly was standing, pulling himself together and looking pleased with himself. "Choose? The hell with that. I'm done here."

"That depends, Ancient One. The destruction of their controller has released your children into the world. What will you do about them?"

With a shrug, Gilly told the God, "The two that were here got eaten by the rift. Why should I worry about the others?"

"Because, Ancient One, your children have made no oath to never kill. Nor any promise to protect. And the one who can never owe you anything stands in their path to thwart them." The God chuckled, "Rise or fall, Unhcegila. It's your choice."

With a curse, Gilly disappeared in a cloud of smoke that left everyone else choking and coughing.

⟨⟨⟨

A high wind spun downwards, carrying dust and smoke along with it and ripping the broken stones from the patio as the hole widened. Behind William someone screamed. It sounded like Aunt Harriet.

Then, before more damage could be done, Dragon was there, his hands moving in circles as his pet flew above him, a huge sphere of shadow and fire swirling between his fingers. Somehow, whatever he was doing was blocking the wind, but William could see it was an incredible strain. "Can I help?"

"Not unless you can do magic!" Dragon shouted back. "Just... have... to hold... on..."

Suddenly he jerked forward, his sphere disappearing, and William leaped forward just in time to catch him, sure the wind would suck him through. Except the wind was gone, faded to nothing as suddenly as it had begun. "It's over?"

Grasping William's arm, Dragon looked up, exhaustion obvious despite his mask. "Not yet. They're free." There was despair in his voice, the sound of a man pushed to his limits and facing far more than he could handle.

When William followed his gaze he saw the strange men, the ones who all looked exactly alike, dropping down from the rooftop, their eyes glowing as if set afire. "What are they?"

"No time. Take this." As he collapsed, Dragon shoved a sword into William's hand, its chill blade shimmering in the light. For a moment he saw Meng within the metal and realized what it was. "They'll go wild. Try to stop them."

Not understanding at all, William rose to his feet and glared at the men, clutching Dragon's sword tightly. He glanced at the blue-masked figure on the floor, knowing what an effort the man had put in to keeping the rift closed. There'd be no help from that quarter, he understood as he rushed into the ballroom to block the strangers' path.

There were people behind William, terrified voices inaudible beneath the flames rising around them. They had nowhere to go, unless he could find a way to break past the men he faced. One reached for him and he reacted, or rather Dragon's weapon reacted, slicing across the man's arm and cutting it off. They were the same as the man who'd tried to kill him before, William realized, allowing the blade he held to guide his motions. At least it knew what it was doing.

Even with the weapon, there were too many of these men for William to fight alone. They moved too fast for his inexperienced self. He took a blow here, another there, and found himself on the floor, the weapon reshaped to a small dragon trying to protect him, with his attacker about to grab him by the throat. And this time there'd be no rescue.

Except there was. The man suddenly jerked back as fire licked his body. As William sat up, staring wildly, he realized Old Smoky had appeared behind the first. "Kids," the man growled, sounding utterly enraged, "should be seen and not heard!" He buried a hand in the chest of another of William's attackers and William heard something inside it shatter.

Within moments the strangers fell, their wooden bodies burning, their chests burst open from the force of the newcomer's blows. Then Old Smoky was beside William, brushing Meng away to pull him to his feet. "Get out of here. It's done."

William looked around, seeing that most of the people in the room escaped. But there were a few left, a man he thought worked for the Mayor, a young woman he recognized as a maid, dressed in unaccustomed finery, some of Tan's men and some of Crogan's. They were trapped, unable get past the flames cornering them against the wall.

They were near the balcony, he saw, near enough that he might be able to help them get out by the doors on the second floor. All he had to do was get up there himself. As he started towards the sculpture holding the balcony up, his rescuer grabbed his arm. "Are you out of your mind? Get out of here. You can't help them!"

"I have to try," William snapped angrily. "There's a chance."

"Are you an idiot? Don't fight me."

The memory of that same voice, saying the same words, the hand clutching his arm and pulling him to safety, nearly floored him. Then he recovered, shoving the knowledge aside for later. "I have to try," he said, pulling free. "You can go if you want. You don't owe me anything."

The man's expression was a terrifying mix of rage, sorrow and fear. "You're just like your mother!"

"From you, that's a compliment." Turning and running towards the statue, he began climbing, slipping and tearing his clothes as he struggled upwards.

"Don't. You don't have to do this!"

William glanced at the figure standing below him and smiled. "Yes, I do. If you can save a life and don't, that's the same thing as killing."

The strangest expression crossed Old Smoky's face. It wasn't afraid anymore, wasn't angry. Just... sad. He was looking at the men and women crouched in the corner, staring at them as if seeing them for the first time. Then, quietly, he said, "This is not what I wanted, Lord of Dreams. Let the record show that I never asked for this. And on your head be it if I can't keep the power contained."

Before William could ask his rescuer what he was talking about, or who he was talking to, the man let his hands fall to his sides and his head fall back to face the ceiling. His eyes were wide, glowing from their depths, and as William watched, his body began to glow. Not with fire, but with the same dark energies that had shone from the rift. Then he opened his mouth and spread his arms.

The fire around them swirled towards the man, surrounding him and streaming down into him as if he were drawing it all into his Self. Then William realized that that was exactly what he was doing, as the flames licking the walls sucked away towards the center of the maelstrom. A howl of agony filled the air, the sound of the rift ripping a life in two.

Within moments the last trickle of smoke faded into Old Smoky's body and disappeared. Silently, he lowered his head and shuddered as the men and women he'd rescued stared at him with expressions of awe and gratitude. He stared back at them wildly, eyes still glowing from the rift. Then, silently, as the last dark glow faded from his body, he collapsed, dozens of crystals from the chandelier scattering atop him, so that he looked like he'd been buried in diamonds.

"Well," John said from the doorway, "Rosamund's not going to be happy about this."

《《《

It wasn't until late afternoon of the next day before anyone could discuss the wild events of the night. At last, though, those most involved gathered in the Krane house's sitting room. Significant by their absence were Crogan, Tiger and Dragon, but Michaels hadn't really expected to see them there. Neither were Rosamund or her mother, for both were under Mrs. McLeod's care somewhere in the undamaged part of the house. Just as well, Michaels thought. He didn't need histrionics.

"So let's get this straight. Krane got himself caught in the rift at the same time his sister did, but part of his mind was caught inside?" Michaels asked.

"I believe so, yes," McLeod agreed. "I can only guess at how the entire incident happened...."

"I remembered." William said shortly. "Uncle Jack found me in the room and turned on the rift device. My mother caught him at it. She pushed him through and tried to save me." He glanced towards the fireplace at the man crouched in front of the blazing logs, wrapped in heavy blankets and looking like he thought it was winter instead of mid-summer. "Then he came, saved me and couldn't save her."

Sticking his hand into the fire and pulling out a piece of charcoal to eat, the man who'd been Old Smoky muttered, "Tried. Rift was eating me up too. She made me escape."

Miss Trendle took notes. "What happened then, Mr. Smoky."

The monster, former monster, according to Mrs. McLeod, started to laugh. "Mr. Smoky? Please don't. That's worse than The Voice." Turing so he could look at Miss Trendle, he added, "I break machinery, or I did. I had no idea how to switch the damned thing off and I thought, if I melted it, that that would be the same thing. It wasn't. The rift wouldn't close." There was a world of regret in his harsh voice.

"Covering it with stone blocked it up," McLeod said. "It plugged the dam so nothing more could get through. But the rift was still there, waiting."

Thoughtfully, Striker added, "So when I bought the house and gave Aunt Harriet all the equipment from the basement, Timothy and Peter were able to recreate the device?"

"I'd say it was Timothy who did most of the work. Peter may have helped, but I suspect he was more a hindrance. There's intelligence in the family, but it tends not to be accompanied by wisdom."

From what he'd been told about the Rancourts and Timothy in particular, Michaels suspected that that was because the Kranes always had someone to defend them from the consequences of their mistakes. "How did he know?"

"Timothy was one of our assistants when we were working on the rift device. He must have realized what had happened to Jack and worked out a way to communicate." McLeod looked thoughtful, "He also must have worked out how to use Old Smoky's... children... as puppets. I'm not sure how he worked out that other device, the one with the phasing ability, but there's no one else who could have done it."

William added, "Once they had the machinery and the puppets, Uncle Jack and Timothy set about trying to get his mind out of the rift and back into his body. They made use of the family's contacts with the south-side's gangsters and put Crogan to work getting the things they needed."

"But all those other jobs? I can understand why they went after you, McLeod, but you can't tell me that wine, or the choker, had anything to do with the rift device," Michaels protested.

It was Francis who had the answer. "No, but the wine provided money to the family and the choker was something Rosamund wanted for Boopsie. And no doubt they went after me because my paper had found out about the situation with William."

"Which, in turn, had to do with something both Rosamund and Aunt Harriet wanted," Striker added. "Rosy wanted a party and Aunt Harriet wanted money. As soon as they found out that the house wasn't theirs to sell and that the Sentinel was printing a story... well, Timothy and Uncle Jack must have wanted to keep everyone from finding out. After the shameful way they treated William and his father when Aunt Gwendolyn and Sebastian Krane died, the last thing they wanted was more bad publicity."

William looked embarrassed. "Neither my father, nor I, ever asked anything of them."

"Doesn't change the fact that you ought to have inherited your mother's property," Striker countered.

Michaels interrupted. "That's for you to work out on your own time, boys. Right now I want to know the rest of it."

"Krane and his crony... oh, I like that turn of phrase...," Old Smoky said and actually flushed at the glare Michaels gave him. "Sorry. It's easy to get distracted in this state. Anyway, they must have figured the party would be the best time to get their people in and reset the rift. Too, I suspect Krane wanted to make trouble for Striker and Jarvis over there. I don't think he liked being thwarted."

Ruefully, William added, "I think he hated me for his being stuck in the rift."

That might be true, but there was no way to find out. The shock of the rift's closing had killed Jack Krane's body. "So, I can't arrest Krane, Timothy is stuck in a table the same way those thugs of Crogan's are stuck in a wall and given Crogan cooperated, I can't do much about him, either. How I'm going to explain this to the public is beyond me."

Old Smoky, or Gilly, or whatever he was going to call himself now that he was stuck in human form, said, "You could always blame communism. That seems to be popular."

"I don't think so," Michaels retorted and added slyly, "Got any better ideas? I can throw a whiskey in the fire if you'd like."

Old Smoky looked thoughtfully into the fire and added, slowly and almost unwillingly, "It wouldn't work. I'm going to be stuck like this for a while. I used up a hell of a lot of my existence getting rid of that fire. Frankly, I'm at a loss for what I'm going to do to keep myself occupied."

"Don't worry your pretty head too much about that, old man. I'm sure I'll think of something."

(((

Maloney eyed his new partner with a jaundiced air. Really, they were looking younger and younger every day. This one was clearly Michaels' idea of just desserts. "Your hair is too long. Get it cut."

Gilly admired the effect of his nice, crisp, new uniform and preened in the mirror, "No can do, boss," he answered and before Maloney could snap at him, added, "It's part of the way this body works. Cut it and it'll just regenerate."

"Then at least try to make it look like you're an officer of the law instead of a punk playing dress-up."

"How about this?" Gilly offered, and his hair seemed to draw itself back into his skull. "I can keep it that way on duty."

It was still longer than Maloney liked but just barely acceptable. "It'll have to do," he said unwillingly. "You're going to have to drive, you know."

"Tiger gave me lessons. Kid can actually be useful, now and then." Gilly grinned, settling his gun in its holster and turning to look down at Maloney. "Ready to go?"

With a sigh for his new partner's forgetfulness, Maloney reached into the man's locker and held out his badge silently. Gilly grimaced, examining the thing for a moment before pinning it to his shirt. "Now are we ready, Officer Maloney?"

"Not quite, Officer Kenneth. There's a few things you need to know before we get into that patrol car." As Gilly cocked his head attentively, Maloney counted off on his fingers. "One, follow me. Two, take notes and don't talk unless I ask you to. And, three, for God's sake, don't trip over your own feet out there."

As Gilly saluted crisply and followed behind him with a suspicious air of meekness, Maloney reflected again that this was some sort of judgment. He just wasn't sure if it was on Gilly, or on him.

THE END

ABOUT OUR CREATORS

Author:

BARBARA DORAN - has been making up stories for as long as she can remember. From playing Ms. Marvel to her best friend's Captain Marvel to writing new stories for old characters (Hannibal King, X-Men, Green Hornet, The Saint, The Shadow and many others), to writing gaming and anime fanfiction online.

After ten years behind the keyboard as a software engineer, Barbara realized that her true love wasn't coding but making stuff up. So when she left that career in favor of dealing with two frequent interruptions of her life (namely her own personal Tiger and Dragon), she decided to use what little time they allowed her to work on writing. Her Long Suffering Husband, without whom she could never have managed such a goal, has been nothing if not supportive.

Along with reading every mystery, SF and fantasy book she could get her hands on, Barbara grew up watching Star Trek, Batman, Green Hornet, along with the usual Saturday morning cartoons. She became addicted to shows like Battle of the Planets and Doctor Who in her teens and discovered Run Run Shaw's martial arts flicks some years later. Those influences, along with a love of folklore and mythology, have become part of the world some small portion of her mind lives in. When, of course, she isn't chasing Tiger and Dragon from one school event to another.

Barbara can be contacted at <BarbaraDoran@sumergoscriptum.com>. Her website is <http://www.sumergoscriptum.com/barbaradoran/>.

Interior Illustrator

GARY KATO - was born in Honolulu, Hawaii in 1949. He graduated from the University of Hawaii with a Bachelor of Fine Arts degree. His comic book work hasappeared in such varied titles as DESTROYER DUCK, THUNDERBUNNY,MS. TREE and MR. JIGSAW. He's also illustrated children's books such as THE MENEHUNE OF NAUPAKA VILLAGE, and the currently available BARRY BASKERVILLE SOLVES A CASE, BARRY BASKERVILLE RETURNS and JAMIE AND THE FISH-EYED GOGGLES. He's also been a contributor to the Children's Television Workshop magazines, 3-2-1 CONTACT and KID CITY.

Cover Artist:

SHANE EVANS –a resident of Kerikeri in New Zealand, Shane has done several other projects for Airship 27 in the past and never fails to deliver stunning colors and renderings for the covers he does.

OCCULT DETECTIVES

They battle demons and monsters, hunt ghosts and defend us against the things that go bump in the night. They are Occult Detectives and they've been a staple of pulp fiction since the beginning of those glorious, garish magazines. Now Airship 27 Productions is thrilled to bring you a quartet of tales starring some of the most unique Occult Detectives ever created; three newly minted heroes and one classic master of mysticism.

From the days of the Wild West, Joel Jenkins offers up his Indian Shaman hero, Lone Crow. Then we have Josh Reynold's colorful Charles St. Cyprian, the Queen's own Royal Occultist, followed by Jim Beard's Sgt. Janus, the Spirit Breaker. And we culminate with a little known pulp classic figure, Ravenwood: the Stepson of Mystery as chronicled by Ron Fortier.

Get ready to take on possessed gunfighters, eerie mesmerizing spirits, a bewitching temptress and a legion of the undead as these four brand new tales usher you into thrilling adventures beyond the realm of the ordinary; your guides....the Occult Detectives.

Situated in the rural back country of Edwardian England is an old, mysterious house whose unique owner earns his living as a Spirit-Breaker, a hunter of ghosts. A former military veteran, Sgt. Roman Janus has devoted his life to aid those haunted, both emotionally and physically by obsessive wraiths whose spirits are still anchored to our world.

Airship 27 Productions is thrilled to present *Sgt. Janus – Spirit Breaker* by Jim Beard. Part detective, part occultist, Janus is himself a man of mystery whose own past is shrouded and the motivations behind his calling kept hidden. Within this volume you will find eight tales as narrated by his clients, each with his or her own perspective on this uncanny hero and his amazing career. Filled with suspense, terror and agonizing pathos, each a solid mesmerizing journey into the unknown world beyond.

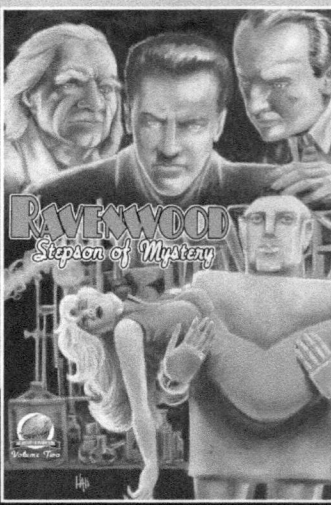